"You got them quiet pretty quickly. They've each got a good set of lungs."

"Part of the design, I'm sure," Gemma said.

She put Lucia back in the crib beside her sister and busied herself with situating them because she wasn't sure she could handle another dose of all that skin. It made her hands itch and her body flush in a way she didn't quite understand. Not that she could deny Dante was a very attractive man—impossible when he was standing there practically in the nude—but her own reaction was confusing her. She loved Dev, after all. And no matter how many times she told herself that didn't mean she couldn't appreciate another handsome—and sexy—man, it was still unsettling.

When she thought she could do so composedly, she straightened and turned around. "It's my job, Officer Mancuso. Next time, you can just go back to sleep," she suggested. *Please.*

"My job, too," he said.

"But you hired me."

"And I'm not paying you."

"I told you I was doing it for the experience."

Of dealing with his very distracting presence?

Justine Davis lives on Puget Sound in Washington State, watching big ships and the occasional submarine go by and sharing the neighborhood with assorted wildlife, including a pair of bald eagles, deer, a bear or two, and a tailless raccoon. In the few hours when she's not planning, plotting or writing her next book, her favorite things are photography, knitting her way through a huge yarn stash and driving her restored 1967 Corvette roadster—top down, of course.

Connect with Justine on her website, justinedavis.com, at Twitter.com/justine_d_davis or on Facebook at Facebook.com/justinedaredavis.

Books by Justine Davis

Harlequin Romantic Suspense

Cutter's Code

Operation Homecoming
Operation Soldier Next Door
Operation Alpha
Operation Notorious
Operation Hero's Watch
Operation Second Chance
Operation Mountain Recovery
Operation Whistleblower
Operation Payback

Visit the Author Profile page
at Harlequin.com for more titles.

K-9 BABY PROTECTOR

JUSTINE DAVIS

Previously published as *Colton's Twin Secrets*

Special thanks and acknowledgment are given to Justine Davis for her contribution to The Coltons of Red Ridge miniseries.

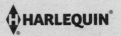

ISBN-13: 978-1-335-50840-9

K-9 Baby Protector

First published as Colton's Twin Secrets in 2018.
This edition published in 2023.

Recycling programs
for this product may
not exist in your area.

Harlequin Enterprises ULC
22 Adelaide St. West, 41st Floor
Toronto, Ontario M5H 4E3, Canada
www.Harlequin.com

Printed in U.S.A.

K-9 BABY PROTECTOR

This one's for readers in one of my favorite states, South Dakota. Don't go looking for Red Ridge, for it's entirely from imagination. But you'll know that. Enjoy the ride anyway. And here's to SD, indeed Great Faces, Great Places!

Chapter 1

Hope.

What a fool's game.

K9 officer Dante Mancuso stood in the doorway of the small apartment, wondering why on earth he felt the slightest twinge of hope that this time it might be different, this time they might actually find something. Anything. Trying to link the Teflon Twins, Evan and Noel Larson, to their multitude of crimes had so far been like trying to break Flash of sniffing.

As if the big dog had heard the thought, he looked up, leaned his head against Dante's leg and gave him that mournful look out of the saddest eyes he'd ever seen. His heart and gut reacted for a moment before his brain kicked in to remind him he was being played.

"Oh, no, you don't," Dante muttered to the blood-hound.

With a long, pained sigh that matched the expression on his wrinkled face, the dog plopped down on the floor.

"You'll get your turn when they're done," Dante told him. The black-and-tan dog gave him what in a person would be a distinct side-eye look. "What? You don't like Mondays or you can't sort out a few extra smells?"

With a distinct huff, the dog settled his head onto his front paws.

A man in uniform stepped through the door, pulling off his shoe covers and latex gloves. Al Collins was fairly new, a lateral transfer from down in Custer, still in training here, and Dante didn't quite have his measure yet.

"I swear, Mancuso, you talk to that dog more than I talk to my human partner."

"Human?" Dante shot a grinning glance at Collins's training officer, Duke Carnahan, a large, muscled man with a forehead and brow line that looked a bit simian, and often served to fool people into thinking him stupid, when in fact he was one of the sharpest cops around. He was also one of Dante's closest friends in the department.

"Keep it up, pretty boy, and I'll have to rip your arm off," Duke shot back.

Dante knew the man was joking, but Duke also looked quite capable of carrying out the threat. "Flash might not like that."

The cop's gaze shifted to the dog, who now looked

half-asleep. "You trying to tell me that lazybones would actually bite me?"

"That lazybones could run you into the ground over any kind of terrain. But when he caught you, he'd just lick you to death. Maybe drown you in slobber."

Duke grimaced. "Ugh. Drown in dog drool? No, thanks. You can keep the arm."

They both laughed.

"Don't see you down here much, Mancuso," Collins said. "Don't like us?"

"Some of the neighbors and I don't get along," Dante answered, his voice carefully neutral.

Collins frowned, but Duke got it quickly. "Oh, yeah. I forgot about your brother."

I wish I could.

Gemma Colton paced the floor of her condo in the building owned by her father, for once taking little pleasure in the sweeping view or the expensive furnishings. She was focused on one thing and one thing only. But it was her entire future.

"Something go wrong at the fund-raiser?"

She turned to look at Devlin. "What?"

"You seem…edgy."

And so, she realized, did he.

Devlin Harrington was the biggest puzzle she had ever encountered in her admittedly pampered life. To be honest, that was half the reason he intrigued her so—her social life wasn't usually so complicated. She was the youngest daughter of Fenwick Colton, and men were usually falling all over themselves for the chance to take her out. But not Dev. She'd never had to chase a man before, but the combination of his good looks, elegant manners, sharp dressing and confident air were irresistible to her.

And so she'd set herself to the task, telling herself it was in part because he was the son of wealthy Hamlin Harrington—who himself was involved with her half sister Layla, which was a puzzle—and a successful lawyer in his own right with his father's company. He was one of the few men where the question of him being after her money—well, her father's money—had never come up, not even with her father, who was paranoid about the subject.

And eight months later, here they were, not an inch closer to where she wanted to be. Oh, they had a relationship—it just wasn't the kind she wanted with him. Because she'd quite fallen for the handsome lawyer, and if it was in large part because even after all this time he still seemed unreachable, she wasn't at all sure what that meant.

If she wanted to see him, it was up to her to reach out. And half the time he had other plans he couldn't—or wouldn't—change. Telling herself he was a busy, successful man was wearing thin.

Quinn's words kept ringing in her head. Her cousin had been kind, gentle even, but her advice boiled down to one thing: you can't force love. But she wasn't trying to force it, she told herself. She already loved Devlin. And he loved her, she was sure, he just needed to move her up on his priority list. And she wasn't certain how to do that; she'd never not been at the top of that list with anyone she'd been with before.

"No," she said finally. "The fund-raiser went fine. Great, in fact. We raised even more than last year." Her chin came up. "Even without you."

He ignored the jab, as he usually did. She could never decide if it was because he didn't see it or it simply didn't bother him. She usually leaned toward the former, since the latter implied he didn't care enough to let it bother him, and she didn't want to believe that.

"I'm sure the animal shelter will be pleased," he said, and he sounded so preoccupied that she was almost certain he was only vaguely aware of what he was saying.

She stifled the childish urge to stamp her foot and say, "Pay attention!" But it was a close thing; Gemma was not used to being an afterthought for anyone.

Especially a man she was crazy about. A man she wanted to build that future with. A man who would fit seamlessly into her world. A man even her father couldn't find fault with.

"Dev!"

He seemed to snap back to reality. "Look, I just couldn't get there, all right?"

She sighed. "It's not that. Not really. Where are we going, Dev?"

He frowned. "Going?"

"You and me. Don't you think it's time we progressed beyond dinner a couple of times a week and only going to official functions?"

The frown deepened. "This is fine."

A pronouncement. Not an "I think," just a judgment

as if the only input required was his. She would have
to break him of that, and soon.

"This isn't my idea of fine. I want more, Dev."

He stood up. "I know," he said softly. He reached out
to cup her cheek, and she thought at last she was getting somewhere. At least she had his full attention now.
But instead he looked almost sad. "I'm sorry, Gemma."

He meant it. She could tell. And her entire mood
shifted. "It's okay. It was just a fund-raiser. There'll be
another one. In fact, the big gala is right before Thanks-
giving, and—"

"No, Gemma."

She blinked. "What?"

He gave her a regretful look. And her certainty about
the sincerity flickered; it was the same practiced look
he gave someone when he was turning them down for
a case, or a favor, or any other request made of him that
he did not want to say yes to. She'd admired how he did
it, at first. But she'd never had it turned on her before.

"I'm sorry," he said again. And again it sounded
genuine.

"It's all right," she said quickly, not quite sure why
she was feeling she needed to scramble to accept something that would have made her angry with anyone else.
But she couldn't be angry with Devlin. She was crazy
about him. "I know it's not your thing, so I'll quit asking if you want."

"It's not that, Gemma."

Anxiety spiked through her. It was an unfamiliar
feeling; she'd had little to be truly anxious about in
her life.

"What, Dev? What is it?"

"I wish I could give you what you want."

"I want you. You know that."

"Yes." He said it sadly but gently. "Yes, I do. And I know you mean it."

"I love you," she said, the anxiety shifting to desperation, as if a snowfield she'd been admiring had suddenly let go into an avalanche.

"You do," he said, sounding a little wondering. And looking almost puzzled. "You really do."

"Yes," she said, feeling a bit better.

"You deserve that kind of love yourself. You deserve a man who adores you." He gave a shake of his head, as if he were surprising himself. "And I'm going to give you the chance to find him. Because you genuinely, truly love me."

None of this was making any sense. "I don't understand."

"I can't give you what you want, Gemma. I don't love you. Not like that."

She stared at him. For the first time she admitted to herself that he was really saying it. But she was still far from believing he meant it.

Chapter 2

With the ease of long practice, Dante yanked his thoughts away from his brother, Dominic, who lived about three blocks from the rather dingy apartment he now stood outside, waiting to search. He tried never to think about him or the rest of his lawbreaking family. He'd long ago accepted that he was the odd one out, the one who had not only chosen not to break the law but uphold it. Sometimes Dominic and his snooty wife, Agostina, looked at Dante as if it were the other way around, or as if his very existence in the Mancuso family was some kind of accusation.

As perhaps it was.

Flash nudged his leg. He looked down at the dog. He knew most people would laugh at him for thinking it, but he would swear this time the dog's solemn expression held concern, as if the animal had sensed where his thoughts had turned. And maybe he had. Like most dogs, Flash was sensitive in areas beyond his prodigious nose.

As he waited, Dante wondered idly if the local judges ever got tired of issuing search warrants in the so far fruitless efforts to relate just about every criminal in Red Ridge to the Larsons. He sure got tired of asking for them, even knowing most of those scumbags were probably part of the Larson operation.

And the ones who aren't are probably related to me.

"Well," Duke said, in the brisk tones of someone changing an uncomfortable subject, "our cursory search was a bust, other than finding out the guy's apparently addicted to chewing gum. Never seen so many wrappers. Oh, and that microwave is a hazmat zone."

"So," Collins said, "I guess you'd better turn the nose loose."

Flash was on his feet before Dante had to say a word. Collins looked startled. "Enough people call him 'the nose' that he's learned it means he's about to go to work," Dante explained.

Collins looked impressed. "Mind if I stick around and watch? Never actually seen him work."

"Just stay out of his way," Dante said, his good-humored demeanor now replaced with the all-business attitude that told Flash he'd brook no nonsense. Bloodhounds were notoriously strong headed, and it took an equal amount of stubborn in a handler to get the best out of them. In the beginning he'd had to outlast Flash on a few occasions to get the dog to understand this was a human who would persist until he did what was asked of him.

But I've got a lot of practice in stubborn.

Dante shook off the moment when his family tried to trample into his thoughts again. Now was all about Flash. That he also made sure the dog had plenty of fun in his life—which meant hours of purposeless sniffing and romping—had brought them to a place where they were a smooth, efficient working team. And it was time to do that work.

He stepped across the threshold, a now eager Flash at his side. He didn't bother to have him sniff the officers who had already been inside so he could tell him to ignore those scents; he knew Flash had already done that. Dante wasn't sure how the dog processed it, but he knew which scents to ignore.

When he gave the command to search, the dog set off instantly. Dante watched, thinking as he often did that if he mapped out the dog's travels, there would be no pattern. And yet to Flash, the paths were as clear as a well-lit interstate. And every inch of those paths must be sniffed at length. In such an enclosed space, Dante supposed it took more time to sort out the trails. He knew the animal's incredible nose could track a scent hundreds of hours old, but the suspect had been in this place not even three hours ago, so it should be hot and fresh.

But as he watched, a different sort of pattern emerged. As if he'd been here to observe, he saw a model of life here in this small apartment emerge. Saw the most frequent paths walked—couch across from the flat screen to the kitchen and back, and almost never to the narrow table in the eating nook. Couch to the bathroom and back. Bathroom to the bedroom in the back, which had been enough to make even the casual-living Dante's nose wrinkle. Did the guy never do laundry? *Poor Flash*, he thought. Although he supposed to the dog the stronger the smell, the headier it was, no matter that to a human it was nearly gagworthy.

He wished there was a way to train the dog to go for the faintest scents first, but he knew that was counter to Flash's every instinct. And so he'd settled into the routine, letting the dog do it his way, because he almost never failed. And if he did fail to find something, it was because there was nothing to find.

Dante watched the dog work in the kitchen now—this was the only time Dante didn't have to worry about the animal's impressive counter-surfing skills, as he never strayed when working—wondering not for the first time if a negative result of a bloodhound's scent work would be as acceptable in court as a positive. If he didn't find something, was that proof in reverse? Would there come a case when a bloodhound's nose would be used in court to prove someone's innocence rather than guilt? He supposed it was only a matter of time, if it hadn't happened already. He should look that up—it was always good to keep on top of things like that so—

Flash pawed at a cupboard door. Dante went still. And then it came—the dog's look back over his shoulder that told him he'd found something. He crossed over to the dog, gave him a pat. He gloved up then crouched and pulled open the door. Bare seconds later he'd shoved aside a saucepan that looked like it had once bounced down three flights of stairs. Then he pulled out the only other thing in the cupboard. And stared as Flash proudly nudged it with that nose.

A five-pound sack of flour.

"Seriously, dog?"

Flash gave him a mournful look. But then, he always looked mournful. Others called it solemn, others dignified, but to Dante it was always mournful. And just now it was as if the dog was hurt Dante didn't trust him.

"All right, all right."

He picked up the bag, straightened up and put it on the counter. Pondered. What the hell would a guy who didn't have even a saltshaker in his kitchen, and nothing in his fridge but beer and leftover pizza, be doing with a bag of flour? Cutting drugs? That made no sense—the stuff was entirely the wrong texture. It looked practically full, anyway.

Collins made a smart-ass comment from the living room about whether they were searching or baking cookies. Dante flipped him a hand gesture. They both laughed.

He studied the bag for a moment longer, then unrolled the haphazardly folded top. Hesitantly—even with the gloves, he was a little wary of what might be in there, judging by the state of the microwave alone, let alone the rest of the kitchen. He was hardly manic about housecleaning, but this was a cut below.

He was glad not to see anything moving, although there were a couple of suspect dark specks amid the white. He bent again, picking up the battered saucepan. Then he pulled out one of the plastic evidence bags he always carried and used it to line the pan. Finally he picked up the flour and started to pour it into the bag-lined saucepan.

"Sarge's car just pulled up," Duke called out.

Dante grunted an acknowledgment, his attention on going slowly. By the time a third of the bag was emptied, he was beginning to get antsy. He trusted Flash implicitly, but—

Something fell out of the bag, sending up a puff of white flour. Dante leaned over to look. And went very still.

It was a phone. A cheap throwaway phone. A burner.

He was almost afraid to breathe. He reached out to touch it with a fingertip, half-afraid he was seeing things. It shifted slightly in the flour. He picked it up.

"Damn," Duke muttered, crossing the room now. He joined Dante, staring down at the phone. "He really is that good."

"Yeah. He is."

He couldn't mean it, Gemma thought. Dev couldn't really be breaking up with her.

"But—" she began.

He shook his head. "I'm going to give you that chance to find that guy," he said again.

Gemma frowned. He sounded as if he were giving her some great gift, not destroying their life together. And somewhere deep inside, where she was the woman who knew her place in this world, she felt a spark of anger.

"That's big of you," she said sharply. "So, what, you're just going to walk away from me? From us?"

"Yes."

"And just what," she asked imperiously, "do you think you're going to find with someone else that I don't have? Just what is it you think I'm lacking, Devlin Harrington?"

Dev looked almost sad. "An ounce of maternal instinct," he said.

Maternal instinct? Her brow furrowed. What on earth did that have to do with anything? Then a memory struck her.

"Is this about your cousin and her baby?"

She found it hard to believe one awkward moment with a tiny, squalling, squirming infant could have brought them to this. Sure, it had been clear she didn't know the first thing about babies, but why would she? She was Gemma Colton, daughter of Fenwick Colton—not to be confused with her distant cousin with the same name, who had had to deal with that awful virus a few years ago in Dead River, Wyoming, the best reason she'd ever heard for not becoming a nurse—and any children she might ever have would be safely ensconced with a nanny.

"That was just the demonstration of what I already knew," Dev said. And now he was sounding sad. "Gemma, keeping Harrington Incorporated in the family is my responsibility. And that requires children."

She might not know much about kids, but that seemed a rather cold-blooded way of thinking about them, even to her. But she loved Dev, and so she plowed on. "So? I want kids…someday." She shoved aside the doubt. "And they'll have a good life," she declared. "The best schools, the best care, a dozen nannies if that's what it takes to find the right one."

"Exactly."

Gemma blinked. "What?"

"I want a woman who will be hands-on with our children. Who will be a great mom. Like mine. She never turned us over to a nanny. Never abdicated her responsibility."

"Abdicated her responsibility? You make it sound like giving up a crown—" She cut off her own words when she heard how snarky she sounded. Secretly, she thought Dev probably had a rose-colored-glasses view of the mother who had died. Kind of like her father did of his first wife, Layla's mother.

Layla.

"Wait, what about your father? Who's to say he and Layla won't have children when this crazy killer is caught?"

Something flashed in Devlin's eyes. Was he not happy about his father being engaged to a woman only three years older than him? Surely he didn't think he would be supplanted by any children they had, since he was already a crucial part of the company.

She herself wasn't thrilled with her sister marrying Dev's father, and not just because it would make things complicated—her father-in-law would also be her brother-in-law—but because she couldn't quite believe Layla loved the guy. Not like Gemma loved Dev, anyway.

And belatedly she remembered she was thinking about complications that would now apparently never arise. Because Dev was breaking up with her. Her ultimatum had gone seriously sideways.

"You can't mean this," she said.

"I'm sorry," he said again. "It's just not a good match. But you'll be all right, Gemma. I wish…" He paused, then said decisively, "I'll let you find the happiness you deserve."

He'd *let* her? She'd had about enough of this royalish munificence of his. She wanted to ask who put him in charge of the world, but didn't.

She'd show him. No one broke up with Gemma Colton. She was the one who did the breaking up. He wanted maternal instincts? She'd show him maternal instincts. She'd make him sorry he'd ever doubted she had them. She'd have him crawling back, apologizing, in no time at all. She'd never been thwarted in her life, not for anything she'd really wanted.

And she would not be now.

"I'll go let the Sarge know you found something."

Dante nodded, didn't even look as Duke left. His attention was fastened on the phone. The screen was tiny compared to his own, and it was obviously bare-bones, but it booted up quickly enough.

The call log was empty. No contacts saved. Neither of which surprised him. He opened the messaging app. His mouth tightened a little at the short list of text conversations. Top name meant nothing to him, nor did the next. In fact, none of the four names did.

But the next three had only phone numbers listed, no names assigned.

And that middle number looked familiar.

He pulled his own phone out of his pocket and quickly called up a file. Scrolled down to a list of numbers…

It was there.

Holy bloodhound nose, it was there. They finally, *finally* had a link to the Larsons. He looked at the patient dog. "Flash, you're a genius."

Okay, Dante thought, *that* look was dignified. And it fairly screamed, "Of course I am." He grinned. His Monday was turning out not just decent, but great. He quickly checked the rest of the bag—nothing but flour. Sealed up the evidence bag. Picked it up. Headed back toward the living room.

Boom.

The front windows of the apartment shattered. Gunfire. Dante grabbed Flash and hauled him back to the kitchen, out of the line of fire. More shots.

His mind was racing. Ran through it in a split second. Three quick rounds. Not fast enough for fully automatic. Large caliber, but not huge. No hope of hitting anyone, so a warning. Then a squeal of tires on pavement. Picking up speed. Maybe—

A horrendous crash from outside echoed through the now broken windows. Metal versus metal, and more glass raining down.

But no more shots.

Can't drive and shoot at the same time.

The ominous silence held. Then he heard shouting from outside. He ordered Flash to stay in the no-nonsense voice the dog always obeyed unless he was on a scent so strongly that his nose shut down his ears.

He made his way into the living room, keeping out of the line of sight of the front windows. Still more shouting, but no shooting. He edged his way over to the window, still in the shelter of the solid wall. Pulled his Glock 22 from the holster, just in case. Risked a quick, darting glance. Behind the relative safety of the wall, he played the scene back in his head.

It was ugly. A big heavy white van had T-boned a small, expensive—and in this case too easily destructible—sports coupe. Crushed it up against a power pole. Signals at the corner were dark, and he'd bet the power was out for blocks around.

The white vehicle was the shooter. Had to be—only one on the street heading the right direction. So the guy he'd glimpsed running from it had to be him. And whoever was in that little coupe had never had a chance, they—

It hit him then. The coupe. The little bright yellow coupe.

He knew that car. There might be more than one in town, but in this neighborhood?

"Dominic," he breathed.

Gun still in his hand, he bolted out the door.

Chapter 3

"He got away," Collins was saying.

Dante registered the words but couldn't speak. He was only barely aware of Flash sniffing around the shooter's car, and he ignored the dog's questioning look as the animal wondered why he wasn't getting the order to track.

"He's hurt, though. He left a little blood on the steering wheel."

Again, Dante didn't react. He was staring at the second gurney being loaded into the coroner's van. When the doors of the van were slammed closed, the coroner's assistant glanced back at him. He supposed someone had told the guy who he was. His connection to the fatalities.

As the van pulled away, he shifted his gaze to his hands. At the blood already dried, staining his shirt cuffs.

"You tried, man," Duke said softly from behind him. "There was nothing you could have done. They were gone the moment that shooter plowed into them."

"They should have stolen a sturdier car," Dante mumbled to himself. Although he'd never been able to prove it, he'd known his brother had stolen the coupe, probably with his wife's help. If for no other reason than Dominic never bought what he could steal, and Agostina had expensive taste.

She had *had* expensive taste.

"Run the VIN, if it's not ground off," Dante said.

"Already did," Duke said. "Matches the logo, comes back to Red Ridge Delivery Service."

Dante registered the name; he'd been so focused on his brother he hadn't even glanced at the side of the van. One of the Larsons' front companies. And suddenly the shooting made sense. Sending a message: don't talk to the cops. *They must not know we already have the guy.*

"I meant that one," he said, nodding toward the bright yellow wreckage, which would now just about fit in the back of the van that had hit it.

"Your brother's?" Duke asked hesitantly.

"Odds are it's stolen," Dante said flatly. Not from here in Red Ridge—the car was too distinctive, he thought. They'd likely done their version of car shopping in a bigger, easier-to-be-ignored-in place.

Duke just looked at him for a long, silent moment. Dante stared him down, silently daring him to say something. Anything that would burst the gates on the dam that was holding back the tangled, messy emotions churning inside him. He and Dominic had never seen eye to eye on much of anything, had had only strained contact for years, but he was still his brother. And they'd had some good years together as kids.

Kids.

Dante's breath jammed up in his throat.

The twins. God, the twins.

"Mancuso? You need the medics? You just went pale."

"I just thought of something," he muttered, all he could manage.

"About the crash, or the shooting, or the investigation?"

They hadn't been in the car. Thank all the gods there be, they hadn't been in the car. "No," he finally got out. "Personal... Family."

Duke eyed him. "Look, get out of here. I'll handle this." Dante blinked. His friend shrugged. "You shouldn't be here anyway, with your brother and all. So whatever it is, go deal with it."

He didn't often let his heart take the lead over his gut-level cop instincts, but this...this was huge. Too huge to be denied. No matter what or who his brother had become, no matter the problems that had caused Dante in his life, this was bigger than any of it.

"Thanks, Duke," he said, called for Flash and ran for his car. He hit the button on the fob for the liftgate and got the dog in the back of the big black SUV. Seconds later he was behind the wheel.

It only took a few minutes to cover the distance to Dominic's. He spent every second of it thinking about the tiny, helpless babies his brother and sister-in-law had brought into the world, perhaps unwisely, just six months ago. For a short while, the arrival of the tiny girls had smoothed things out between them all, but it sadly hadn't lasted, for even that small pair of miracles apparently couldn't change Dominic's chosen path. He continued with his crooked ways, and Dante had had to back away once more.

The place stood out on the quiet street; Agostina's taste for flashy things didn't stop at vehicles. Amid the wood-sided houses with big trees, lawns and carefully tended flower beds in the neighborhood, the tiled roof, stone walls and concrete yard stood out glaringly. And even if they hadn't, the statuary would have done it. He'd thought Agostina was going for the feel of a palazzo in Florence, although he knew she'd never set foot in Italy. Problem was she'd missed it by a very long shot; the statues were cheap copies lacking the life and vitality of the originals. He was all for respecting his Italian heritage, but this didn't look impressive or grand, just completely out of place.

The house was locked, which he'd expected. But the fact that no one answered the door made him wonder where the girls actually were. Agostina might not be the nicest person around, but surely she wouldn't have left those two tiny children home alone.

He walked around the side of the house. Most of the windows were shuttered, or masked with the showy ceiling-to-pooling-on-the-floor draperies his sister-in-law had chosen. Every possible point of entry was secured with high-quality locks, which he also expected.

He took the flat stone path around to the back of

the house, where the kitchen looked out on yet another courtyard full of statuary he thought would make a meal rather unappetizing. This was where Agostina had chosen to put the more brutal art—gods fighting with each other, warriors running through their enemies or beheading them. He'd expected—maybe hoped—she would lighten up a bit after the twins arrived, but there had been no visible changes yet.

And now there never will be.

He pried loose one of the larger stones from the pathway and used it to break a window in the kitchen door. He wasn't worried about an alarm system; the very last thing his brother would have wanted was to have the police responding to his house when he wasn't there. He'd told Dante more than once that while his brother was welcome in his house, the cop was not. And certainly not that ugly, drooly thing he called a dog, Agostina always added.

He knew he was thinking about those things to avoid fixating on the images that were etched into his mind, probably permanently. When he'd first reached into the crumpled vehicle to touch his brother, he'd already known. The unnatural angle of Dominic's head had warned him, and when he'd been unable to find a pulse, it only confirmed what his gut was already telling him. And one look at his sister-in-law had told him there, too; Agostina must have hit the windshield hard. She'd always hated seat belts, for they wrinkled her elegant clothes. And even becoming a mother, having two innocent souls depending on her, had made no difference.

So you avoided wrinkles but ended up blood-soaked.

He shook his head sharply as the kitchen door finally swung open. He stood just inside for a long moment, simply listening. The house was quiet.

Dead quiet.

He looked around the kitchen, hoping to find a notepad or something, maybe with a helpful phone number. No such luck. He repeated the action in the large room adjacent, which looked more like a museum than a home. He made his way to where he knew Dominic's office was; there, at least, his brother had refused to allow his wife's taste to dominate. It was a functional room, with a large desk holding a computer and a file cabinet behind it. He could only imagine what might be in there. Dominic wasn't stupid enough to keep paper records of his illicit activities, was he?

He walked to the desk, again looking for some kind of clue that might tell him where his nieces were. Nothing.

He sat down, booted up the computer. It was, as he'd expected, password protected. He tried the obvious ones first—names, birthdates, including the twins'. No luck. There did not appear to be any password-generating software present, although it didn't have to be on the machine itself. He was sure Katie Parsons, the RRPD's tech whiz, could crack it in a matter of hours, but he wasn't sure he wanted to go there yet.

Right now all that mattered was finding the girls. Once he knew where they were, that they were safe, he'd be able to think straight. It would be something to focus on, something productive. He and Dominic had no other family left—at least not out of prison—except an elderly uncle and some cousins back in New York. Now he just had to—

The knock on the front door was faint all the way back here, but definite. It was followed by the loud clang of a doorbell that sounded disconcertingly like church bells from a cathedral. He made his way carefully, watchfully down the hall and through the drapery-darkened living room to the rather grand foyer. A glance out a window had told him there were no police cars in sight, but then, a good cop wouldn't park in view anyway. And he still didn't believe Dominic would have risked a burglar alarm, and there had been no control panels visible anywhere in the house.

The sidelight windows next to the door were a rather garish stained glass portrayal of…something, but they enabled him to see onto the porch, although distortedly. A short someone, with a frizzy-looking shock of gray hair. And a rather shapeless dress.

He put a hand on his weapon, and with the other pulled the door open. An older woman stood there, and her expression when she saw him was one of surprise. He saw her eyes flick to the K9 unit patch on his jacket.

"Oh! I knew it was the police, I saw the car…but you're Dominic's brother, aren't you?"

"I… Yes."

"I thought so. I recognize you from the picture, although you look very different out of uniform."

Picture? Dominic had a picture of him? Somewhere this woman would have seen it?

"Who are you?" he asked carefully.

The woman smiled briefly, and in that moment she

looked like someone's kindly grandmother. "I'm Louise Nelson. I live next door. But I'm very glad you're here. I got a phone call a while ago, and my daughter is ill. I have to go to her."

"I'm…sorry," Dante said, not sure what else to say, or why she was telling him, a total stranger, about this. Then, because it was his nature as well as ingrained, he asked, "Can I do anything? Drive you somewhere?" *With my luck she'll say yes and the daughter lives in Sioux Falls, about as far east as you can go and still be in the state.*

She looked startled. But then she smiled again, and it was steadier this time. Worry, he realized. She was worried. "No, but that's so sweet of you. You're as nice as Dom said you were."

It was his turn to be startled. "He…did?"

"Oh, often." She hesitated, then added, "He said sometimes you were too nice for your own good."

Well, that was his brother, all right.

Had been.

He wondered how long it took to start thinking in past tense.

But she was frowning now. Looking at his hands. He'd pulled his jacket on over his bloodstained shirt, but the cuffs still showed. "I was…at an accident scene a while ago," he said, and she seemed to relax. And thankfully did not put his sudden appearance at this house he never visited together with that bit of information and realize who was in that accident. It was not something he wanted to talk about. He hadn't even begun to process it himself.

And he needed to find Zita and Lucia, that was the most impor—

"So can you come over and get the girls?"

He blinked. "What?"

"I'm really sorry, but I have to leave as soon as possible."

"You have the twins?" he asked, feeling a little slow on the uptake.

"Yes. I watch them now and then. I enjoy having little ones to take care of again for a while." She smiled again. "My husband's with them now, so they're all right, but he's hopeless with babies beyond keeping them from getting hurt."

"I'm afraid so am I," he admitted. *Hopeless, meet helpless. What the hell am I going to do?*

"Oh, you can't be that bad. Otherwise Dom wouldn't have told me to call you if anything happened and I couldn't reach them."

And again he felt a little slow. Shock, maybe? "He told you to...call me?"

She nodded. "He said you were the reliable one in the family."

He almost laughed. Except he wasn't sure there was any laughter left in him.

A few minutes later, he was staring down at two impossibly small humans, sleeping snuggled up to each other in a single crib.

"They're doing so well for being born early," Mrs. Nelson was saying. "They'll be caught up soon. They're so cute."

She kept talking, but Dante had tuned out. Because

one of the babies had opened her eyes and looked at him. And smiled. It gave him an odd, melting feeling inside.

It was followed by an icy chill.

She didn't know that her short life had just changed forever.

Chapter 4

"Well, now there's a sight fit for a horror movie."

Dante didn't get angry at Carson Gage's comment as he walked into the Red Ridge PD building. In fact, he almost welcomed it; everybody else wanted to pour out sympathy he didn't want. But then Gage had lost his own brother, a brother he hadn't been close with, to the Groom Killer, so if anyone knew about walking in these shoes, it was Gage.

Besides, the detective was right. What else would you call a guy with eyes the color of an overripe tomato, hair that had yet to see even his fingers run through it, a jaw that was more stubbled than usual, and under his jacket with the unit logo, a T-shirt he thought he'd probably pulled on backward in his bleary-eyed haste this morning?

The fact that this character out of a horror flick was also lugging two baby carriers, occupied, only made it all scarier. To him, anyway.

"Longest night of my freaking life," he muttered to Gage.

"I can see that." And Gage was looking at the twins warily. They stared back, wide-eyed and uncertain. "Uh…what are you going to do with them?"

"Hell if I know," Dante muttered.

One of the girls made a string of sounds that—purely coincidentally, he was sure—had the same cadence and number of syllables of his muttering. He groaned inwardly but made a mental note to watch his language. He had no idea when babies started to talk, but he didn't want their first words to be swear words they'd picked up from their uncle.

He stared down at the two innocent faces. He had no idea when babies started to talk. He had no idea when they started to walk.

He had no idea, period.

Not to mention that the twins had gone through most of the bottles Mrs. Nelson had provided, and he had no idea what to do when the food ran out.

His desk phone rang. Since it was practically behind her head, Lucia gave a start. Her face scrunched up in the expression he'd learned during that long night meant she was about to erupt into a screeching wail. Quickly he reached into the bag Mrs. Nelson had sweetly packed for him and pulled out a bright pink stuffed rabbit. The moment Lucia saw it, her expression changed. The wail became a coo. And after a moment she moved a tiny hand toward the toy.

Breathing again, Dante tucked it in beside her and answered his phone. "Mancuso."

"Hey, Dante, it's Frank." Dante cradled the phone between ear and shoulder as Frank Lanelli, the day-watch dispatcher, spoke. "I've got a caller on the main PD line asking for you by name, but with everything—I'm really sorry, by the way—I thought I'd check with you before I put him through."

"Thanks," he said, meaning it, and appreciating the businesslike approach. "Who is it?"

"Name's Fisk. He's a lawyer."

Dante frowned. Rarely did a lawyer's call mean good news for a cop. "Any idea what he wants?"

"Maybe," Lanelli said, and for the first time Dante heard hesitancy in the efficient man's voice. Frank had been with the department for decades and was the solid linchpin that kept things moving, keeping more in his head at one time than Dante would have thought possible.

"Hit me," Dante said with a sigh.

"He says he's your brother's lawyer."

"Damn." His eyes flicked to the twins as soon as the word slipped out. But Lucia seemed happy with her rabbit, and Zita was merely watching him with apparent interest. "All right, put him through."

While he waited a freight train of possibilities barreled through his mind. Criminal lawyer? Was there some case pending? Was his brother a suspect in something? Had Dominic been arrested and he just hadn't heard about it yet? Oh, God, had they been fleeing a scene when the shooter had hit them? They had been careful about where they did their thing; Agostina had always said you didn't dirty your own pool.

But you never minded dirtying someone else's, did you? You always—

The click of the call going live cut off his fruitless thoughts.

"Mancuso," he said again.

There was a brief pause before the caller spoke. Startled by the name? That he was still using it, despite the connotations his brother had hung on it? *Believe me, I've thought more than once about changing it.* But he'd chosen to keep the name. Both as a reminder of growing up dirt-poor and wanting, and maybe, in some crazy way, thinking he could clean it up a little.

"This is James Fisk," the caller said. "I've just gotten word about your brother. My condolences."

"Thanks," Dante said shortly. If the guy was really Dominic's lawyer, he probably already knew he and his brother weren't close. And he didn't have time to waste on words he didn't want to hear anyway. "What did you need?"

"It's more what you need." Dante nearly smiled at that. He'd lived most of his life in a determined effort never to need a lawyer. So far he'd succeeded. "I have your brother's will."

"Oh."

"I don't know if he told you—"

"He didn't." Whatever it was, Dominic hadn't told him. Because he never did. And Dante was happier with it that way, because it let him hang on to the tiny bit of brotherly feeling he still had.

"Well. Then. Everything is left to his wife, or if she is also deceased, to his daughters."

"Of course," Dante said, although he couldn't help wondering how the girls would feel if they ever realized how said property had been obtained, with the proceeds from a career of criminal activity.

"You understand, then?" the man said, sounding relieved.

"Understand?" Dante asked, puzzled about what could be confusing about this. Then it hit him. He almost laughed. "Wait, you think I expected my brother to leave me something? No way in—"

He cut it off with another glance at the twins, who were being rather cooperative, both having apparently gone back to sleep.

Why not, after all? They were awake most of the night...

"Well, he did, in a way."

Dante frowned again. "In what way?"

"The children."

"What?"

"I'd say making you their legal guardian is leaving you something, wouldn't you?"

Dante sank down into his desk chair. He had no choice—his knees had suddenly gone weak. "What?" he repeated numbly.

There was a long, silent pause. "He never told you?"

Dante searched for words and finally said, very carefully, "My brother made me the twins' guardian?"

"Yes."

"Why?" It came out as bewildered as he was feeling. "We weren't… We didn't…"

"He told me you were the only one he would trust. Because, he said, you were the only one who would see to them properly."

What the hell did that mean? "Look, Mr. Fisk, I can't—"

"I understand things are a bit…chaotic at the moment. I'll send you a copy of the relevant portions of the will, but there are some other papers to sign and be filed. So if you could manage to come in to my office, or I can meet you somewhere, if that's impossible."

This is all *impossible.*

"Give me your number," he said, almost automatically. He scrawled it down and hung up without saying anything other than goodbye. Stared at it for a moment. Then looked at the sleeping girls, the picture of innocence now, nothing like the twin demons who had kept him running all night.

What the hell did he know about babies? Nothing. He knew nothing about little kids, either. And half the time—more than half, in fact—he was convinced he understood absolutely nothing about the female of the species at all, so how was he supposed to raise two of them?

A flood of images rushed through his mind, of toddlers wreaking mayhem, emotional teenagers doing the same. Girls. Clustered in packs, whispering. God, that time of the month. Warning them about that kind of boy.

Teaching them how to put that boy on his knees? Now that might be something I could contribute.

But the rest? No. No way.

Why, Dominic? Why me?

He couldn't do this.

He had to.

...the only one who would see to them properly.

What the hell did that even mean?

It was too much. Panic filled him. He couldn't be responsible for this. He could deal with thieves, armed robbers, murderers, the scum of the earth. But he couldn't be responsible for seeing that these two helpless babies had a good life.

Zita opened her eyes again. Smiled again. He pictured handing her over to some stranger to raise. Or worse, refusing the task and handing her over to the system. He knew too well, better than a civilian, that no matter how well meaning, there were too many gaps, too many holes in that system. Holes big enough for these two to fall right through.

"They kinda look like you."

Dante jerked out of his swirling thoughts to stare at Gage. "What?" Seemed like the only word he could manage lately.

"When they're frowning, anyway," Gage gibed at him.

He started to make an insulting hand gesture, a reflex among cops who had worked together awhile. But he stopped before it formed. That, too, would have to stop.

He remembered at Mrs. Nelson's, looking down at...he wasn't sure which one it had been, now, Zita or Lucia, who had opened her eyes and looked at him, but he remembered thinking how her life had changed forever and she didn't even know it.

But now he knew something else.

So had his.

"Maternal instinct," Gemma said rather huffily as she stared down at the artistic pattern worked into the surface of her latte.

"What?"

She raised her gaze to her brother's face. And she couldn't help but smile. She'd been terrified Blake was going to die just two months ago, after that horrible incident at the train station. And she'd already missed him while he'd been off building his fortune, but she completely understood his need to prove something to their father.

But now he was almost recovered, and much, much happier as he, Juliette and their daughter were building a life together. She envied but didn't begrudge him, because she loved him. She'd even come to like the bright, clever little girl who was his daughter. She didn't mind children at that age, where they were beginning to talk and you could communicate with them.

An ounce of maternal instinct...

Devlin's words came back to her. Her jaw tightened. Just because she didn't want children *yet* didn't mean she had no instincts. And there had to be a way to convince Dev of that. That she could be what he wanted.

"Gemma, what's wrong?"

She blinked. Blake had gone out of his way to meet her for coffee—the least she could do was pay attention. They were still finding their way in their own relationship, after his five-year absence.

"Sorry. Just...distracted. How are Juliette and Pandora?" That would do it, she thought. And the smile that warmed Blake's face, that lit his green eyes, proved her right.

"Besides wonderful?" he asked.

"Already knew that," Gemma said with a wave and a grin. "How about Sasha?" Juliette's K9 partner, a clever beagle, had been instrumental in the case that had brought them all together.

"She's a character," Blake said. "I think she's glad to be back to work, though."

"Toddler getting to her?"

"No, they get along great, but Juliette says it's a learning curve." Blake let out a compressed breath, as if he'd thought of something sad. "Not as much as one of the other K9 guys, though. Juliette told me he just inherited his twin nieces, six months old."

Gemma blinked. "Inherited?"

Blake nodded. "His brother and sister-in-law were killed in a traffic accident yesterday."

"That's awful!"

"Yeah. Juliette says Dante's going crazy, trying to deal. He says he knows nothing about kids and less about babies."

"No paternal instincts?" The words were out before she could stop them. It irritated her that Dev had gotten to her so deeply that she couldn't seem to shrug it off.

"Not on five minutes' notice, no," Blake said, looking

at her in apparent puzzlement at her sharp tone. "Anyway, he's in a panic, looking for a nanny."

Gemma stared at her brother, beyond startled at the idea that flashed into her head the moment he'd finished the sentence.

"A nanny," she said.

Blake nodded. "No way he can do it alone, and he knows it. And he's a cop—never knows when he might be late, or get called in after hours."

"So he'll need someone with…strong maternal instincts."

"Yeah." Blake lifted a brow at her. "What is with you today? All this parental instinct talk? If you're worried about me and Pandora, we're okay. I've already fallen for her like the proverbial ton of bricks."

"I know. It's not that. It's me." She gave him a wry smile. "You know, it's always about me."

Her brother studied her for a moment. "Some might believe that. But you've got a heart of gold, Gemma. You're always willing to give away what you've got or raise money for good causes."

"Maybe I need to get more hands-on."

"Like?"

She knew it was crazy. Completely. Yet she couldn't think of a better way to prove Devlin utterly, totally wrong.

"That cop who needs a nanny," she said, slowly, as her common sense tried to rein in the insane idea. "Who is he?"

"Dante Mancuso," Blake said, lifting his coffee cup. "Word from Juliette is he's a good guy. Pulled himself up from the proverbial wrong side of the tracks and made something good of his life."

"I'll do it."

"Do what?" he asked, taking a sip.

"Be nanny to those babies."

Chapter 5

Blake made a strange sound, as if the coffee had suddenly gone bad. Or as if he'd choked on that last swallow.

"You...*what*?"

"I'll take the job," Gemma said.

He stared at her. She stared back, her mind set now that she'd voiced it. He started to speak. Stopped. Started again. Stopped again. Then, in a tone she could tell was purposely level, he said reasonably, "If they tracked people who know even less than he does, you'd be on the list."

"I can learn," she said stubbornly.

"You're smart, and you've got drive," he agreed. "Nobody raises money for charity like you do without it. But that's a lot different than dealing with babies."

"Nobody's born knowing," she pointed out.

"No. But they usually have time to learn before it's in their lap, so to speak."

"So I'll learn fast."

"Why would you want to do this?"

"Maybe I don't like not knowing anything about... the whole baby thing."

Her brother studied her for a long, silent moment before saying softly, "Does this have anything to do with Dev Harrington?"

She stiffened. "Why would you ask that?"

"Look, I don't know the guy, but—"

"Exactly."

"I just don't like to see you hurting."

She lifted her chin. "I'm not hurting. I'm mad."

"Uh-oh. Mad like when you painted my shoes red, or mad like when you broke that window in Dad's car?"

"Mad like when Anna Witton called me a useless socialite," she muttered.

Blake smiled at that. "And look what you turned that into," he said softly. And she knew he meant that was when she'd begun her philanthropic efforts, determined to prove the former mayor wrong. Well, and to show her father she was good at something. And she had found, to her surprise, that not only was she good at it, she loved it. It gave her a sense of fulfillment that nothing else in her life ever had.

Even Dev.

She brushed away that traitorous thought as she made her way back to her car after Blake had to leave for an appointment. And for a few minutes she sat tapping a finger restlessly on the steering wheel of her racy little red coupe.

You can't be serious about hiring that useless little socialite.

Mayor Witton's words echoed in her mind. She'd proven her wrong—more than wrong.

And now, she thought determinedly, she would prove Dev wrong, too. So wrong he'd have to admit she'd be the perfect wife—and eventually mother. She'd just postpone the mother thing as long as she could.

She started the car and left the parking lot with a bark of tires.

It was noon before Dante had a chance to check and verify that yes, he had pulled his T-shirt on backward this morning. Which explained the irritating rub of the collar against his neck all morning. A morning spent doing everything but work. A dozen phone calls and he was no closer to finding the help he needed. All the nanny agencies he'd tried were more than ready to send people out for interviews. Tomorrow, or the next day. He didn't think he'd live that long.

The girls had finally gone to sleep, but only after he'd brought Flash in and the big dog had settled down beside them. He'd noticed very late last night, when it seemed the wailing would never stop and he'd expected the neighbors in his condo building would be pounding on the door any second, that they quieted when the bloodhound wearily lumbered over and sat in front of them as if he were staring them down with those mournful eyes. And as long as he stayed, they kept quiet. Dante had spent the rest of the night dozing on the floor beside his partner; what little sleep he'd gotten he owed to the animal. Who had featured in the snippets of wild dreams he remembered, born of some children's tale where a dog had served as a nanny.

"If only," he muttered now as he looked at the odd trio.

He caught himself tugging at the neck of his shirt again. He glanced around the office; there was nobody else here at the moment. He quickly tugged the shirt out of his jeans, pulled it up to where he could slip his arms out of the long sleeves, and turned it around the right way. Like everything else since yesterday, it got tangled, and by the time he'd gotten his arms back through and reached to pull the shirt back down, he was no longer alone.

For an instant he thought he'd somehow dozed off. Because the woman standing across the office gaping at him was something out of a particular type of male dream. Tall, willowy and dark eyed, long hair in loose waves with streaks of golden brown that framed her face… And that face. *Damn.*

He shook his head sharply, half expecting her to vanish. She did not. Instead she just stood there as if as stunned as he. She wasn't quite as tall as he'd thought, because a good three inches of it was the heel on the shoes that matched the soft, silky gold shirt she wore with tan slacks.

She matched her hair, he thought numbly.

And then he realized he had frozen in the midst of reaching for the hem of his shirt. And she was staring at his bare torso.

His abs contracted involuntarily. Hastily he tugged his shirt down, forgoing tucking it in for the moment. He felt another—lower—involuntary response, but quashed it rapidly. This woman, whoever she was, was way, way out of his league. He could tell that from the designer clothes and expensive jewelry.

She's probably just stunned—and offended—to walk in and find a guy with his shirt half off. She looks the type.

Which brought him to the question of how she'd gotten in here. Normally civilians didn't just walk in. They had to get past Lorelei Wong first, and the woman was a very efficient guardian of the gate, as it were. Usually.

"Can I help you?" he asked with businesslike politeness.

"I…" She swallowed, as if she were as rattled as he was. But damned if he was going to apologize for his appearance when she was the one who was in a usually restricted area. He waited silently.

Her gaze flicked to the corner where the two baby carriers sat, guarded by the lugubrious-looking Flash. Then she looked back at him and said, with a hesitancy he found surprising, given her appearance, "You're… Dante Mancuso?"

Possibilities raced through his mind. Was she some child services rep? He felt an unexpected jab of panic; was she here to take the girls? Some deep-down part of him suggested he should be relieved at that, but it was swamped immediately by the horrific thought of these two innocent babies winding up in the system.

Then he discarded the thought; this woman was too

expensively dressed. Unless she was some wealthy do-gooder dabbling. But she knew his name.

And she was still staring at him.

"Who are you?" It came out a bit abrupt, but he was running on too little sleep and too much chaos.

"I'm... Gemma. Gemma Colton."

Colton. Oh, great.

He could have guessed by her appearance, but he already knew which branch of the famous—and infamous—Colton family she had to be from. Because he knew she wasn't from his colleague Brayden Colton's sketchy side of the family tree, or Chief Finn Colton's ranch-grown side. That left only one possibility: the überwealthy, often annoying Fenwick Colton. Personally he'd always found the loud, brassy man an irritant, although he often wondered how he'd turned out such decent kids as Patience, the K9 unit vet. And Blake, who had had the sense to get out from under his father's thumb and make his own way—nothing like coming home a huge success and almost as rich as the old man.

Blake. A vague memory tickled his weary brain. The fund-raiser last year, when he and Flash had drawn the short straw and had to put in an appearance. Not onstage, thankfully, but just to mingle and be seen. The fund-raiser organized by Blake's sister. That's how he'd always categorized her, as Blake's sister, and if he'd ever heard her full name, it hadn't registered.

It registered now. He hadn't seen the event organizer that night, but if he'd had to imagine her, he would have come pretty close to the woman before him, in her ex-

pensive outfit, including the spike heels and the perfect hair.

"What do you want?" He'd tried for a neutral tone,
but he hadn't quite made it.

He saw her gaze flick again to the babies. "I... Blake
told me you needed a nanny."

Blake? Dante's fellow K9 unit officer Juliette must
have told him. He wasn't surprised; he was sure he was
the talk—or the joke—of the department by now.

"You know someone?" he asked, daring to feel a
spark of hope.

She nodded. Then, after a moment's hesitation that
surprised him—the rich Coltons were not generally
known for a lack of confidence—she said, almost
meekly, "Me."

Dante stared at her elegance, the aura of wealth and
the above-it-all air she projected, probably without even
trying. And he couldn't help himself. For an instant the
panic, the worry, the grief vanished.

And he burst out laughing.

Chapter 6

Gemma barely reacted to his laugh, although it was rare that she, Fenwick Colton's daughter, was laughed at. But she knew that was because nobody wanted to get on her father's bad side.

And she was self-aware enough to know how the idea of her as a nanny would appear on the surface. A nanny should be motherly looking, she thought, with some vague idea of ballet flats and one of those huge diaper bags slung over her shoulder.

She also knew she was staring, which was silly now that the lean, muscled abdomen that had struck her breathless was covered. But the image played back in her mind so vividly he might as well still be standing there, shirt rucked up around his arms, bare chest and that lovely six-pack open to her view.

She forced her gaze up to his face, wondering oddly if this was how a guy felt when he caught a glimpse of female flesh he normally wouldn't have. If so, no wonder they stared.

He didn't look much older than she was. The Italian heritage his name implied was obvious; he had the dark hair and eyes and the kind of face that made women with any heritage look twice. Not to mention the body...

Yes, whatever else Dante Mancuso was or wasn't, he was certainly a lovely example of the male of the species. Even though she guessed he wasn't at peak just now; the dark circles under his eyes spoke of a rough night.

And grief, she remembered suddenly, her brain seeming to finally shake off the shock of her first sight of him. He had inherited this problem—two problems, she amended—because his brother was dead.

"I'm sorry about your brother. Were you close?"

His expression went cool. "Thank you, no."

It took her a moment to realize that was two answers, not one. Her gaze shifted to the babies again. Then why...?

"If you'll excuse me, I have more calls to make." He turned toward his desk.

"I told you, I'll take the job."

He stopped, turned back to her. Looked her up and down, assessingly, and not at all in the way she was used to. Not for her figure, her hair or her clothes, or anything else she was used to being assessed for.

"I don't think so."

He clearly found her lacking. That was also not something she was used to. And it was far too close to Dev's assessment of her for her not to react. She drew herself up, and her chin rose. "You don't think I can do it?"

"Do you know the first thing about handling one baby, let alone two?"

"Do you?" she countered.

"Not even the thing before the first thing," he said, so easily it unexpectedly charmed her. "That's why I need someone who does."

"I—"

A piercing wail from below cut her off. Her head snapped around to look at the babies. It was the one on the left, clearly very unhappy. The big dog—a bloodhound, she remembered from seeing them at one of the charity functions—lifted his head and looked at the baby dolefully. The other baby, impossibly, continued to sleep. Perhaps she was used to her sister's outbursts, Gemma thought.

Her gaze flicked back to Dante, who was wincing. Other heads in the office were turning, and from far across the room came, "Tone it down, will you, Mancuso? On the phone here."

Moving on impulse, Gemma bent down and unstrapped the crying infant from the seat and picked her up. The wailing continued. She tried to rock her in her arms, but she only seemed to get louder. Prodded by vague memories of having seen it done, she lifted the baby—who was astonishingly solid and warm—to her shoulder. She felt the little legs kick, saw the tiny hands flail slightly and tightened her grip, pressing the tiny girl to her.

It felt strange. Different. Foreign. And yet…amazing. Something about that warmth, the weight, the shape of her. She cooed at the tiny child, not even caring if it helped or not, only feeling it was the thing to do. She patted the tiny back.

"Higher up," came a call from behind her, and she glanced around to see the receptionist who had been grinning as she had let her past the desk.

She followed the instructions, and moments later the baby let out an outsize burp. With it came some milky liquid that flowed down the shoulder of her blouse. And she was stunned to realize she didn't even care. Even if the $500 garment couldn't be cleaned, she didn't care. Because the baby in her arms felt so good, and, wonder of wonders, she had stopped crying and was looking at Gemma through bright, innocent eyes. And Gemma felt something stir deep inside her, something like awe, amazement and wonder all rolled into one blossoming explosion of warmth.

And then the tiny being closed her eyes and almost immediately dropped off to sleep. Trusting. Added to what she was already feeling, it was almost overwhelming.

She looked up met Dante Mancuso's dark eyes, which seemed almost amused now. Or surprised, perhaps. "Please," she said softly. "Let me do this."

He hesitated. Looked at her for one more moment, at the way she was cradling the tiny girl in her arms. But it was the cop who spoke. "You're Fenwick Colton's daughter. You have no experience with this, no references, and as far as I know, this—" he nodded at the tiny child in her arms, that sweet, warm weight "—is as close as you've ever been to taking care of a baby. And I'm just supposed to just say, 'Sure, move on in,' and turn my nieces over to you?"

Move on in.

She hadn't thought of that. But it only made sense he'd need a live-in nanny. She almost frowned; Dev wouldn't like that.

Devlin Harrington, she told herself fiercely, *dumped you. And this is the fix for that. He can hardly say you wouldn't be a hands-on mother if you show you can handle twins!*

"You know Blake. Call him, ask him."

"He may be a billionaire whose word is golden, but he's also your brother," Dante pointed out.

"Okay, then call Juliette. Cops trust each other, right?" She could see by his expression that she had him thinking now. Actually considering. And she pressed her case. "You don't even have to pay me. I'll do it just for the experience."

"I could talk to Juliette," he said, but reluctance was still clear in his voice. In that moment, as if conspiring to help her, the second twin woke, seemed to realize she was missing out on interesting things, and began a wail that put her sister to shame.

"And," Gemma added, with more bravado than confidence, "I'll start right now."

Dante's eyes closed wearily for a moment, and Gemma had an inkling of the kind of night he'd had. It touched her, in an odd sort of way she would never have expected. She tried to imagine.

When he opened them, he said decisively, "I'll call Juliette. If you can keep them quiet long enough for me to do that, we'll talk."

Gemma had no idea what to do to accomplish that. Trying to think, she put the sleeping twin she was holding—how on earth did you tell them apart?—back in her carrier, and set it down beside her sister's. She reached for the crying twin. The big, droopy-eared dog's head came up, and she hesitated.

"That's Flash. Flash, meet Gemma." The dog looked up at him, and Gemma would have sworn he was asking a question. "Gentleman for now," was Dante's answer, given in commanding tone.

With an odd sound, a sort of combination sigh and groan, the dog gave her a studying look, took a deep sniff and settled his big head back down on his paws.

"For now?" she asked, a little warily, as she picked up the crying baby and repeated the earlier procedure, which seemed to work, and thankfully without the spitting up this time.

"Withholding final judgment pending further evidence," he said.

That seemed fair to her. It was just the dog part that threw her. "And he…gets that?"

"In his own way, yes. It means you'd have to do something he really, really didn't like for him to come after you."

She blinked. Glanced again at the dog, who looked for all the world as if it would take an explosion to bestir him from his selected spot.

"Don't let him fool you," Dante said in the tone of

someone who knew perfectly well what she was thinking. "What he might lack in speed he makes up for with stamina and sheer power. And he's got a mind of his own. You're going to have to earn his trust, too. He decides for himself when you've crossed a line."

She drew herself up. "Does he let you know when you've crossed a line?" she asked sweetly.

If her manner registered, he didn't let it show. Then again, he was a cop and probably had a lot of practice with keeping his thoughts unreadable.

Except when his life was blasted to bits.

She remembered not only why she was here, but what had happened to make him need help, and felt bad about her tone.

But he answered her easily enough. "Yes. He just cuts me more slack, because he knows that while I'm a just a dumb human, I usually catch on eventually."

As she watched him pull out his cell phone and walk across the office, tapping out a text message, probably to Juliette, she found herself thinking that Dante Mancuso was very far from a dumb human.

"I won't lie, buddy, she's spoiled," Juliette Walsh said in Dante's ear. "But she's also got a heart of gold, is quick to learn and very determined. And she's got depth to her. For a Colton, she's…a tiny bit naive about some things. Don't know how she managed that."

Depending on what those things were, Dante wasn't sure a little naïveté wouldn't be welcome. "All I really need to know is can I trust her to take care of the twins?"

"She would never intentionally hurt anyone, but I

doubt if she's ever even babysat in her life," Juliette said frankly. "Blake could probably tell you that."

He had the thought that calling Blake might be a good idea anyway. They could share the novelty of instant parenthood, although the situations were very different.

"He's the one who told her about...my situation."

"I did mention it to him, sort of in passing. Thought he might know someone who could help."

"Thanks," Dante said, meaning it. "Although I bet he never expected his little sister to volunteer."

"That," Juliette said with a laugh, "I can practically guarantee. But Gemma can be a real sweetheart, Dante. She's surprisingly easy to be around, even for us ordinary people."

"How would you know? Nothing ordinary about you," Dante teased, and she laughed again. It was infectious. She was so happy these days it fairly flowed over the connection. And he had a suspicion that once that damned Groom Killer, as the ever-helpful media had tagged the serial killer terrorizing would-be grooms in Red Ridge, was caught, some wedding planning would be starting.

"And one more thing," Juliette added. "If she says she'll do something, she'll do it, unless outside forces prevent it. She truly, honestly tries to never break a promise. Their father broke too many, I think, so she's hard over the other way."

Dante went still for a moment. Juliette could have been talking about him. He knew all about long strings of parental broken promises, and his reaction had been the same: if he gave his word, his promise, he'd go to whatever lengths necessary to keep it.

"Thanks, Walsh."

"No problem."

"Stay happy, will you?"

She laughed, and it was a light, airy sound that was full of delight. "Blake'll see to that."

He stared at the phone when the call was done, contemplating for a moment the unlikely way and place Juliette Walsh had found—or rather refound—the love of her life. And as unlikely as it was, he believed his brother had genuinely loved Agostina, at least as much as he was able. Dante was the one who was out of step on that front. He'd never met a woman he thought he could spend the rest of his life with. And cops were generally lousy marriage material anyway. What kind of woman would want to put with the crazy hours, the callouts, the grimness of it all, let alone the fun of knowing every time your husband walked out the door he might never come home?

That had even been one of Dominic's arguments when Dante had signed up for the police academy. After the shock had worn off, anyway, and after his outrage at the problems this would cause for the family. Especially when Dante had bluntly told his brother not to think he'd now have an in with the department, that he had every intention of becoming and staying an honest cop.

Dominic had never forgiven him for that.

And now he never would.

Chapter 7

As the memory of the scene she had walked in on played back in Gemma's head, she had to admit Dante was also damned sexy. Not as sexy as smooth, suave Devlin, of course, but in a different, rougher, edgier way.

Not that that type appealed to her. Which did not explain her first reaction to the sight of his bare torso, but she decided not to think about that now. She had other things to deal with. Like keeping these two quiet. She dropped down to sit beside the two babies and the dog.

You two are going to be my résumé. When Dev sees I can handle this, he won't have doubts anymore. Then everything will go back to the way it should be.

The dog lifted his head again, looking at her steadily. She knew she was being fanciful, but there seemed a world of wisdom in those deep-set canine eyes. She felt the urge to pet him but didn't know if that would break some K9 protocol. Funny, she'd heard all her life about the Red Ridge K9 unit, had raised money—a lot of money—for them, but she knew very little about the animals themselves. Maybe she'd held herself apart because they had been the pet cause of her father's first—and, if she were honest, most beloved—wife. Maybe the only one he'd really loved; she'd figured that out fairly young.

She glanced across the office at Dante, who appeared to be waiting for a response to a text to Juliette asking for a convo. Then, tentatively, she held out a hand for the dog to smell. He didn't seem impressed, but then she remembered the deep sniff he'd taken earlier.

"No harm," she whispered to him. With some idea that it might be less objectionable than a pat on the head—this dog, with his almost noble mien, did not seem the type for such saccharine gestures—she reached out and stroked one of the long, dropping ears with the back of her fingers. It felt surprisingly thin and delicate, and amazingly, incredibly soft. And it curled at the tip, inward and back, in a way she had spent many hours trying to get her hair to do just right.

One of the babies giggled. Or at least that's what it sounded like. It startled her, and her head snapped around. It was the baby she'd just put down—she'd have to learn how to tell them apart, so she didn't call them by the wrong names—and she was watching her and Flash with obvious interest.

She felt another gaze, knew it was Dante. She looked up at him and smiled.

He went very still. But before she could decipher the

look on his face—normally she wasn't much for stubble, but she had to admit on him it looked good—he turned away. For an instant she wondered if it had been an expression of male reaction, but then she heard him talking into his phone as he walked away, toward the window, and laughed inwardly at herself.

God, you really do think it's always about you, don't you?

She looked back at the two girls. And for the first time felt overwhelmed at what she'd done. Felt the fierce urge to back out, now, fast, before she got in any deeper.

...an ounce of maternal instinct.

Dev's words rang in her mind. And her determination returned. She'd set out to prove him wrong, and she would. Somehow.

She stroked that soft ear again. And to her surprise, the big head nudged her hand. She looked at the dog. The dog who had already gotten one of the girls to giggle.

"Will you help me, Flash?" she whispered to him, scratching behind that ear now. "You've obviously got the knack."

The dog gave her another long, considering look, and then turned toward the two babies, as if he understood exactly what she meant. With a sigh that sounded nothing less than long-suffering, he plopped his head back down on his huge paws.

Gemma chose to interpret that as acceptance, if not an outright offer to help. It would have to do.

Jolted out of useless meanderings, Dante turned to walk back toward his desk. And stopped a few feet away at the sight of Gemma sitting cross-legged on the floor, one hand holding one of the dangling, beaded earrings she'd been wearing in front of one of the twins, who was batting at it happily as her sister slept on, and the other hand stroking one of Flash's ears. The dog looked as close to blissful as he ever did.

It wasn't much to go on, he knew that. But the combination of that recognition that he and Gemma had chosen a similar response to parental unreliability and this image of her, the twins and Flash before him made up his mind.

"I hope you can learn to tell them apart."

Gemma looked up at him, smiling widely. All the Colton polish and elegance was still there, but that smile made her seem...real. "Oh, I can already do that."

He blinked. "You can?"

She nodded. Gestured at the sleeping twin. "She's a little smaller, but that might not last, so I looked for something else. And see, her right eyebrow has a little point on top."

He looked where she was indicating. And indeed saw a point in the shape of the tiny brow, where the other one was a smooth curve.

"I...never noticed." Odd, he usually had a cop's eye for details, but he'd missed this.

"It's a girly thing," Gemma said blithely, as if she never would have expected him to notice. "Besides, I'd guess you've been a little busy."

That was an understatement. Dante thought. Everything was a blur from the moment he'd picked up the girls from Mrs. Nelson. "Frankly," he said drily, "I'm amazed we all survived."

Again that smile. Genuine, he thought. That's what it was. "I just hope you can tell me which is which."

"I… They have little bead things with their names. Elastic. On their ankles." He grimaced. "They come off, though. Thankfully not at the same time so far."

She laughed. It wasn't the light, airy thing that Juliette's had been, but rather a deeper, huskier sound that seemed to make the back of his neck itch.

"Let's see, then," she said, with her free hand tugging at the tiny bootie of the twin so entranced with her earring. "Ah, ah, sweetie, that earring would be just too easy for you to swallow, so I'll just hang on to it while you play."

He remembered wrestling with the tiny cloth foot coverings in the wee hours, remembered with an odd twinge of…something, that moment when he'd caught that impossibly tiny bare foot in his hands and marveled at it. That these two tiny beings were connected to him, were of his blood, his DNA, even if once removed, filled him with awe. And the burst of protectiveness that had flooded him in that instant had shocked him.

How could his brother stay on that crooked path when he had these two tiny girls depending on him? How could he not be changed, simply by their very existence? How could he—

It had hit him again then, with renewed force. And he wondered if he would ever get over the jolt of having to think of his brother in the past tense.

"Ah," Gemma said softly, yanking him out of the painful memory. "So you're Lucia," she said. "With the affinity for flashy things. I'll remember that." She looked at the sleeping twin now. "Which makes you Zita, of the pointed brow. Sounds like a mythical name, doesn't it?"

Dante was smiling. Widely. And he wasn't quite sure why. Sure, it was in part because he was feeling better about the impulsive decision he hadn't even told her he'd made yet. And because he liked her voice. But it was more than just that. It was how she was speaking to them, not in baby talk or cooing, but lightly, with humor, as if they could understand.

And perhaps they could, the tone if not the words. For Zita had awakened as if in response to her name, although she couldn't really know it yet, could she? Or maybe she could. He sighed, seeing yet another internet search in his future. He really needed to learn where they were at six months, where they should be and what he should be watching for from here on out.

Here on out. Which meant the rest of his life. For the rest of his life, he was responsible for these two. Not just care and feeding, which suddenly seemed simple in comparison to protecting, nurturing, teaching…

It all crashed in on him at once, and he sank down in his desk chair. Gemma looked back up at him.

"Are you all right?" she asked, sounding startled. "You look a bit…pale."

"*Ashen* is the word you're looking for," he said shakily. "Because it all just hit me."

"All?"

"That my brother is gone." He looked at the girls. "That the rest of my life is no longer mine."

She looked from him to the girls and back. "No," she agreed quietly. "I guess it's not."

"I don't even know why he did it. Why he chose me for them."

Any more than he knew why he was telling her this. He never spilled his guts like this, not even to his friends, let alone a virtual stranger.

"You're his brother," Gemma said, sounding a little puzzled.

"Yeah, but…" He drew in a deep breath, steadying himself. "Never mind."

"You're probably feeling what Blake felt when he found out about Pandora. Shocked, and a little terrified."

"That fits," he muttered wryly. "Especially the terrified part."

"He said learning he was a father stunned him even more since she was already here." She waved at the girls. "Like they are. No months of waiting to prepare, get used to the idea."

"I'm only their uncle," he said, not even sure why.

"But you're going to have to be more."

He shifted his gaze from the girls—now giggling quietly at Flash, who was looking at them, head tilted and wearing his most quizzical expression—back to Gemma.

She's got depth to her…

He was seeing that now. Never in a million years would he have expected to be having this kind of conversation with the spoiled youngest daughter of Fenwick Colton.

"I always thought I'd have kids. Someday. But not now."

She gave him a look that bordered on surprise, but only nodded. Then, after a moment, she said softly,

"Maybe it doesn't matter *when* you become a father, only that you do."

He stared at her. She was rattling him, this pampered yet unexpectedly sweet heiress, and he didn't know what to think of her. Quickly he looked at the babies. They were making soft sounds now, simple ohs and ehs and ahs, but in turns, looking at each other, as if they were carrying on some sort of secret twin conversation. As perhaps they were.

"Maybe if they were boys," he muttered. "I'd know something about that."

"Then it's lucky you have me, isn't it?" Gemma said airily.

Dante looked back at her. She looked…at home on the floor next to his desk, Flash at her side and the two girls in front of her. He caught himself picturing this same tableau in his living room, maybe before the fireplace, the flames throwing a soft glow over them.

He yanked himself off the uncharacteristic and unwanted path. He wasn't sure she was qualified, or that she wouldn't get bored and walk out within the week. But he needed help right now. And just because she seemed to screw up his thinking was no reason to refuse her offer.

Desperate times called for desperate measures.

"Okay," he said, surrendering to what now seemed inevitable. "You're hired." *For now, at least.*

Chapter 8

I always thought I'd have kids. Someday. But not now.

Dante's words played back in Gemma's mind, words that had so exactly mirrored her own thoughts. He'd sounded so bewildered. Lost. Even a little afraid, which struck her as the most poignant of all, since he was a cop. But her half sister Patience, the veterinarian for the Red Ridge K9 unit, had once told her being a cop didn't take away the fear, it just taught you how to go on in the face of it.

She couldn't imagine that kind of life. As Fenwick Colton's daughter, she had rarely had reason to be afraid, as a child or now. Even the disruption of her parents' divorce hadn't lasted long; she'd seen little of either of them anyway by then. Her life had gone along smoothly, staff and servants seeing to her needs, her father dropping in occasionally with some glitzy new woman on his arm and a guilt gift for Gemma in his hands. She'd learned to arrange—okay, manipulate—everything to her liking, and she planned to keep it that way.

She would make Devlin Harrington see sense, he would realize he loved her, they would get married, and eventually—that "someday" Dante had mentioned—there would be children of her own. She would show Dev he was wrong about her, they would put it back together and then she'd find a way to stall his rush for children. The plan fell into place easily in her mind. She would make it happen. She wanted Dev, and she'd never been thwarted when she really, truly wanted something.

Funny, though, how Dev wanted children so much but would have to wait to have them, and Dante, who hadn't, suddenly had two. Of course Dev's father would want his son's children to be his own. And mere nieces wouldn't be enough for him. He would want Dev to have a son, or sons. He'd said as much the first time she'd met him, last year, before she and Dev had started dating. It was some party or other, and he'd spoken expansively of expanding his empire, and those plans included the next generation of Harringtons. Male Harringtons, sexist that he was.

And all of that had been blasted right out of her mind when she'd turned around and seen Dev for the first time. It had taken a few months of carefully arranged but apparently coincidental meetings before he finally asked her out. She'd heard rumors he'd been intent on another woman for a while, but she'd won in the end. She always did.

But what his father had said came back to her now. And for a moment, looking at the two sweet, innocent faces as Dante gathered up what seemed a bewildering array of their accoutrements, she felt a qualm. *Mere* nieces? How could anyone look at these two and think they were mere anything? Less than anyone?

She shook off the unsettling feeling. Dev might want to do what his father expected of him, but that didn't make him like his father. He didn't think that way, she was sure.

Mind eased now, she eyed the grocery bag Dante had stuffed all the baby things into. That would never do. She'd have to get a better bag. Not one of those cheesy plastic things, but maybe a nice, big designer leather bag she could adapt.

And she would need to go home and pack her own things. But that should wait until she saw what her living situation would be. She hoped her room would have a big enough closet.

It only took until they got down to Dante's car for things to start to unravel.

"Does he go with you everywhere?" she asked, nodding at the dog lumbering along beside them.

"Pretty much," Dante answered. "He's got a kennel here, and I can leave him over at the training center if I need to, but mostly he's with me. He's my partner."

"What about on dates?" she asked, not certain why she'd asked. Why it even mattered. She told herself it was only curiosity and idle chat to keep the conversation going. Which it did, but in a way she hadn't expected.

"That's easy. Then he's my sorter."

She blinked. "Your what?"

"He sorts the good from the useless. I go by how they treat him."

"You mean if your date doesn't like your dog—"

"It's a one-date string."

"Love me, love my dog, then?"

"Pretty much," he said again.

Gemma smiled, and she wasn't quite sure why. The Red Ridge K9 program had been a part of her life for as long as she could remember, yet she herself had never had a dog. And it had always been pounded home to her that these were working dogs, with a job to do, not pets.

As they reached his vehicle, Dante nodded back toward the building. "And if you hadn't reached out to him in there, I never would have taken a chance on you."

"So I needed his…stamp of approval?"

"In a way. If you couldn't get along with him, there was no point. It's a package deal. As I said, he's my partner."

"Smells like it," she said when he opened the big SUV to put the carriers in the back seat. He paused, gave her a look that said…she wasn't sure what. "I wasn't complaining," she said hastily, "It's not a bad smell. I just noticed."

"Most bloodhounds have their own scent. No getting rid of it." His mouth quirked. "Some people think it smells like Cheetos."

She laughed, the description instantly clicking. "So that's why I suddenly wanted something crunchy!"

He grinned at her, and it transformed him. In that moment when the worried, weary expression was gone, she realized it wasn't just that trim, muscled body that was attractive, that overall, Dante Mancuso was quite a package, dog partner not withstanding.

"You don't happen to have an engineering degree, do you?" he asked with a glance at the back seat of the vehicle.

"Um…no." She did, in fact, have a degree in business, at her father's insistence, but she'd never pursued the MBA he'd wanted her to. She hadn't wanted to end up like her sister Layla, with no other life except work. But that was not something she wanted to discuss. "Why?"

"Because that's what it takes to get these things fastened right," he muttered, lifting the first carrier into the seat and starting to wrestle with the seat belt. She saw a pile of things on the floor—a large stack of towels, a clipboard with some sort of checklist and, making her smile, a bag of dog treats. She guessed the things had once been on the seat itself, but all had been cleared for the new occupants.

She watched him finally get it done, picked up the other carrier—Zita of the pointed brow—and walked to the other side of the SUV.

"I think," she said as she lifted it in and began to copy his actions, "it'd be easier to just leave these in and put the babies in and out."

"Occurred to me," he said. "Now just figure out how

to maneuver both babies, their stuff and Flash into my condo without ever leaving any of them alone to get into trouble, and you'll have something."

She frowned. Straightened up and glanced at the dog, who had jumped heavily into the back of the vehicle. "Isn't he a little big to live in a condo?"

"Yes," Dante said, and it was clearly heartfelt. "That's why I spend hours at the dog park or in the hills with him on slow days. If he isn't worn-out by nightfall, he'll remodel it for me."

"You have to take him inside? He won't just follow you?"

"Always." His tone was dry. "Unless there's a scent trail too exciting to resist. Like a mouse having run by a week ago."

"It sounds," she said carefully, "like a lot of work."

"It is. But it's worth it." He looked the dog himself, and there was no mistaking the affection in his expression. "We've been working together for three years. He's put away more bad guys than any partner I've ever had. And he's saved a life for every one of those years."

Her eyes widened. "Really?"

He nodded. "Five lives, actually. Found a family of three lost hiking, just hours before they probably would have frozen to death. Found a guy who literally fell off a cliff, and a woman caught by a rock slide. Add in the burglar he found hiding in a tree, the armed robber he tracked to the storage room of a convenience store and all the evidence he's sniffed out and he's got a clearance rate we all envy. So he's worth the work and then some."

"Wow," she said, honestly awed. She'd known, of

course, how useful the animals were, but she'd never had an itemized list for a specific animal quoted to her before. "But now you have all the work of these two added on."

"And I have a feeling they're going to make Flash look like a cakewalk," he said wryly.

She looked at the two innocent faces, thought of the harried mothers she'd seen—and that was with just one baby. And she had a feeling he might be right.

What had she let herself in for?

Never mind. You said you'd do it and you will. This is the perfect chance to prove to Dev that he's wrong about you.

And once she'd accomplished that, things would happen just as she intended. Of course, Dante would have to find another nanny then, but at least he wouldn't be in such a panic. Oddly, that made her feel as good as the thought of her impending marriage—because she *would* get that all fixed up—to Devlin Harrington did.

"Oh."

It was all she said, but Dante read the undertone easily. "Not the big, ritzy place you expected to be living in?" he asked, an edge in his voice.

"It's fine," Gemma said, recovering. "Nice, even."

"Gee, thanks."

"It's just…small for four."

In fact, the condo, the front one of six in a remodeled brick building that had once been a warehouse, was spacious for what he'd paid for it. More importantly, it was only two blocks from the park with the fenced area for dogs and a couple of miles from both open range, the K9 training center and the PD. But ritzy it was not. The furniture had been chosen for comfort, not style, and there wasn't a lot of it, since Flash needed some room just to turn around. And while he wasn't a slob, he sometimes got in a hurry and tossed a shirt here or shoes there. Fortunately, there were only his hiking boots tossed in the entry today. And then he resented that he'd even thought the word *fortunately*. This was a job, not a date to be embarrassed in front of. She'd just have to take what there was, like it or not.

And he laughed inwardly at the very idea of dating a Colton. The Fenwick branch of the famous family was way out of his league. He liked the ranchers better, but Finn Colton was his boss, and he didn't fish in that pool. Not that there were any fish—Finn's sisters were both spoken for, anyway.

Who you kidding? You've got the most in common with Rusty Colton and the Pour House bunch. Same side of the tracks, that's where you're from.

Not that he didn't like Quinn, and feel bad at what she'd been through with the bombing near her father's dive bar. Or Brayden, a fellow K9 officer. And he admired Shane Colton, who'd gone through the hell of a wrongful murder conviction and had come out stronger and making a good thing of his life.

Of course, then there was Demi. Speaking of murder.

He wasn't assigned to the Groom Killer case that had the entire Red Ridge PD on edge. No one liked to admit Rusty Colton's youngest daughter, a tough girl with a hair-trigger temper that had likely gotten her into this worst kind of trouble, had managed to elude them for months now. But the first victim was her own ex; Demi had become the prime suspect in the murders of several grooms right before their weddings and was still at large.

He wasn't sorry not to be in that ugly mash-up. Besides, the Larson twins were giving him enough trouble. He'd stake his badge—and Flash's—on them being dirty as hell, but they were also smart and slick. They—

"—sleep?"

Dante snapped out of his reverie. "What?"

She gave him a rather odd look but repeated her question evenly enough. "Where are you going to have the babies sleep?"

"I…don't know. Last night I kept them in my room, in case they woke up and were scared, being in a strange place."

She looked surprised, first at him, then the twins. "Do you think they even realize?"

"I don't know. I just felt better, being close. A decision," he added sourly, "I came to regret about the eleventh time they woke me up."

"What did you do then?"

His mouth curved ruefully. "I let myself get played and ended up holding both of them the rest of the night."

That smile again. With a touch of surprise, perhaps at his admission. He was beyond being embarrassed at this point. Desperation did that to you.

"What do they sleep in at home?"

"I don't know." And he was getting damned tired of

having to say that. When she gave him an odd look, he shrugged. "I told you, my brother and I weren't…close."

"But he left you his children."

"Yeah." *He told me you were the only one he would trust. Because, he said, you were the only one who would see to them properly.* Mrs. Nelson's words echoed in his head, right next to the dull, tired ache behind his eyes. *Not doing so great so far, Dom.*

"So he trusted you to take care of them."

"My brother," he said carefully, "was never the most careful guy around."

Thankfully, she let it drop. She looked at the bag Mrs. Nelson had given him—diapers, wipes, powders and some other things that he had no idea what they were or were used for.

"Where are the rest of their things?" Gemma asked.

"The rest?" God, he was tired of feeling stupid. He was tired, period.

"Clothes, toys?"

"Oh. At home, I guess." She looked at him consideringly. As if she were trying to decide whether she should ask what was on her mind. "Go ahead," he said. "I can't feel any worse."

"All right," she said, briskly. "Where did they live?"

"Over on Brookside Drive."

"A house?"

He thought of the out-of-place building. "In a manner of speaking."

"Maybe it would be better to stay there, where all their things are, the place they know." He suppressed a shudder at the thought of living in that house. Apparently he didn't suppress it enough, because she said quietly, "When you said you and your brother weren't close, did you mean...estranged?"

He sighed. "I don't know what you'd call it. We spoke, but not often. And when we did, it almost always ended in an argument."

"So you didn't see eye to eye on much?"

"Anything," Dante said. "Or close enough." Why the hell was he telling her this? Just because she asked didn't mean he had to answer. "Look, that's got nothing to do with the job at hand."

She hesitated, then nodded. "All right. But you at least need to go there and get the rest of their stuff."

"Stuff..." They couldn't possibly need more than he'd already been lugging around, could they?

"Babies need a ton of it," she said. "I have two friends with babies, and I swear, they need a moving van to follow them around."

He found himself chuckling despite it all. He was feeling inept and incompetent, and neither were feelings he was used to; he'd worked too damned hard making sure they didn't apply to him. But that was his work, and this was something entirely different. This was... He didn't know what this was, besides life altering. In all senses of the phrase.

Chapter 9

"I can't face the idea of living in my dead brother's home," he said to Gemma, also realizing for the first time that he had no idea if Dom had even owned the place. He was guessing yes, because he couldn't see any landlord allowing the decor choices Agostina had made, but maybe it was somebody long-distance who had no idea. "But I guess I should go see what's there."

He wondered if he sounded as tired and lost as he felt. Apparently he did, because when she spoke again, it was in that same brisk tone. "When did you last eat?"

"I had toast this morning and grabbed an apple at lunch."

Her expression told him what she thought of that. "No wonder you can't think. You need to eat. Is there any food here?"

"Just some leftover steak from…before."

"It's a little early, but…" She looked thoughtful. "Any onions? Peppers?"

He frowned. "A half, I think, from the steak. And canned peppers."

"That'll do."

She set down her purse and strode toward the kitchen. He saw her look around, noting the block holding knives and the crockery pot full of other utensils he was too lazy to dig into a drawer for every time, even for the very basic cooking he did. She turned to the fridge and quickly found the rather large piece of steak; he always fixed two meals' worth because it saved him from cooking one night. Or grilling, at least, on the small patio out back. She also took out the half an onion.

"Skillet?"

"Under the cooktop."

She looked, pulled it out and set it on a burner. Then went back for the bottle of cooking oil he kept there, because it made the most sense to him.

"Seasonings?" she asked.

He shrugged. "Assuming you don't want cinnamon, I'm afraid salt and pepper is pretty much it. But there's garlic salt."

"The best kind," she said, grabbing the two containers.

"So…you cook."

She give him a sideways look. "Was that supposed to be a brilliant observation or an insult?"

He blinked, then shrugged. He'd been doing a lot of that lately. "Maybe just an assessment of further job skills."

To his surprise, she grinned at that. "You want a cook and a nanny?"

"Right now," he said with grim honesty, "I want to not be dealing with this."

"Can't blame you for that," she said, looking across to the dining alcove where the twins were ensconced on the table he'd found in a furniture store that had once been broken into. He'd gone back later, after Flash had tracked the small-time junkie who hadn't had time to blow the cash he'd stolen, and bought it, having to forestall the grateful owner from simply giving it to him. He'd liked it for the clean lines and solid feel, and the cheerful, bright colors of the mismatched cushions on the matching chairs.

"It's not that I don't...want them, or..."

He trailed off, shaking his head.

"I get it," she said. "How could anybody be ready for something like this dropping on them? Especially if you weren't close."

"It's not their fault," he said, feeling suddenly like he needed to defend those two innocent babes. "And... when I thought, this morning, that they really are connected to me, that we share DNA, it...was the weirdest feeling."

He half expected her to laugh at him. Or say something banal or full of false reassurance. Instead, to his surprise, as she began to heat the oil, she said, "I don't really cook. I have about a half dozen dishes I'm really good at, because our cook taught me. But outside of that, I'm hopeless."

Our cook. Of course. Why would Fenwick Colton's

daughter ever have to learn to cook? She would have had a cook on staff all the time and would expect that to continue.

"Well, six meals plus a night of takeout, and we're through a week of dinner," he said lightly.

Something in her smile made it belatedly hit him that she'd been returning honesty for honesty. He'd let out that weird feeling of connection he'd gotten, and she'd confessed she couldn't cook. Interesting, he thought, in much the same way he did when a suspect said something unexpected.

"You'd probably get tired of the same thing every week," she said as she chopped the onion with relative efficiency.

"Nah. I'm not picky."

She dumped the onions in the skillet. Then she picked up the can of peppers and looked around. He leaned over and opened a drawer, pulling out a can opener. She looked at it doubtfully, and he wondered if she'd ever even used a manual one. He took the can from her and applied the opener, then handed her back the can, hanging onto the sharp-edged lid. She turned to the sink and drained off some of the liquid, then added the rest of the contents to the skillet. It was already starting to smell edible, and his stomach rather fiercely—and loudly—reminded him he'd had only toast and that apple today.

She glanced at him, and he couldn't define the smile she gave him then. Nor the feeling it gave him.

"You might want to feed the babies while I'm fixing this. They're starting to fuss."

"Oh. Right. There's stuff in the bag Mrs. Nelson gave me."

And as he went to get them, he was thinking that Miss Gemma Colton was just full of surprises.

Gemma stared at the house as they pulled up. Dante hadn't been kidding when he said it stood out.

"No wonder you don't want to move in. If your place is your style, you'd never be happy here." He looked surprised but didn't speak, so she went on. "It might look at home in Florence, maybe on the outskirts of Rome, but here it just looks…garish."

"I think that's what she was going for. The Italian part, not the garish," he added hastily, as if he'd just remembered the woman he was speaking of was dead.

"You have a key?"

"I do now," he said. They each took one of the baby carriers, and as they walked toward the big, heavy front door, she pondered all the layers in that answer. He did now, so he hadn't before. Not even in case of emergency? She guessed most people with a first responder for a relative would choose that person to have access in case of emergencies. Who better? So apparently Dante had been serious when he'd said they weren't close.

And yet his brother had left him his children. Officially, he'd explained on the way over here, according to his brother's attorney.

They'd left Flash at his place for this trip, and she'd had to smother a smile at how he'd explained to the dog why.

"May need the space in the way back for...stuff, buddy, so you need to stay here."

"You think he understands?" she'd teased.

"Don't know," he'd answered. "What I do know is that if I don't tell him, when we get back it'll look like a bomb went off."

She'd looked from him to the dog and back. "I don't know why you think you don't know anything about handling a baby."

He'd looked startled, but then he'd grinned at her.

Dante Mancuso had a killer grin.

She could admit that, she told herself. Just because she loved and was going to marry Dev didn't mean she couldn't notice that other men existed. And that some of them were great looking. Or really built. Or had killer grins.

Some even had all three.

"Gemma?"

His voice snapped her out of the memory, and to her own irritation she felt herself flush slightly. There was no reason for that—her thoughts had been perfectly normal.

He'd opened the front door and was holding it for her. She stepped inside, and the illusion of stepping into another world was complete. The pattern of statues of marble and other materials continued inside. She glanced at the twins, who were quiet. Because they were happier here? She looked back at Dante and decided not to bring that up.

"Your sister-in-law did all this?" At his nod, she said, "She must have really missed Italy."

"Far as I know, she'd never even flown over it."

Gemma's brows rose. "She did a lot of research, then."

"I guess," Dante said, looking around as if he'd never thought about it that way.

"Was it your brother, then, who wanted the style?"

"I don't think so. He never cared much. And he liked keeping things…inconspicuous."

Her brows rose. "This is hardly that."

"Exactly." She thought she saw his jaw tighten before he said, "My brother didn't like drawing attention because his dealings weren't always on the up-and-up." He grimaced. "Just like the rest of the family."

She studied him for a moment. Obviously this wasn't something he tried to keep secret or he wouldn't have told her, someone he'd just met this afternoon. "And yet you became a police officer."

"I always was the misfit," he said drily.

She laughed at that, but she wasn't certain he'd meant it to be funny. "Then maybe they're lucky they ended up with you."

He stared at her, looking suddenly thoughtful. She turned and walked through the elaborate house to a room in the back. Here the decor was more typically a nursery, although a bit heavy on the pink frills. She took out her phone and checked the screen, then went around picking items he in turn stacked near the door.

"You made a list?" he asked.

"I didn't want to forget anything important," she said. He didn't need to know she'd sent a desperate text to Juliette asking what the essentials were. The list she'd sent back seemed impossibly long; how could such tiny beings require so much? The pile grew. Diapers, wipes, lotions, ointments, powders—it seemed endless. She found one of the diaper bags she'd feared—bright pink again, with huge purple flowers—and filled it, vowing to replace it at the earliest opportunity.

At last it was down to the big things.

"The twins slept together?" she asked, looking at the single crib.

"I don't know." He jammed a hand through his hair. Nice hair, she thought. She bet it felt good to touch. Dev kept his so short she'd forgotten what it felt like to—

Stop it! What are you doing?

"If there's no second child's room, they must have," she said.

"I don't know," he repeated. "And I'm getting damned tired of saying that."

She looked at him, saw the frustration in his dark eyes. Nice eyes, too, with the annoyingly long, thick lashes some guys were blessed with.

Stop it!

"Then do something," she said, her own rebellious thoughts putting an edge in her voice she hadn't meant to show. "Go make sure there isn't a separate room." She glanced at the list on her phone. "And see if there's a playpen somewhere. And we'll need to find the rest of their bottles and such." Something else Juliette had said hit her. "I hope she wasn't breastfeeding too, or this will be even harder."

He turned on his heel and left without a word. With him went the odd tension she'd been feeling. Which was strange, because she'd thought it was the insanity of what she'd done that had her so stressed. Surely the enormity of taking on two babies—she glanced at the girls, who seemed content in what were familiar surroundings—was enough to stress anyone.

She crossed the room and opened the closet. It was stuffed with frilly pink things, mostly matching sets. The Mancusos apparently had really gone in for the identical part. She wondered how the girls would feel, later, when they grew up a little. Would they want to keep that identical thing going, maybe enjoy fooling people? Or would they reach a stage where each wanted to be an individual, different from her sister?

She didn't want to think about what might happen if one wanted to cling to the matching and one didn't.

"Don't invent trouble that hasn't happened yet," she muttered to herself as she selected clothes, mostly play things, although a couple of the adorable frilly dresses made the cut as well.

"I found something that looks like the pen they kept Flash in when he was a pup." His voice came from the doorway.

She laughed at the bemused tone in his voice. "That must be it."

"Load it up?"

"Load it up."

He nodded. Looked at the crib. "In the master bedroom it looked like they had them in there at night, at one point. There's a basket-looking thing in there."

"Probably, when they first came home." She tried to

sound knowledgeable. "They say to keep them close at first."

"Found some canned stuff, labeled formula. Is that food?"

"Yes. And a relief," she said, meaning it, "that they're already used to it."

"Bunch of baby bottles, too. I didn't see much actual baby food, though. A few jars."

"They may be just starting on solid food. They're about the age for that, along with their own room." *Thanks again, Juliette.*

He just looked at her for a moment. He didn't speak, but she could almost see him reassessing, thinking that she knew more than he'd thought she did.

"I found something else, too," she said, pointing to the tall dresser in the corner. He glanced over, his brows lowering as he spotted the set of three framed photographs. He took two steps that direction, then stopped. Stared. She saw the moment he realized the pictures were of each of the newly born twins and...him. As if his brother had wanted Dante's face to be familiar to them.

He turned on his heel and came back. She couldn't read his expression, and he didn't speak until he shifted his gaze to the crib.

"Guess I need to break that down."

"Yes. Oh, and I found the double stroller," she said, gesturing toward the corner of the room.

"I'll get it."

"You'll have to figure out where you're going to put everything."

He looked around the room, eyes slightly unfocused, as if he were seeing the whole house in his mind.

"I can't," he said softly. "I know it would make more sense, but I can't."

She knew he meant live here. "I understand. Losing your brother and sister-in-law like that, and—"

"There are other reasons not to stay here," he said, suddenly back to the sharp focus of a cop. "I'll start on the crib."

"I'll gather up the food and bottles."

And as she did she thought about his reaction to seeing that picture—his own picture—in his nieces' room.

Chapter 10

It took every inch of cargo space in the back of his big SUV. He had studied the pile for a moment and then begun packing it in, very efficiently using up the space. He only had to rearrange something twice, which she thought rather amazing given the varying sizes and awkward shapes they were dealing with. Last to go was a large box full of various toys, which he looked at for a moment. Then he looked at her.

"There was a ton more," he said. "How'd you choose?"

She shrugged. "I just held each one up in front of them and packed the ones that brought the most smiles and giggles."

The slow smile that curved his mouth made her feel a warmth inside that was unlike anything she'd felt before. That smile held a sort of approval, appreciation and acknowledgment she didn't think she'd ever seen aimed at her before. She had gotten all three after a successful charity gala came off well, or a fund-raiser made the goal, but that had never made her feel the way Dante's smile did.

And somehow that rattled her more than even taking care of two six-month-old babies.

She worked, Dante thought, harder than he ever thought she would. Helping him lug all the stuff into the condo, moving it around and all the while somehow managing to keep the twins from causing chaos, by decibel level if nothing else. She talked to them constantly as she went, in that same light, chatty tone that had intrigued them in his office, and it continued to work now.

He supposed he should have known. Her siblings, full and half, were no slouches. Blake had built his own fortune, Patience was a dedicated vet to the Red Ridge K9s, Bea ran a successful bridal salon—or at least, she had until all these groom killings had started—and Layla was a VP at Colton Energy, and word was it was not nepotism; she was hands-on and very good.

But word had also been that Gemma, the youngest, was more than a bit spoiled and had only dabbled here and there. But then she began fund-raising for her various animal charities and had apparently found her calling. Since she'd raised a great deal of money for the K9 unit in particular, Dante figured he owed her respect if nothing else. Not to mention she did a job he would hate to do.

Once they had everything inside, his condo seemed

to have shrunk by half. And Flash was looking very aggrieved.

"Sorry, buddy," he said softly to the dog, who gave him a pained look. "Neither one of us is cut out for this, are we?"

"And yet you're doing it." Gemma had come up behind him. He'd known it, from Flash's glance and his own innate cop-honed awareness of his surroundings, plus there was that just enough scent of something flowery, spicy...something.

Something that likely costs hundreds per bottle, he reminded himself, hoping it would quash the odd reaction he had to it.

It didn't.

He turned on her then, letting a bit of the edginess he was feeling into his voice. "I'm their uncle. That's why I'm doing this" *No other choice.* "Why are you?"

"I told you, for the experience."

"And why do you need the experience of—" he gestured at the chaos around them, including the two babies in the playpen they'd set up and put them in first thing "—this?"

"Maybe I'm just curious."

"And maybe that's not a good enough reason. If this is just some rich girl's whim that you're going to get over by tomorrow—"

"I am a rich girl," she said, admitting it so easily he was surprised into silence. "A trust-fund baby, and a few other names people throw around. It would be silly to deny it," she added, as if she'd read his thoughts. "But this is not a whim. I need to do this, to prove I can be a good mother. When the time comes," she added, a little hastily.

He studied her for a moment before he said softly, "Prove to who?"

She studied him in turn, then took in quick breath. "My boyfriend."

His brow furrowed. He'd heard something, mentioned in passing, about a Harrington and a Colton. But he thought it had been Hamlin Harrington, the head of Harrington Incorporated. He couldn't believe it. The guy had to be at least sixty. Only one reason he knew why a woman her age would marry a man that much older than her. But she was no gold digger—she didn't have to be.

"Not the old man," he said in disbelief.

"No!" she exclaimed. "That's my—" She broke off, apparently thinking better of what she'd been going to say. Instead she said in a bit of a rush, "My boyfriend is Devlin, his son. And his father insists he have kids. So the company will always be in family hands."

Dante had never met either Harrington, had only seen pictures in the *Gazette*, and once in person when the senior Harrington arrived at that fund-raiser where he and Flash had had to put in an appearance. He wondered now if Gemma had been there that night. Wondered how he could have missed her if she had been—she was the kind of woman who drew all the light in a room.

"Anyway," Gemma said, sounding in a rush to get it out now, "Dev has this silly idea I wouldn't be a good mom, the hands-on kind he wants. So I have to show him he's wrong. Then we'll get back together and everything will be like it's supposed to be."

He stared at her, a little stunned. "Wait. Are you saying he...broke up with you because he didn't think you would be a good mother to kids that don't exist yet?"

He saw a tinge of color rising in her cheeks. "He's wrong," she said, rather urgently. "And he'll see that. And then we'll get married and someday have those kids."

"And you're all right with that?"

She frowned. "What do you mean?"

"Gemma, you can earn respect. Admiration. Even caring. But you should never have to *earn* love."

"It's not like that, it's just—"

"Sounds like it to me. Like you have to prove to him you're worthy before he'll deign to love you."

"Dev loves me! And I love him."

He just looked at her.

"He does," she insisted. "It's just his father's expectations that messed things up."

"Because he let them. You're setting yourself up for a broken heart, Gemma."

"What do you know about it?" she snapped.

"I know a bit about family expectations. And going against them."

"This is different," she insisted.

"Why? Because it's you, and you're special?"

She looked stung. With reason, he thought. That had come out a little snarky.

"You're awfully free with advice, Mr. Mancuso," she

said coolly. "Where's your girlfriend or wife helping you out with this, if you've got this all solved?"

"Not something I'm looking for," he said, his tone equally cool.

"Might want to rethink that," she said, gesturing at the twins who were, oddly, trying to pass a stuffed unicorn back and forth, with great concentration.

"Getting married just to have someone to help take care of them would be the worst thing I could do for them. And that wife." Her brow furrowed. He added, his tone carefully measured now, "Not to mention the insult to that woman if, for instance, I asked her to prove she could take care of them before I'd marry her."

"That would be..."

Her voice trailed off, and he knew she'd seen the parallel.

"I rest my case," he said.

"Why don't you just mind your own business?"

"Why don't you—"

In unison the twins wailed, and he had the sinking feeling it was because their voices had gone up a bit. Guilt flooded him. He started to move, but Gemma beat him to the girls and picked one up. He grabbed the other and hoisted her to his chest. It only made the wailing more piercing. He patted her, bounced her, everything he'd ever seen a parent do. Nothing. He held her back a little, looked at her scrunched-up, unhappy face. Zita of the pointed brow, he noticed. Realized he was grateful to Gemma for noticing that, no matter what.

Lucia calmed first as Gemma cooed to her. He half expected her to shoot him a triumphant glare, but she didn't. She merely came over to him, standing close enough that Lucia could reach out to her sister. Zita seemed to realize she was now wailing alone, and the volume decreased slightly. Lucia leaned out in Gemma's arms, her tiny hand flailing a bit, but looking for all the world as if she were patting her sister's arm. The wailing subsided into a hiccuping of sorts, then into silence as Zita reached for her sister's hand.

When it was quiet again, Dante looked at Gemma and said, "Thanks."

"My job," she said brightly, patting Lucia's chubby cheek.

"Still," he said.

She gave him a smile that lightened his guilt that they'd set the girls crying. "Maybe you could put that crib back together? It's probably getting close to time to put them down."

"Where should I put it?"

"Where do you want them?"

"I don't know." He groaned as soon as he said it. Rubbed at eyes that felt as if he hadn't slept in a week.

"Maybe you should shorten it to *IDK*."

His gaze shot to her face. She was clearly suppressing a laugh. And suddenly the pressure lessened.

"Well, I don't," he said, but he was shaking his head ruefully.

She looked at him curiously then. "When that someday came, when you'd have kids, how did you imagine it? What kind of relationship?"

The words were out before he thought. "Better than I had with my father."

For a moment she looked away, but then she shifted her gaze back to his face. "Well, then. We have some common ground."

The simple declaration relieved him much more than it probably should have. Considering he had no idea how to accomplish that goal.

"Where are they now, your parents?"

"Dead. A while ago now. We weren't close, either." *And for the same reason.*

"I had a nanny," she said, and it seemed almost a non sequitur until he realized it wasn't, really. "I saw my parents rarely, maybe a couple of times a week. And when I did, they were always going somewhere. So Mrs. Hicks, the nanny, was the closest thing to a parent I had. Then my parents got divorced, Dad bought me in the deal and—"

"Bought you?" The way she'd put it startled him.

She shrugged. "I was still young enough to be useful when he needed to put on the solid-family-man image. And my mother didn't care. I got a huge trust fund that nobody else can touch, and she got a nice payout and went off to live in… Majorca or someplace."

Dante let out a low whistle. "And I thought my family was bad."

She smiled, as if her description hadn't been the coldest thing he'd heard in a while. "I wasn't supposed to mind, because we were rich and I could have anything."

"Almost anything."

"Some things you can't buy, isn't that what they say? Like love?"

"Yes." He studied her for a moment, then decided to

risk it. "And sometimes the price isn't money. Sometimes it's…doing what someone else thinks you should, whether it's right for you or not."

Something flashed in her dark brown eyes. Temper, maybe. "Let's not talk about Dev again."

He shrugged. "I meant my brother, who thought I should give up this stupid cop idea and settle down into the family business. And when I wouldn't—couldn't—he pretty much disowned me."

"Oh." She looked abashed. But she held his gaze as she said, "And yet…" and waved toward the girls.

"Yeah. And yet."

"So…he didn't love you, but he trusted you?"

"Apparently."

"Did he ever understand? Why you became a cop?"

"No. And I gave up trying to get him to."

She sighed. "I envy you that. I can't seem to give up trying to win over my father."

And your boyfriend.

He managed not to say it. But in the silence she stared at his face, and he realized he might as well have shouted it.

He shook his head. "You were right. It's none of my business."

"True." She gave him a faint smile. "But I appreciate the concern." She glanced around at the gathered things once more. "And we are no closer to a working arrangement, are we?"

"Options," he muttered. "The master, the guest room or the den, which right now is my office. That's pretty much it. So it's just deciding what will work best."

She lifted a brow at him. "You'd give up your room?"

"I can sleep anywhere. If," he added wryly, "they'll sleep."

"I suppose what I should really ask is, do you want to be involved at all?"

"What?"

"Do you want to be involved hands-on with them, or would you prefer they just be presented to you periodically, clean and tidy, for inspection and conversation?"

He thought he might be gaping at her. "Inspection and conversation?"

"True, they're not talking yet, but they seem to like to pretend they are, which is the first step, I think. They—"

"I get that, but…inspection? Is that what you had to do?"

"In a manner of speaking, yes."

Dante shook his head. And a moment later he was laughing, he couldn't help it. "And to think I used to envy you Colton kids."

She colored up rather brightly this time. But when she spoke it was brisk again. "If you would rather not be bothered, I would suggest putting them in the guest room, with me. It might be a setback, however, in their sleeping through the night on their own."

He didn't like the way she said "rather not be bothered." He hadn't wanted this, certainly hadn't had it in his game plan, but now that it had happened, he didn't want Zita and Lucia growing up thinking they were a bother.

"What about the den?" he said. "Then we could both get to them, if necessary."

"But you said you have an office in there."

"It's just one corner, and I can move the laptop out of there if I need to. There's a pocket door so it can be closed off. And it's between my room and the guest room, so at least one of us would likely hear them in the night."

After a moment, she nodded. Then she looked at him. With that smile again. The genuine one. Not the practiced one he would have expected, the kind he'd always classified as that "heiress" smile, smooth, polished and utterly fake.

"I think we have a plan."

Dante smiled back. He couldn't quite believe how relieved he felt. He might not be sure how good she would be at this, but she couldn't be any worse than he was, so that counted for something. And no longer being alone to deal with this counted for a lot more.

He was still smiling as, just as he had finished getting the crib together and was putting it in the den, his cell rang. He pulled it out and saw it was his boss, Finn Colton. The chief was a hands-on guy and worked all shifts to, as he said, keep his hand in, so it wasn't so unusual that he was calling after hours.

"Mancuso," he said.

"How's the daddy thing going? My cousin any help?"

"Word gets around fast," Dante said drily.

"I won't mention the betting pools already starting on how long she'll last."

Dante looked through the doorway to where Gemma was changing the girls into pajamas, or whatever it was they slept in—she seemed to know. "She might surprise you."

"Hope so, for your sake."

"So…you didn't call just to check on my domestic situation, did you?"

"Afraid not. That phone you found in the bag of flour? With the text to one of the Larsons' known numbers?"

He could hardly forget that long-sought prize bit of evidence that could be the key to bringing the Larson brothers down, no matter how his life had been turned upside down since. "Yeah?"

"It's gone."

Dante blinked. "What? It should be in the evidence room. Duke and his partner booked it in for me after the…accident."

"I know. And Ron remembers them doing it and where he put it. But it's now missing."

The property officer, Ron Fox, was organized to the point of obsessiveness and never made mistakes. "But no one has access to that room except…"

"Exactly," Finn said grimly.

Dante swore, low and harsh. "One of us?"

"Seems it has to be."

Great. Just what they needed. A crooked cop.

Chapter 11

Gemma looked up from the list—yet another—she was making on her phone of things she'd need to bring here from home. Her new boss was brooding again. Sitting in the chair opposite the gas fireplace, he was staring into the flames. His long legs were stretched out before him, his elbows on the arms of the chair and his fingers steepled before him. He looked dark, intense and totally at odds with what Juliette had told her.

Dante's a good guy. Everybody likes him. He came up the hard way, from the wrong side of town. He's all the more honest because of it, and people admire that. He's tough because he's had to be, but he's the first guy you go to if you need a favor.

To her, that said a lot.

But right now, nice guy Mancuso looked more like

a man with a mission. Odd, how she could tell it wasn't the twins—who, after an uncertain start in the strange room, had settled down the moment they were in their crib together—on his mind right now. The atmosphere around him was completely different; there was nothing hesitant or uncertain about this man. This man was focused and intent...and angry. It was suppressed, but she could see it in the set of his jaw, the tight cords of his neck, the dark, lowered eyebrows.

This wasn't the guy who'd just become, for all intents and purposes, the father of two baby girls and was floundering.

This was the cop.

She took advantage of his absorption to study him for a moment longer. She noticed again his thick, dark hair, wondered if whoever his stylist was had instinctively known how to cut it to get it to look so perfect. Then she remembered how she'd seen him shove his fingers through it several times, and concluded he probably went to some old-school barber and that was just the way his hair grew. Another unfairness, she thought, along with those impossible eyelashes. And he was clearly a guy who could shave in the morning and have that roughly attractive stubble by late afternoon. She'd always thought she preferred men clean shaven, but she might have to reconsider that.

As she watched he tapped his steepled forefingers against his lips, clearly still deep in thought.

Yeah, those lips, too. What a mouth.

He jolted her out of cataloging of his assets by lifting his gaze suddenly and locking onto her, as if he'd somehow sensed her scrutiny. Maybe he had, with some weird sixth sense cops had.

"Bad news?" she asked rather hastily, needing to distract him before he came right out and asked why she'd been staring at him.

He frowned. "What?"

"That phone call. You've been a bit...preoccupied ever since."

"Oh. Yes. Work."

"The twins seem to have settled in."

"Yes."

"Would you be all right with them for a while?"

The frown came back. "Bailing on us already?"

She found it interesting that he was already calling himself and the girls "us." She was finding a lot about this man interesting. But that's all it was. She was curious about the guy she was now working for, and that was only natural, right?

"I need to go home and get some things. Clothes and stuff."

His gaze slid down her body. For an instant she thought—with a smothered gasp of what she was certain was outrage—that he was checking her out.

"Better shoes," he said when his perusal got to her feet, blasting that idea right out of her head.

Better shoes? She couldn't help glancing at his feet and the worn pair of black military-style boots he wore. What did he know about shoes? These were $600 pumps she'd bought at a designer boutique in San Francisco!

"Wouldn't want you falling off those stilts while you're carrying the girls," he drawled.

She blinked. He hadn't had a drawl before, had he? And then she met his eyes, saw the glint of humor there. And the calculation. As if he was waiting to see how she'd take it.

She realized the corners of her mouth were twitching. Felt a matching humor rising. He did have a point, after all. She was used to heels, but she was not used to heels while carrying two tiny squirming bundles that tended to throw her off balance.

"I'm thinking steel-toed construction boots," she said with an echoing drawl. "That jar Lucia knocked over onto my foot hurt."

"Coulda been worse." He was grinning now, and she couldn't help it—she laughed.

"Yep. The jar could have broken and I'd have a real mess to clean up." She wrinkled her nose. "Ew. Mashed peas."

He laughed in turn, and the seriousness of the last half hour or so vanished. For a moment they just looked at each other, and Gemma became oddly aware of her own breathing, her own heartbeat. She didn't know why, nor did she understand the odd sensation stealing over her—a strange combination of heat and chill that made the back of her neck tingle.

Just as the silence became unbearable, he spoke. Softly. "Go get what you need. We'll be okay."

She nodded, glad of the break in this unexpected tension. She stood up. "I won't be long."

He rose, too. Walked over to the kitchen, opened a drawer and pulled out a key on a ring with a small metal animal attached. He came back and held it out to her.

"A coyote?" she asked, looking at the ornament.

"It is the state animal, after all." He gave her a crooked smile. "Besides, I kind of admire their adaptability." He drew back at his own words. Glanced toward the den. "Guess I need to work on that myself."

She took the key. "I'll return it when I get back."

He shook his head. "Keep it. You'll need to be able to come and go on your own. And I'll show you how the alarm system works."

"Just like that, you give me a key and the alarm code?"

He gave her a startled look, then laughed. "You going to steal something? I don't have anything Fenwick Colton's daughter would want."

She barely managed not to retort, "Don't be so sure," and spent the entire drive back to her own condo wondering what on earth was wrong with her.

Sleep. He needed sleep. That had to be it. The only explanation for the crazy way he'd felt when he'd looked up to see Gemma staring at him. Because for a moment there, he'd thought she hadn't been looking at him like he was the guy she now worked for.

He shook his head, hoping to clear out…whatever this was. He'd been told, more than once, that he could get pretty intense when deep into a case. And nothing could be deeper than finding out that someone at Red Ridge PD was dirty. Hell, that was probably why she'd been staring at him, afraid he was going to explode or something. Now that was an explanation that made sense. As much as anything could to his weary brain right now.

He rubbed at his eyes. It didn't help much.

So he started to chew on it. Like Flash on a bone, he worked on it awhile, turned it over and started again on a fresh spot. Over and over. But no matter what angle he looked at, the crux of it stayed the same. The Larsons had gotten to somebody. Whether it was a payoff or coercion, whether they'd offered someone so much they couldn't refuse or had something on somebody or threatened someone they loved, the end result was the same. Whether it was a onetime threat or bribe, or they had somebody inside already on their payroll, it was still the same. Whoever it was had stolen the one piece of evidence they had that connected the Larson brothers to the criminal web he knew in his gut they ran.

He hated the whole idea. Hated what it meant to the trust they all had to have in each other. Hated the thought of having to look at everyone he relied on to have his back and wonder which one had gone bad.

He was way down in the rabbit hole when his cell rang. Yanked back to reality, he picked it up. The boss again. Maybe it had all been a mistake, the phone just misplaced?

Wondering when he'd started believing in fairy tales, he answered rather sourly.

"Mancuso."

"You sound like I feel."

"I'll bet."

"I'm pulling you off the Larsons," Finn said bluntly.

Dante blinked. This made no sense. He was deeper into that case than anyone—he had more contacts, informants and threads to follow, so he couldn't just stand down. Even if the only concrete evidence they'd found so far was suddenly missing. He knew Finn Colton wouldn't give up that easily. But the chief also didn't make capricious decisions, so he waited. Silently.

"No protest?"

"I have a loud one. Just waiting to hear your reasoning."

Finn laughed. "Don't think I don't know that's a compliment. And I'm about to give you one, although you probably won't think so."

He already didn't, but again he merely waited.

"Look, you need time to…adjust to being a guardian to those girls. Am I wrong in thinking you haven't had much contact with them before now?"

His nearly nonexistent relationship with his brother was hardly a secret—in fact, he'd made a point of being sure everyone knew it, because everyone also knew Dominic had had his fingers in a lot of unsavory places.

"No," Dante said warily, wondering where this was heading.

"Okay, then, like I said, you need time with them, to get your life rearranged."

"That," he said drily, "is an understatement." And Finn would know, given the turn his own life had recently taken. Setting up a fake relationship to try and smoke out the Groom Killer and to see that turn into the real thing had to be…as crazy as hiring a Colton heiress as a nanny.

"So, officially, you're now on half days."

Dante went still. "Officially?" Was Finn implying

there was an unofficial purpose to all this, some off-the-record op?

"And work those half days from home. You can still show up here when you need to, but bond with those girls."

Dante held the phone away from his ear for a moment, looking at it, wondering if he was hearing right. Then, carefully, he put it back and asked, "If you're pulling me off the Larsons…work on what?"

"Finding who's dirty."

For an instant he couldn't breathe. Him? "Isn't that what IA is for?"

"Eventually. But I'd much rather present Internal Affairs with an already-cornered rat."

"Chief—"

"You've got the perfect cover. You really do need the time to get your life reordered. Nobody will question that. And if you're off the Larson case, their rat might be less careful around you."

He couldn't deny it made a certain amount of sense.

He also couldn't deny the last thing he wanted was to be digging around in the lives of his friends and colleagues, looking for dirt.

"I know it sucks, Mancuso. But it has to be done. And now, before word gets out about the phone going missing. Right now only you, Ron Fox and I know. We've got to use that."

Dante drew in a deep breath. "Yes, sir."

"Run everything through me. You can use Parsons for routine stuff—she can keep her mouth shut." Dante knew the department's tech whiz could and would do exactly that. "Whatever else you need, let me make the request. I've already got the feed from the evidence room cameras. I'll send it to you."

"Copy."

"Anyone asks, you're working on the Groom Killer, because we need more bodies on it and I decided the Larsons could wait."

"Yes, sir." He thought rapidly. "I'll bring Flash in. Have him take a sniff around the evidence locker the phone was in. That way it'll be cataloged in that brain of his."

"Good idea. Whatever it takes, you find him. I don't like people dirtying our house."

"Agreed," Dante said, wholeheartedly this time.

"Oh, and Mancuso?"

"Sir?"

"Here's the real compliment. Next time that sergeants' test is up? Take it."

Dante was still staring at the phone when he heard the key in the lock. He was so taken aback by this turn of affairs that the sound startled him.

And suddenly another side of this new arrangement hit him, and it was almost as troublesome.

He was going to be spending a lot more time around Gemma Colton than he'd planned on.

Chapter 12

None of this was going as she'd expected, Gemma thought.

When Dante had told her he'd been put on half days at home until he was settled in with the babies, she'd almost expected him to say he didn't need a nanny after all.

She was surprised at the depth of her disappointment at the thought. And not just because she would lose her chance to prove Dev wrong; she'd been looking forward to getting to know those two tiny girls, how they were the same, how they were different. She had already planned to use their nap times to do internet searches for all the information she could find on raising twins. And tomorrow she'd planned on calling Mrs. Moncrief, one of the big donors she'd lined up for the K9 unit fund-raiser last year, who had mentioned she had twin grandsons. But now, if Dante didn't need help...

He quickly disabused her of that notion.

"I'll still need time to work, and sometimes I'll have to go check something out. Plus there's Flash—he needs his routine, too."

"Routine?"

"Yes. If we're not on a case, of course. If we are, it all goes out the window."

"What's his...routine?"

"To the dog park first thing in the morning. Half hour at least of sniffing and chasing."

"And bathrooming?" Gemma suggested wryly.

"That, too," Dante said with a half shrug. "He'll use the patio in an emergency, but he thinks it's undignified."

Gemma smothered a laugh, half at what he'd said and half at the fact that he was obviously serious. She glanced at Flash and realized if there was a dog who could do a pained-with-the-indignity-of-it expression, it was probably this one.

"Anyway," he went on, "the park's a lot easier, with the bag station right there to clean up. Then home and breakfast. Another longer foray midday, or a stop at the training center for an off-leash run if I can fit it in. Then a good, long tug-of-war session before dinner. Then back to the park once more at night, and he's good."

He said it so matter-of-factly she felt compelled to say, "He's almost as much work as the babies."

"Nah. No diapers. Do have to wash his face a lot, though."

She blinked. "What?"

"Those wrinkles serve a purpose in his work, but they also have to be kept really clean. And he's not a… er, tidy eater. Or drinker."

She glanced toward the kitchen. "Hence the big rain mat under his water and food bowls?"

"Exactly."

She looked back at him. "You don't have two kids, you have three."

He blinked, then smiled wryly. "I guess I do. And this one drools more."

"The towel," she said, realizing suddenly. "That's why you have all those towels in the car, and one in your back pocket." She said it before she realized he might ask why she'd been looking at his back pockets. And the only answer she had—that she'd been ogling his backside because it was a particularly fine one— would embarrass them both.

But he didn't even blink. He laughed. As if it had never occurred to him she might be appreciating. Which interested her even more.

"You mean the one that makes me look like I work in an old-time gas station? Pretty much. Half my laundry's his." Then, with a sideways look at her, he asked, "Want to change your mind?"

She looked at Flash again. "Is he my responsibility, too?"

"Nah. He's mine. And if anything happens, everybody knows to see that he gets to the training center. Patience will look after him. Or Micah Shaw, the other bloodhound handler. Flash and Chunk get along fine."

"Okay."

Belatedly the real meaning of what he'd just said hit her. *If anything happens.* He meant if anything happened to him. And he was a cop, so that was more than a throwaway comment—it was a genuine possibility.

"What?" he asked, and she realized she was staring at him.

"Nothing," she said hastily, looking away.

But her realization stayed with her, and most of the time when she was unpacking her things in the small but workable guest room, she was wondering why on earth anyone would pick this job, what it was about some people that led them to put their life on the line so others could not think about the ugliness in life. She was guiltier than most, she supposed—her upbringing had sheltered her from most of that. The K9 unit had always been on the periphery of her life, but she'd never thought about the real nitty-gritty of it all.

And the idea of Dante getting hurt—or worse—was unsettling in a way she didn't quite understand.

It must be the idea of the twins being orphaned all over again. Who would take them then? Was there other family? Dante had said they all skated on the wrong side of the law, so could they be trusted with those two precious babies? He'd thought about what would happen to Flash but probably hadn't even had time to think about what would happen to the babies.

She dropped the sweater she'd been about to slip into a drawer on the bed and walked back out to the living room. Dante was on the couch, his laptop on his outstretched legs. She saw some kind of video running, although it was in black and white and oddly choppy. The moment he realized she was there—which was the instant she stepped out of the hallway—he hit a key and blanked the screen.

He'd obviously retrieved the computer from the den, so she asked first, "Are they still asleep?"

He looked up. "Yes. Thankfully."

She nodded, hesitated.

"Problem?" he asked. "Room not grand enough?"

She stiffened. Glared at him. "That was nasty. And uncalled-for."

She saw him let out a breath. "You're right. Sorry. I guess I'm a little on edge."

"With reason," she said, surprised that he'd apologized so easily. Dev never, ever apologized. He'd buy flowers or take her to dinner, but he never actually said the words. It didn't matter, she always told herself. He was showing it, not saying it, and that was more important anyway. Wasn't it?

"There are bath towels in the cabinet in the bathroom," he said.

"I saw. Am I sharing them with the dog?"

He laughed. "No, that's too much closeness even for me. I keep his separate."

"Will he be insulted if I say that's a relief?"

"I doubt it." He tilted his head, looked at her curiously. "Have you ever had a dog?"

"Not really. I've been around them but not had one of my own."

"Cat?"

"No."

She managed not to say she hated the shedding, fur all over her clothes. She wouldn't have even hesitated to say it before, even if it did sound a bit prissy, but she found she didn't want him to thank that of her. She wondered if Flash shed. She supposed so—almost all dogs did, didn't they?

"Prepare for a shedding storm, then," Dante said, startling her. This wasn't the first time he'd echoed her actual thoughts. Was the guy a mind reader? Or was this some kind of cop trick? "And I'd suggest you not sit there," he added, gesturing at the large, overstuffed chair nearest the fireplace. "It's that color for a reason. It's his."

"Oh." That was kind of sweet, actually. And it did almost match the dark color of most of Flash's coat. "I didn't know. I haven't seen him in it."

"He's not comfortable enough yet, what with all the changes. The girls, you," he said. "He wants to be on the ground, where he can move more quickly."

She glanced at the big dog, who at the moment was on the floor near the doorway to the den. He didn't look like he would do anything quickly.

"Yeah," Dante said, "I know he looks like a lump, and he'd lick you to death sooner than bite you, but he can move when he wants to."

"Good to know," she said rather faintly.

"He's not used to sharing his space." He gave her a slightly wary look. "And frankly, neither am I. So if I seem a little jumpy, that's why."

"It is…going to be close quarters," she said carefully.

"When things level out a bit and I get a handle

on dealing with the twins, you'll get some time off," he said, as if he were trying to sound encouraging. "Enough to go see friends, or go shopping or whatever."

She didn't get angry; it wasn't the first time she'd encountered this assumption of what her life must consist of. It seemed almost universal, that concept of the life of a twenty-six-year-old heiress. And up until she'd started to work on the fund-raisers, she couldn't deny it was close to the truth. And he was so sincere about assuring her it wouldn't always be this chaotic, she couldn't help but tease him a little.

"And when might that happen?"

He looked as if he were actually calculating, as if there were some kind of formula that would work when there were two—no, three, sorry, Flash—other beings with their own ideas involved.

"A couple of weeks, maybe?" he finally said.

"You sure about that?"

His mouth quirked. "Hopeful?" he suggested.

"Overly optimistic," she suggested in turn.

He let out an audible sigh. "Probably."

"Don't panic until, say, six months. If you haven't gotten it together by then, you may need to get a real mom."

She said it with all seriousness, but he finally heard the undertone. For a moment his brow furrowed, but then he let out a chuckle. "And where do I go to do that?"

"'Rent-a-Mom'? There must be an app for it."

He really laughed then. "You make it sound like a dating app."

"There's that, too. Post a photo of yourself and I'm sure a long line of women would jump to apply."

His gaze sharpened. Then, a little too neutrally, he said, "Like you did?"

She felt herself flush. Again. She, who rarely got embarrassed. "I," she said with an edge, "applied to help with the children. Not be a…a girlfriend applicant." Although she was certain he'd have no shortage of those if he wanted.

Belatedly, the implications of what he'd said before hit her. He wasn't used to sharing his space.

"Speaking of girlfriends, is there one I need to meet? And is she going to be…unhappy with me being here?"

"Not an issue," he said. Answering but not answering.

"She doesn't exist, or she won't be upset?" She was pushing, she knew, but it suddenly seemed crucial to know. And she didn't dare think about why.

"She doesn't exist," he snapped, "and if she did and got upset, given the circumstances, she wouldn't exist any longer."

It took her a second to work it out. And it didn't surprise her that Dante Mancuso wouldn't put up with a woman who didn't get that this sudden acquisition of two orphaned babies had to be the most important thing right now. And that pleased her for reasons she didn't yet fully understand.

"I'm glad to hear that," she said softly.

She left him to figure out which part her answer applied to and went to check on the girls. And every step of the way she was denying to herself that her answer had applied to both.

That she was glad that phantom girlfriend didn't exist.

* * *

Was it insane that the first thing he'd noticed was that she'd indeed lost the stiletto heels? Which of course meant he'd noticed her feet were bare. And small. And nicely arched.

And when the hell had feet become a thing?

Dante rubbed a hand over eyes gritty from lack of sleep. When he'd dived into this finding-a-nanny project, he'd only thought of how desperately he needed help. And to be honest, in the back of his mind, he'd had someone more…motherly in mind. Maybe even grandmotherly. Like Mrs. Nelson, who'd been watching them before. Maybe he should have called her—maybe she could have used the job. But then, she had that sick relative. But maybe they were recovered now, and—

"They're still sleeping," Gemma said quietly as she came back, sliding the pocket door partially closed, leaving it open enough that they could hear if the twins woke and started fussing.

"It's a miracle," he said wearily, not looking at her.

"It's after ten. Maybe you should be sleeping while they are. While you can."

She had a point, he had to admit. "Good idea."

He slapped the laptop closed and stood up. Flash lifted his head. "Leash," he said. The dog lumbered to his feet.

"You're taking him out now?" she asked.

"It's now or 3:00 a.m." He smiled wryly. "And believe me, him howling at that hour will wake up not just the twins but everybody within about five square miles."

"Oh." She looked at him consideringly. "When you got Flash, did you ever think about getting a house? With a yard?"

"Yeah," he admitted. "Still do. But he's adapted pretty well, as long as he gets his exercise. He seems happy." Or at least he had, before the girls—all three of them—had disrupted his life.

She watched the dog amble over to the door and pick up the heavy leather lead with the heavy-duty clasp. He brought it back and sat politely at Dante's feet.

"He's very well trained," she said.

"Yes. Whether he decides to obey that training when not actually working is less certain." When her gaze shot to his face, he grinned. "Flash has a mind of his own. He obeys best when he's getting something out of the deal."

"Like a treat?"

"He'd much prefer a hot scent to trail, but a walk will do."

She shook her head as if in wonder. "You really do have three kids." But she was smiling when she said it.

And, he thought as they went out into the fall chill, she had a very nice smile. Especially when it was the real one, not the practiced fund-raising smile he'd seen in pictures, the one she had down pat.

He gave himself a mental shake. He needed to be thinking about the job at hand, not his new nanny. But he still hadn't quite wrapped his mind around the idea someone at RRPD was dirty. And that on top of the rest was going to take some serious sorting out.

Flash was pulling ahead, having found something interesting to smell along the narrow sidewalk that led to the park. But it wasn't the fierce "I've got it!" pull of a hot trail he knew he had to follow, it was merely the ordinary pull that said, "Hmm, what's that?" Dante smiled at himself, at his tendency to assign human thought patterns to what was likely a very different process in the canine brain. But he and Flash had reached the kind of understanding that got the job done; the dog knew when it was time to work, and at those times Dante was in charge. The rest of the time, it was a toss-up as to who was the boss.

"Enjoy it while you can, dawg," he said to the big bloodhound. "This time next month it's going to be freezing out, and by Christmas we won't make it out of the teens and you'll likely be plowing through snow."

Flash seemed unconcerned, although Dante knew that once it dropped below twenty degrees the animal was no more interested in being outside than he was. If only because he knew it meant those silly thermal dog boots he hated. Again, very undignified.

By the time the dog indicated he'd had enough for the night, Dante was wishing he'd worn his heavier jacket. And his own sheepskin boots.

"Wimp," he told himself. "It can't be much under forty."

Once inside and with the door closed, he looked around and saw no sign of Gemma. Deciding she must have gone to bed, he unhooked the dog's leash. Flash lumbered toward the fire, where he usually stayed until Dante called him to his bedroom; the dog's bed was tucked in between the nightstand and the gun safe. But as he slipped off his jacket and hung it on the rack near the door, Dante noticed that the dog headed for the den. He followed, blowing a little on his hands and making a mental note to add gloves to the wardrobe tomorrow night, and got there just as the dog emerged once more. And to his surprise, behind him was Gemma.

He glanced past her toward the crib. "They're fine," Gemma said. "They woke up a bit ago—no idea who woke who—but went back to sleep pretty quickly after a wet diaper and a burp were dealt with."

"Oh." His brow furrowed. "How did you know which needed which?"

"Process of elimination," she said cheerfully. As if she'd been doing it for years. Maybe it was just something women were born knowing. Even women like Gemma Colton. "And Flash is so funny," she added. "He just came in, looked at me, then walked over to the crib and looked at the twins for a minute, like he was making sure they were there. Then he kind of sighed and walked back out."

"Probably trying to figure out if they're staying."

She reached out and scratched the top of Flash's head. The dog allowed it. "Poor guy. No wonder he's confused. His whole life's been turned upside down and he doesn't know why."

"I do know why, and I'm still confused," Dante said drily.

She gave him a wide smile at that. "Come on," she said, heading for the kitchen. He followed, curious. She walked to the microwave and keyed in a ten-second cycle. At the beep she reached in and pulled out a mug, which she handed to him.

"What—" He stopped, staring into the mug. "Hot chocolate?"

"I saw it in the cupboard earlier and thought it might be nice after your walk in the cold. Better than coffee at this hour, anyway."

He cupped his hands around the steaming mug, savoring the heat. "I… Thank you." He took a long sip, and it felt wonderful going down, spreading warmth from the inside. "Thank you," he repeated, a bit more fervently this time.

She smiled, that genuine, sweet smile again. "You really take good care of your dog."

"He's not just a dog—like I said, he's my partner."

"I think I'm beginning to understand what that entails," she said with a glance to where Flash was sprawled before the fire. "I'll be glad when he's comfortable enough with the girls—and me—to get back in his chair."

"He will. Eventually." *I hope.*

"Does he sleep with you?"

Dante nearly choked on the hot chocolate as he stared at her.

Chapter 13

It was said innocently, Dante thought, it was obvious what she meant, and yet his mind, as if the safeguards had been lulled by the warm, sweet drink, careened into craziness in an instant. *No. The space is open. Want it?*

His hands tightened on the mug until he was surprised it didn't shatter. Only when he was sure he would not betray himself did he answer.

"His bed's in my room, yeah."

"And he stays in it?"

"Unless invited otherwise."

He saw a faint tinge of color in her cheeks, and for a moment had the crazy idea that her thoughts might have veered into insanity just as his had. But she spoke again without a trace of it in her voice, so he decided he must be wrong. *Wishful thinking?* No. No, damn it. That way definitely lay insanity.

"And when would that be?"

"After a job well done. Or on really cold nights."

She blinked. "Um…central heating?"

"We sleep better in a cold room."

She frowned. "Just how cold do you let it get in here at night? Do I need an electric blanket?"

I could keep you warm.

He nearly groaned aloud as the words formed in his mind, followed by images of her in his bed, snuggling up for that warmth, preferably naked. Having to work way too hard not to say the words aloud, he said instead, "Down comforter, maybe."

"Oh."

She looked so serious he relented. He'd been going to anyway. "It doesn't usually drop below sixty in here overnight. I'll bump the thermostat up to sixty-five. That warm enough for you?"

She smiled again. "That's fine. I just thought you meant you turned off the heat altogether. That wouldn't be good for the babies, either."

Chagrin flooded him. He'd actually forgotten. "Damn," he muttered. "I'll leave it where it is. If I get too warm, I'll go sleep on the patio." *Or too hot.*

"So the Italian blood doesn't tell?" she asked, eyeing him.

He laughed and was back in control. "The blood may be Italian, but the thermostat was born right here in South Dakota."

She laughed in turn. "So we're both natives. Ever wanted to leave?"

"I did, for a while. Thought I wanted the big city. Hated it. Came home."

"Big cities are nice to visit, but I wouldn't want to live there."

He leaned on the kitchen island. "That surprises me. I would have thought you were all about the city."

Irritation flashed in her eyes. He'd clearly hit a nerve. "You seem to make a lot of assumptions, Mr. Mancuso."

"Maybe I do. But with all the Coltons connected to the department, word gets around when you're off on a city jaunt. Not my fault the Coltons are famous around here."

She grimaced. "And then there's the infamous branch."

"The Pour House crew?" he asked, lifting a brow. "I didn't forget them. I'm a lot closer to coming from that world than yours."

"They're not so bad," she said, surprising him yet again.

"Brayden's a good guy," he said. "And Shane got a raw deal."

She smiled at him, and it was the best smile yet. "Yes. And Quinn is…really good people." The moment she mentioned the caterer's name she blushed, and he wondered why.

They were, of course, avoiding the most notorious Colton of all, the murder suspect who'd managed to elude capture for the better part of a year. But then, surprising him yet again, Gemma brought her up.

"I don't believe Demi killed Bo Gage or any of those men," she said firmly.

Dante went still. Was this family loyalty, even if they were only cousins? Or did she know something? "Why?" he asked.

"She's a Colton, and she wouldn't commit murder just because some guy dumped her. She's a lot tougher than that."

"There's a lot of evidence," he cautioned her, knowing that was all he could say.

"I don't care. I just don't believe she would ever do something like that."

"So this is a...gut feeling?"

"Don't you dare laugh!"

"I wasn't," he said. "I've got a lot of respect for gut feelings. Most cops do. But they're not evidence."

Gemma gave a sad-sounding sigh. "No. I guess not."

And it wasn't until much later, lying awake in bed long after he'd thought he'd be sound asleep, that he replayed in his head what she'd said about Demi. *She's a Colton, and she wouldn't commit murder just because some guy dumped her.*

But Gemma had upended her entire life because some guy dumped her. Not to get revenge, but to prove him wrong.

He wasn't sure what that meant, if anything. And while he was still dwelling on that, he finally fell asleep.

Why doesn't someone quiet those screaming children?

Gemma rolled over, pulling the covers up over her shoulders against the chill.

Chill? It shouldn't be cold. Was her heat not working? Had the power gone out? What—

Suddenly she bolted upright, heart hammering at the strange surroundings. It all came flooding back in a rush. Especially the part about who should quiet those crying babies.

She got up quickly, throwing on the robe she'd put at the end of the bed. Sliding her feet into her fluffy-lined slippers, she hurried toward the noise.

"Okay, you two, who started it?" she asked in that light, cheerful tone she'd discovered usually interested them enough to distract them. It worked again, but only with one of them. Zita, she thought, noting the eyebrow. But Lucia kept wailing, so the problem must be with her. She patted Zita, and the supportive crying faded away. Then she picked up Lucia, and it didn't take long for her to realize a change of diaper was required.

She went through the process, chanting the proper order of wipes, drying, powder in her mind. Then she fastened the clean diaper securely and redressed Zita in her inevitably pink onesie.

"You, my sweet, need a little color variety," she cooed. "Pink is all well and good, but a girl needs a change now and then." She picked up the now quiet baby and finally turned her head toward the door. And realized they weren't alone.

She nearly gasped aloud. She was glad she had the baby to hang on to or she probably would have clapped her hand over her mouth to cover her gaping. Because apparently Dante Mancuso slept naked. He'd grabbed a towel and wrapped it around his hips, so at least he'd been that mentally functional. But that damned towel looked like it was about to slip those last crucial inches at any second if he so much as breathed.

And damn, but the man was built. The glimpse she'd gotten that first time at the RRPD office was nothing compared to this display of taut muscle, broad chest, narrow hips and flat belly. And long, strong legs.

Only the fact that he was obviously still half-asleep made the sight bearable at all.

"I like the way you talk to them," he said, giving her a matching sleepy smile that was somehow charming despite all that distracting…maleness. "You don't gush or baby talk them."

"They seem to like it," she said, proud that her voice was steady.

"You got them quiet pretty quickly. They've got a couple of good sets of lungs."

"Part of the design, I'm sure," Gemma said.

She put Lucia back in the crib beside her sister. Busied herself with situating them, because she wasn't sure she could handle another dose of all that skin. It made her hands itch and her body flush in a way she didn't quite understand. Not that she could deny he was a very attractive man—impossible when he was standing there practically in the nude—but her own reaction was confusing her. She loved Dev, after all. And no matter how many times she told herself that didn't mean she couldn't appreciate another handsome—and sexy—man, it was still unsettling.

When she thought she could do so composedly, she straightened and turned around. "It's my job, Mr. Mancuso. Next time you can just go back to sleep," she suggested. *Please.*

"My job, too," he said.

"But you hired me."

"And I'm not paying you."

"I told you I was doing it for the experience."

Of dealing with his very distracting presence? Her reaction to him put an edge in her voice, and she gestured at his precariously placed towel. "And that might work for now, but eventually you're going to need to... wear something around the girls."

His expression changed. "Am I bothering you?"

She did not care for the note of not quite smugness that had come into his voice. She put on her best look of Colton superiority and let her eyes slide down his body to the towel. And confirmed what she'd thought she'd seen; he was no more immune to her presence than she to his.

"Maybe I should be the one asking you that," she said coolly as she let her gaze slide back up his body to his face. She might have hesitated to taunt some men, but on a gut level she knew Dante was made of stronger stuff.

He didn't deny the obvious evidence the towel couldn't quite hide. And for some reason she didn't quite understand, she appreciated that. "Why ask," he said with a shrug that threatened to unveil everything, "when the answer's obvious? You're a beautiful woman, and it's been a long time for me."

The compliment made her flush, which was ridiculous, because she'd heard it many times before. That wasn't conceit, simply fact. She took little notice most times, because she knew perfectly well that to most people, their assessment of her beauty was directly correlated to their assessment of her wealth. But with this man, she wasn't so sure.

"Why?" she asked, trying to divert the conversation.

His brow furrowed. "What? Why am I not jumping you? Are you that certain of your deathless appeal?" That stung a bit. She managed not to look at the towel again, but he answered as if she had. "That's just biology. It doesn't run me."

No, this man wouldn't be casual about such a thing. Because he was a man, not a boy with no guardrails. If he came after a woman, she'd know it wasn't just a passing whim, a temporary urge of that biology. And somehow that knowledge made her ache a little inside.

"I meant why has it been a long time?" she clarified, denying that feeling. "You must have them lined up at your door."

He looked startled. Then he gave her a crooked grin. "Time was," he said. "But funny how putting on a badge changed the minds of most of the girls I knew, back in the day."

She supposed he meant the ones who were like his family, not on the right side of that badge and what it meant. "If that's all it took," she said, ending with a shrug.

"Yeah." He studied her for a moment. "Must be kind of the reverse for you."

She blinked. "What?"

"They avoid me because of my family, but guys probably come after you because of yours."

She stared at him. Once more he'd come so close to

her earlier thoughts that it was almost uncanny. "Yes," she whispered. "They do."

"Guess that's why they say fair is just a weather condition."

He'd gone from startling her to making her laugh in the space of a half second. Disconcerted, she scrambled for something to say.

"You know, eventually you're really going to need a bigger place, because they will need their separate space."

He sighed. "Yeah. I know."

He suddenly looked so weary she hastened to say, "Not for a while, though. I'll do some research on when they recommend twins start sleeping apart."

"I… Thanks."

"And now that they're settled, I'm going back to bed."

For a moment he didn't speak, and the silence spun out into something different than just quiet. "Yeah," he finally muttered.

He turned and left without another word. She started toward her room, but when she got to the door, she looked down the hall just in time to see him going into his. He obviously got rid of the towel the moment he was inside, because she saw a corner of it whip through the air in the instant before he closed the door. As if he'd yanked it off angrily.

Or in frustration.

That made her smile, but only until she was back in bed and she realized that he wasn't the only one fighting down a physical response. She frowned, pulling her knees up to wrap her arms around them. This was not like her. She never reacted like this. It made no sense.

That's just biology. It doesn't run me.

But right at the moment, it seemed to be running her.

She sat there for a long time, trying to understand. She finally decided that it had to be that she was missing Dev. It was the only answer that made sense. Not that it explained the way the sight of Dante affected her. That still made no sense. Dev was just as handsome and much more polished, yet what she felt around him was rather tame compared to the crackling hum she felt around Dante.

Gemma flicked off the light and lay back on the pillow. By the time she finally felt sleepy again, she had convinced herself it was simply that she hadn't seen Dev for a couple of days. When she saw him again—when she would present her proof that he'd been wrong, that she would be a great, hands-on mom—things would get back to normal, back to where they should be.

But when she at last fell asleep, it wasn't Dev she dreamed about.

Chapter 14

"Hey, Mancuso, I thought you were on daddy leave!"

Dante turned, ready to fire back at the ribbing. He was already edgy, and it wouldn't take much to push him over. For a guy who claimed his body's natural responses didn't rule him, he'd slept—or not slept—like utter crap last night. But when he belatedly—which showed him how tired he was—realized it was Katie Parsons, he bit back the words. Not because she couldn't take it, but because she was the department tech ace, and he needed her just now.

"Yeah, yeah," he muttered. Then his gaze slid to her hair; she'd taken last week's blond and turned the tips a rather bright and obviously unnatural blue. "Interesting," he said.

"Don't like it? Where's your sense of adventure?"

"Dead, apparently," he said, too tired to even enumerate the number of levels that was true for.

"Yeah," she said sympathetically, "my sister was a wreck with just one baby. I can't imagine two."

He gave a rueful shake of his head, but then cut to the point. "I need a favor," he said.

"I don't babysit," she replied hastily.

He smiled while wondering what the girls would make of the two-tone hair. "Got that covered, thanks."

"I heard," she said, eyebrows rising. "Gemma Colton? Really?"

He'd known word would get around quickly, but he hadn't expected to have to deal with it the minute he walked in the door. "Yeah, really."

"Wow. I never would have thought… She's really doing it? I mean, is she any good at it?"

"They're still breathing," he said drily. "Which is more than I could guarantee if it was just me."

Parsons looked suddenly contrite. "I shouldn't be joking. I'm sorry about your brother and sister-in-law."

"Me, too." And it was the truth, even if he was just as sorry at how Dom, even in death, had managed to blow up his brother's life. Again. "Listen, I need you to run a correlation check for me."

"Sure. Chief said you might need stuff. What?" She sounded almost eager. Probably the sympathy thing.

"Work schedules and cases caught since Monday morning, tagging those with evidence booked in."

True to form, she didn't question; for her the job was the challenge—she didn't need or want all the pieces, just her part. It made her invaluable, and trusted. "Give me fifteen," she said. "Only because I have to drop something off at the chief's office first and that'll kill five."

He grinned at her. Only Katie Parsons could blithely promise something like that for a department the size of RRPD in essentially ten minutes. "I'll stop by on my way out."

She was as good as her word, and when he had finished grabbing some things he needed from his desk and then threaded his way through the various greetings ranging from expressing condolences to those who treated him like it was any other day—he preferred the latter, he found—and reached Katie's small domain, she had the data he'd asked for ready.

"Want me to email it, or you want it on a flash drive?"

Dante hesitated. Then Finn's words echoed in his head. *Right now only you, Ron Fox and I know.* And it was someone inside, probably with access to the department network.

"Flash drive," he said. "And you never did it," he added.

She gave him a scornful look. "Of course not."

She inserted a drive about the size of his thumbnail into a slot and started the transfer. She had a drawer full of the things, he knew, just for such instances. But when the files had finished, she didn't disconnect it. Instead she glanced up at him.

"What?" he asked.

"Do you want… I have some video…"

It was unlike her to be so hesitant, and that gave him a clue. "The crash?"

She nodded. "It's from the convenience store cameras, down on the corner, so it's not close or clear, but..."

"Yes. Please."

It was all he could manage. She copied the file over, then ejected the drive, stood up and handed it to him.

"I really am sorry. My sister and I aren't particularly close, but I know how I'd feel if she died."

He couldn't think of a thing to say, so he only nodded, then patted her arm rather awkwardly. It seemed to be enough, because she smiled then went back to work.

He would be very glad, he thought, when this passed. Everybody knew he and Dominic hadn't been close, which only made it more difficult to know what to say. Which was why he preferred the ones who didn't say anything, saving him from having to think of something appropriate to say in return.

Oddly, it had been Shane Colton, whom he'd run into on his way out, who'd hit the right note, saying only, "Condolences, if you need them. If not, forget it." Then again, maybe not oddly; if there was anyone who knew about the vagaries of life and family, it was Shane. He'd learned the hard way, coming up from the Pour House branch of the family.

When he got back home, it was to an empty place. Very empty. A note on the kitchen counter told him Gemma had taken the girls out for a drive. Thoughtful of her to let him know, although he wondered why she hadn't just texted. This must be why she'd asked him to help her move the car seats to her vehicle; she'd wanted to take them out.

Or needed to get herself out.

For a moment he just stood there, listening to the quiet and wondering how the hell things had changed so much so fast. How could a place that had seemed comfortable and like home for years now seem like it was…missing something? In the space of three days? His life had been T-boned as completely as his brother's stolen car, and it—*he*—would never be the same.

He wondered if the twins would even remember their parents. Did permanent memories even exist at their age? And when they were older, when they inevitably started asking about them, what the hell was he going to say? The truth, that their parents had been petty criminals, and most of their other relatives were either dead or in prison?

He walked into the den, stopped and stared down at the crib. His nieces. His family. His blood.

Then maybe they're lucky they ended up with you.

Gemma's words suddenly came back to him. At the time he'd blown them off as just something you said in a difficult situation. But now they seemed to take on new meaning.

If the twins' lives had continued as they'd been, centered around Dom's various criminal efforts, what would have happened? How would they have turned out? Would they have followed in their parents' footsteps, into that shady world that had been the Mancusos' for decades? Or would they have rebelled, as he had? Or maybe one of each?

They would not be in that world now. He would see to that. And suddenly the girls represented more than just the total disruption of his life. They represented a chance for him to make peace with his family and who they were. And to see that the Mancuso name didn't always stand for the wrong side of the law.

Had Dom known this? Had he chosen Dante instead of someone else for that reason, or simply because there was no one else? He didn't know. Wouldn't ever know.

But accepting his responsibility as the chosen guardian for his nieces suddenly took on a whole new meaning.

Gemma was very glad Dante's condo was on the ground floor. She couldn't imaging lugging all this stuff and the twins up a flight of stairs. Even in her low-heeled snow boots.

She had to set one of the girls down—Lucia this time—to wrestle with the key to the front door. But before she could get the lock turned, the door swung open from the inside.

"Hi," she said, rather breathlessly.

"Hi," he returned, already reaching for the carrier she'd set down. "Get inside, it looks like it's about to rain."

She hurried past him, smiling at his concern. He really was a nice guy, she thought. A gentleman. She'd bet if he was with a woman, she'd never feel like he'd forgotten she was around, like Dev sometimes seemed to.

"Hey, little one," he said, smiling at—she checked the eyebrows—Zita, the one he'd just unstrapped from her carrier. The baby batted out at him. He caught her tiny hand and kissed it. Zita giggled.

Girls of all ages, apparently.

She gave herself an inward shake. It had been a sweet, loving gesture toward his niece.

"Where'd you go?" he asked, crouching down to tickle Lucia's chubby cheek. Gemma wasn't used to being questioned about her whereabouts—Dev never asked, and for a moment she wondered if it was because he didn't care enough about her to want to know.

Dante only wants to know where you took the girls—he's just being a good guardian.

She wasn't sure why it mattered that she tell herself that, but it seemed to.

"Shopping, first," she said, gesturing at the big new leather bag she'd picked up. When he looked at it, puzzled, she nudged it open to show him the clever organizer inside that now held diapers, wipes, lotion, spare clothes and everything else the website she'd read said was essential at all times. "Better than the pink baby ducks," she said.

"They did look…unnatural." He was smiling now. She smiled back. She was starting to feel more confident.

"Then I stopped by my father's place." He stood. His eyebrows lifted in obvious surprise. Then lowered quickly. She knew perfectly well many people's reaction to her father and quickly added, "He wasn't there."

"Oh. Then why…?"

"I traded cars."

He blinked. "What?"

"My little coupe was way too hard to get them in and out of." She gestured toward the parking area out

front, where the luxury SUV now sat in the space assigned to the condo.

"That's yours, too?"

"It's more of a family car. We can all use it when we
need the room or the four-wheel drive."

"Oh."

They got the girls into the playpen, held up a suc-
cession of the toys she'd brought and gave them both
the first one they'd reached for. Which fortunately had
been different ones.

Dante disappeared for a moment, then came back and
handed Gemma something. She took it, realized it was
a garage door opener and looked at him questioningly.

"Park in the garage. You'll need to for you and the
girls—it's getting colder."

"But what about you?"

"Flash and I can tough it out," he said with a crooked
grin that did odd things to her pulse rate. "Especially
now that I'll be here more." The bloodhound's head
had come up at his name. Dante looked at him. "Sorry,
buddy. I'll preheat the SUV for you—that's the best I
can do."

The dog put his head down and let out a very put-
upon-sounding sigh. Gemma laughed, glad to be able to
hide the odd feelings that were rocketing around inside
her. Giving them the garage, going out in the cold himself to preheat his own vehicle for the dog's comfort…
yes, Dante Mancuso was a very nice guy.

"I… Thank you," she said.

"Let's switch the cars now," he said.

She glanced at the girls. "They should be okay alone for one minute, shouldn't they?"

He stopped in the midst of reaching for his keys. Looked at the playpen. Sighed. "Damn."

"What?"

He slowly shook his head. "No. I've heard it too many times from distraught parents. 'I only turned my back for a minute.' 'I was only outside for a minute.'"

She could only imagine the circumstances under which he'd heard those words. She stared at the tiny girls. "I think I'm only beginning to realize the enormity of what got dropped on you."

"You're not the only one."

"You have to rethink everything, don't you?"

"When to sleep, shower, take a leak— Sorry," he said, cutting himself off and looking embarrassed, as if he'd said something crude.

"I did grow up with a brother," she reminded him. "And we were pretty close. I've heard worse."

"I can't imagine it from Blake Colton."

She waved a hand. "Ha. He's like that now, but at fourteen he discovered every vulgar word in the language. Most of it, sad to say, from our father."

He gave her the curious look she'd come to recognize. "He's your full brother, right?"

She nodded. "That and age are probably why we were so tight. It's a complicated family."

"I'll bet."

She looked at him consideringly. "No more complicated than yours, though, it seems."

He grimaced. "Maybe. But still a world away."

"Juliette speaks highly of you."

He gave her a level look. "I like her, too. We have a lot in common. From the same side of the tracks."

"And you both pulled yourself out of it," she said. "That takes work."

"What it takes is stubbornness."

"That, too," she agreed easily.

"So about the cars," he said, returning to the subject abruptly enough to tell her he didn't care to discuss his past with her. "I'll go move mine out into a visitor space, come back, you go put yours in the garage, come inside, then I'll move mine into the assigned slot."

She nodded, gave the girls a glance. "Who knew such tiny things could drive you crazy with simply parking a car?"

He let out a low chuckle, and his tension vanished. "I'm going to need a degree in logistics."

Flash stirred, trudged out to the kitchen for a drink. "Too bad you can't get him to carry the girls. Or at least one of them."

Dante looked at the dog, then suddenly looked thoughtful. "You know, I'll bet it could be done."

"Seriously? I was only joking."

"No, I mean it. He carries his own supplies when we're hiking, including water and food, and I'll bet they don't weigh any more than what he's used to."

"But they wiggle. And make noise."

"He's pretty unflappable. He just gripes."

She couldn't help smiling at the way he talked about the dog as if he were human. She was the first to admit dogs had their own personalities—she just hadn't ever been around one enough to attribute human characteristics to him. But she had to admit, Flash invited it.

They got the cars rearranged easily enough and the girls seemed entertained by their rapid switching, although the consistent presence of the dog seemed to keep them settled.

"He has a calming influence on them, doesn't he?" she asked when they were done.

"Seems that way. Whatever it is, I'll take it. Heck, I'll take any help I can get."

"Obviously," she said, making sure she was grinning when she said it. And as she'd expected, his head snapped around. And slowly, he smiled. And it was a very good smile.

"You," he said with a slight shake of his head, "are not at all what I expected."

"That's okay. Neither are you."

For a long moment they stood there, gazes locked. She had no idea how long—her perception of time, indeed, even her surroundings seemed to have faded away into vagueness. She realized she was aware of her heartbeat in a strange, intense way. She felt the strongest urge to take a step toward him in the same moment he leaned in slightly, as if feeling the same urge.

His cell phone rang, shattering the moment. She should be glad of that. She had no business feeling… whatever this was for a man who wasn't Dev. So she should be grateful for the interruption.

She wasn't sure she was.

Chapter 15

"Mancuso."

He was surprised at how steady his voice was when he answered. He had no idea what that had been a moment ago, but it had been…intense.

"Dr. Maria Sprague, at the ME's office," the voice in his ear said.

Damn. He hadn't even looked at the screen, he'd been so rattled, or he would have been prepared. "Oh. Yeah." He shook his head sharply. Braced himself, knowing what this had to be. "Go ahead."

"I've got the autopsy results on Mr. and Mrs. Mancuso," the woman said gently. "I've emailed the full report to you, but I thought you'd want to know there's no evidence of any COD except the injuries from the crash."

Hearing the names jabbed at him, but he clenched his

jaw, then released it, regaining control. He'd watched that damned video of the crash enough times he'd already known this in his gut. And, as much as was possible given his brother's dealings, he was sure they hadn't been targeted.

"Any contributing factors?"

"No. They both had a small amount of alcohol in their system. Well under the limit, probably no more than a glass of wine an hour or so before."

"Nothing else?"

"Not that's immediately obvious. I've sent out for toxicology tests, of course, but I don't expect there will be anything unusual. I'm very sorry, Officer Mancuso, but it seems to have just been a tragic accident."

If you didn't count the shooter who caused it.

He fought down the memory of hearing those bullets shattering glass, then looking out and seeing the crash the shooter had caused. The crash that had decimated his brother's car, and his nieces' lives.

"Thanks, Doc."

"They can be released to whatever funeral service you've selected whenever you wish."

Dante said something, he wasn't sure what but it had probably been an oath. And a moment later, he was standing there with his silent phone, staring into space.

"Are you all right?"

Gemma's quiet voice yanked him out of whatever space he'd been spinning out into. "What?"

"Bad news?"

"What?" he repeated, then shook his head sharply.

"No. I mean yes." He took a deep breath and tried again. "Bad, but not unexpected."

"You just looked a little…shell-shocked again."

He finally looked at her. There was concern in her eyes that he would swear was real. But there was only one thing at this instant that he was absolutely certain was real.

"A funeral. I have to plan a freaking funeral."

She reached out then, touched his arm. "I'm sorry. I won't say I know how you feel because I don't. But I am sorry."

His emotions were so tangled even he didn't know how he felt, so he appreciated that she didn't claim to.

"I don't even know where to start," he said, hoping he didn't really sound as helpless as he thought he did.

She looked as if she were thinking, considering. She did a lot of that, he'd noticed. Gemma Colton might be a beautiful heiress who'd rarely had a care in life, but she was certainly no airhead.

"Who does the planning if…forgive me, if something happens to one of your officers?"

He blinked. "I don't know."

"That might be a place to start."

For a moment he just stared at her. "I… Thank you. That's a good idea."

She hesitated, then said, "I'm fairly good at organizing."

Those galas, beautifully coordinated fund-raisers, popped into his mind. "I know."

"If you get me the contacts, I could make the calls. It would be easier for me, I think."

He nearly gaped at her, so unexpected was the offer.

"I've never done a funeral, but I think the principles are probably the same. Contact the people who handle things, arrange the location, put out the information, make sure the crucial people know."

Again he just stared at her, unable to think of a damned thing to say.

"I can do it while the girls are napping, or while you're with them." When he still didn't speak, she shrugged. "It was just an idea."

She started to turn away. He grabbed her arm. Finally found his voice. "I… You'd do that?"

"Like I said, it's what I do. And you've said you weren't that close, so there's no reason you absolutely have to do it yourself. You'd only have to tell me what you want."

What I want…

The thoughts that crashed into his mind at that moment were unexpected, unwanted and entirely inappropriate for the moment, because they all involved this also unexpected woman standing bare inches away, looking at him with a gentle, caring concern he never would have expected in Gemma Colton.

Only then did he realize he was still holding her arm.

And that she hadn't tried to pull away.

He let go, suppressing the urge to yank his hand back as if suddenly burned. He looked away from those soft, warm eyes. He had to look away.

"What I want is for none of this to have happened," he muttered.

"Of course. Who wouldn't? But it has."

Again, the matter-of-fact words helped him get a grip, at least on his tangled feelings about his brother, the twins and planning a funeral. They weren't so much help on that other thing.

"Devlin Harrington is a lucky man," he said, his voice a little rough. "And if he lets you get away, he's a fool."

It was her turn to stare at him, and he couldn't miss the color rising in her cheeks. And the smile she gave him then changed from pleased to perplexed so quickly he couldn't help wondering what she was thinking.

What you should be wondering is what the hell you're thinking.

There was no way her boss's words should have had that kind of effect on her. She'd taken to thinking of Dante as only her boss—or tried to, at least—because it helped slow down stupid reactions like the one she'd had when he said that about Dev.

She had thought, once, about going out with someone else and flaunting it in Dev's face, but she'd been so stunned by his unexpected ending of their relationship she hadn't pursued it. Besides, she didn't want him angry.

And maybe you're just not sure he'd be jealous at all?

She brushed away that thought. He'd been clear about why he'd broken up with her, but he'd been so very gentle about it that she knew he loved her and hated doing it. So as soon as she had proved his assumption wrong, everything would be fine. He could go to his father—because she suspected the senior Harrington was behind it, and she knew too well how rich, powerful fathers liked to control everything—with proof she'd be just what he wanted, a good mother, and all would be well.

Dante made a couple of calls to find out who handled arrangements if an officer died or was killed. The result was a list of numbers provided by, he'd said, Lorelei Wong, the civilian who, along with whatever sworn officer was assigned at the moment, handled front-desk duties. Gemma remembered the woman with an amused glint in her eye behind her silver-framed glasses, who had given her directions and let her through the day she'd walked in on a bare-torsoed Dante three days ago.

Three days ago. Had it really only been that long? So much had happened, it seemed much longer. He wasn't the only one whose life had been upended.

She shook her head, made herself focus on the list. Funeral homes, cemeteries, florists, news outlets and a long list of numbers for what looked like every sheriff's office and police department within a thousand miles. The last two threw her until she remembered the source of the list. And visions of every police funeral she'd ever seen, with officers from all over the country coming to pay their respects to their fallen, flashed through her mind.

She felt a sudden chill. She'd watched the coverage of those events, marveled at the turnout and the ceremony. She'd raised money for the Red Ridge K9 division and had met many of the officers. She'd admired all and liked most.

But she'd never personalized it until now.

Until she'd met Dante.

In that moment the thought that he risked his life every day invaded her mind and left little room for anything else. That could be him one day. And he knew it. Yet he did it anyway.

She fought off a shiver and made herself focus on the list. She was good at lists. With that thought in mind she began making one, of questions that had to be answered before arrangements could begin. Maybe it would be easier on Dante if she wrote them down, so he could answer without having to talk about it. Obituary—they'd need that written. Choice of mortuary and cemetery. Burial or cremation. Either way, together or separately. Maybe there was a will or document specifying their wishes.

And maybe it was the inherently grim nature of the task, but when she had finished an image, washed over her. An image of Dante lying dead, that lean, muscled body bloodied, the life gone from those amazing eyes, nearly swamped her. How did anyone live with that? He himself, or anyone who loved him?

She dropped her pen, wrapped her arms around herself. She almost wished the twins would wake, start fussing, anything to take that vision out of her head.

You would have to be, she decided, an utter fool to fall in love with a cop.

Chapter 16

It should have occurred to him, but it hadn't until Gemma had handed him her list of questions. He'd been surprised, not by the questions but by her selection of that method. When she'd quietly said she thought it might be easier for him to write rather than talk about it, he was amazed at how relieved he was.

She's got depth to her.

Juliette was obviously right.

It wasn't until he'd read the bit about a document specifying their wishes that he remembered the large envelope he'd shoved out of sight when it had arrived via a messenger service. He'd expected it to be from the PD, maybe more info from the chief. But when he saw the law office logo in the corner, he'd known it was the copy of Dominic's will. He'd had no desire to look at it and had stuffed it in a drawer in his desk in the den.

But he got it out now—taking care not to wake the twins—and settled into his usual chair by the hearth to read it. He was used to reading legalese, so it only took a paragraph or so to get into the mind-set. It wasn't that long, just a few pages, and when he was done he sat in silence, still holding the papers.

It was a joint will, not unexpected in itself because Agostina had never wanted to bother with such things. She—

"Dante?"

He looked up to see Gemma holding out a glass to him. The amber liquid glowed in the light from the fireplace, which she had also apparently turned on. He hadn't noticed any of it, which told him how out of it he'd been.

"I think this process needs a drink," she said.

He took the glass; obviously she'd found the bottle of Scotch in the cabinet. And she was right—he felt like he needed a drink just now. Maybe several.

"Thanks."

She only nodded. She sat down opposite him—no drink for herself, he noticed—then said, "You looked surprised a couple of times, reading that."

He let out a breath. "I'm surprised it—" he gestured with the will "—exists at all. Then again, I'm not. Nobody expects to die at thirty-one, but my brother didn't lead the kind of life that promises living to a ripe old age."

She looked thoughtful. "And I suppose having children changes more than your life. It changes how you have to think about death."

Definitely depth.

It hit him suddenly that now he had that responsibility, that he would have to make some legal changes on top of everything else. As a cop he had even more reason than his brother to think about the twins and what would happen if he were killed. He had a will, drawn up his first week on the job. Not that he had much to leave, except this place, whatever death benefits there were and a few material possessions. He'd directed whatever there was to go to the K9 unit, since he wasn't about to leave it to his brother.

And yet his brother had left the most important things to him.

"I just don't get it," he muttered.

"Families," she said wryly. "Seems they all have their... quirks."

"I could have done without my brother's. But I'm sure he'd say the same about me."

"Your quirk was being a law-abiding citizen?"

"Yeah." He looked down at the papers again. "He owned the house. Outright. That surprises me."

She looked surprised in turn. "As in paid off? Even my father doesn't ever do that."

Her phrasing registered, and he wondered how many houses Fenwick Colton owned. Probably a ski chalet somewhere, an apartment in New York City and maybe a nice tropical getaway for when the Dakota winters got to be too much. And who knew what else.

He shoved the thoughts out of his mind. "Yeah. Maybe he was a better crook than I thought."

"You say that so easily."

She sounded merely curious, so he answered, "I've had a lot of years to learn to accept it."

"The family business, you said."

"Yes." He was getting uncomfortable talking so much about himself and decided it was her turn. "Not something you joined, either."

"Me? Heavens, no. The corporate world drives me crazy."

"Did your father want you to?" He was curious, because she hadn't talked that much about herself, which surprised him. But he was beginning to realize he'd just might have bought into a stereotype.

"He already had Layla, my oldest sister, and she lives for the business. He tried to push my other two sisters into it, but they went their own way. Bea has her shop, and you know what Patience does."

He nodded. "We're lucky to have her. She's a great vet."

"He really tried to push Blake, him being the only son, but Blake fought back harder than any of us. And went off and made his own fortune."

"Literally," Dante said, rather drily. "But I asked about you."

She shrugged. "I think I was the lucky one. After all that, he didn't try much with me. By then he had other things on his mind, I think. Or maybe he just realized I wouldn't be any good at it."

He had his doubts—he'd seen her organize, seen

the results. But he said, "It's easier to be good at something you love."

"Like you love being a cop?"

He nodded. "It was the only thing that ever called to me."

She gave him another of those looks. Gemma Colton, it seemed, had a very lively and curious mind. "Did you ever wonder if it was a reaction to…your family? Like it was with Blake?"

"Often," he replied, a little surprised since he barely admitted it to himself.

In fact, he was a little surprised at this entire discussion. Never in a million years would he have ever pictured himself having such a conversation with the likes of Fenwick Colton's offspring. But he'd been surprised by a lot of things about Gemma. Including his own reaction to her.

Especially his own reaction to her.

She was quiet for a moment, then nodded toward the papers he'd dropped in his lap. "Did you find anything helpful?"

"Yeah. Dom left instructions." Along with some other surprises that were probably going to present a moral dilemma for Dante down the line. He was glad his brother had provided for his daughters, but there was every likelihood the money in their trusts had been ill gotten. He shoved that out of his mind for later, even as he wryly acknowledged he'd been doing that a lot lately. "He even…had a cemetery chosen already. For both of them."

"That makes it easier, then."

She smiled at him, and suddenly he wondered if that had been the whole point of this unexpected conversation, if she'd purposely distracted him from the grimness of it by getting him talking about other things. A week ago he would have scoffed at the idea of the youngest Colton heiress having such sensibilities, but now it seemed completely possible.

"Thank you," he said quietly.

"I offered," she said as he handed her the page with the details.

"I didn't mean for that, although I do thank you. I meant for the diversion."

She stared at him as if startled. "Dev usually just tells me to be quiet."

One corner of his mouth quirked upward. "Already gave you my opinion of your ex."

She looked disconcerted then. And said rather too firmly, "He's not my ex. Or won't be, soon."

"Hmm."

"It's true," she protested. "Dev is—"

He was rescued from hearing her glowing opinion of Devlin Harrington by a sudden burst of crying from the den.

"Saved by the wail," he muttered as she got up.

She gave him a sharp look but only gestured with the page of instructions and said, "I'll get on this first thing tomorrow."

She disappeared to deal with the twins. He wondered idly, because it distracted him from the weeping, if he should pay her for doing the organizing. That was what she did, after all. And he realized he didn't even know if she got paid for that sort of thing. She certainly didn't need the money, but it was a skill that deserved remuneration. He already owed her enough—he didn't want this piled on top of it.

He'd offer, later, and hope her rate wasn't more than he could afford. And if it was, well, he'd think of something.

Now if he could just stop thinking of other things. Things he had no business thinking about Colton Fenwick's daughter and Devlin Harrington's girlfriend. Ex or not.

But the guy really was a fool if he didn't realize what he had.

Chapter 17

"Are we done?"

Attorney James Fisk leaned back in his chair. "I believe we are. Unless you have any questions."

"Seems pretty straightforward." Dante nearly laughed.

"Something funny?"

"Just using the word *straightforward* about my brother."

"I understand that things were...difficult between you."

He did laugh then. "That's putting it mildly." The man seemed intelligent enough, so Dante guessed he knew that his client hadn't walked the straight and narrow. But even crooks needed lawyers. Probably more than anyone. "You ever handle his...criminal cases?"

The man's expression never changed. "I don't do criminal law."

"Then maybe you don't understand—"

"I understand. And however difficult your relationship, your brother admired you greatly."

Dante blinked. "What?"

"That was quite clear from our discussions. He admired your strength, your determination." Dante stared in shock as the man hesitated, then went on. "He once joked that he had no idea where your integrity had come from, since it did not run in the family."

When he got back to the car, Dante was still trying to process the lawyer's words through his disbelief. Somewhat on autopilot, he drove to the K9 center, where he had dropped Flash off to ramble around the large, fenced enclosure, sniffing to his heart's content.

He admired your strength, your determination.

Dom? Dom, who had never stopped ragging on him about his chosen path, his decision to walk away from generations of family history? It seemed impossible. But what reason would the lawyer have to lie? Not that they didn't lie—as a cop he knew that well enough, but he couldn't see why the man would, not about that, and not now.

When he nearly missed the turn he needed, he yanked his wandering mind back to reality. Flash came to his whistle easily enough, not even giving him that woeful look for abandoning him, as he sometimes did. He spotted trainer Danica Gage waving from the back of the building and returned the wave, then gestured at Flash. She nodded in understanding, saving him a trip inside to let them know he'd picked him up. A prized dog and a puppy had been stolen not long ago—by the Larson twins, Danica believed—so now no dog left without her knowledge.

He loaded Flash into the SUV, then got back in himself. He sat for a moment, pondering. The urge to go to the PD was automatic, and he had to remind himself he wasn't supposed to be there.

He felt the pressure building inside him again. It had been there since he'd looked at the wreckage of Dom's car. It had multiplied a thousandfold when he'd learned he was now responsible for two six-month-old babies. Add in the theft of the one piece of proof they had against the Larsons, and he was ready to blow.

He hammered a fist against the steering wheel in helpless anger. He wasn't used to feeling helpless, and he hated the sensation. If it hadn't been for Gemma...

Gemma. Damn, what a surprise she had turned out to be. When he'd gotten up this morning, there had been evidence in the den that she'd been up with the girls at least once. He hadn't heard a thing, and Flash hadn't awakened him, so he'd asked when she appeared in search of coffee. He'd poured her a cup and sipped at his own as she explained she'd woken up with a feeling and had gotten in there just as Zita was starting to fuss, needing a change.

"You're getting good at this fast," he'd said, and she'd beamed as if he'd presented her with a medal.

A medal she can show to ol' Devlin Harrington to prove her worth?

He grimaced at the thought. She deserved better than someone who'd dump her like that.

He started the car and headed home. He had an obituary to write.

Gemma sat on the floor with the twins under Flash's watchful eye. She was trying to keep them quiet for the moment, because Dante was at the kitchen bar, working on an obituary for his brother. Or at least, that was what he was supposedly doing; she hadn't seen him write a word yet.

She lifted the stuffed rabbit, bent its ears at a funny angle and hopped it toward the girls while making silly "Dum-de-dum" sounds. Lucia smiled while Zita giggled delightedly.

She saw Dante's head come up at the sound and looked up, afraid he'd be angry at the interruption. But he was smiling at the twins. Then she saw him take a deep breath, and he rubbed a hand over his jaw wearily.

"Not going well?" she asked.

"Not going, period. I don't have any idea what to write."

She stood, leaving the girls trying very hard to hand the rabbit back and forth, and walked over to him. "Just the basics, then. I read some online this morning."

He looked at her rather oddly. "You read obituaries?"

"Just to get an idea, you know? There are a lot that just give names, dates, where they were born, lived, family names, and the funeral info."

He grimaced. "Sounds better than 'Dominic Mancuso, full-time crook, and his equally crooked wife.'"

"Those who need to know that probably already do, don't you think?"

He stared at her. After a moment he said softly, "How did Harrington not turn to you for help on everything?"

Gemma nearly gasped at the jolt those words gave her. Color flooded her cheeks. She'd gotten lots of compliments in her life—on her looks, hair, clothes, jewelry, style and, later, more satisfying ones on her organizing and genuine caring for her animal causes. But she had never had her breath taken away by one before.

Because Dev never wanted her advice, and rejected it if she gave it.

She was glad he'd begun writing, quickly, because if he kept looking at her, she didn't know what she would have done. He consulted a small piece of paper at his elbow that had some notes scribbled on it. In a couple of minutes, he had it done, leaving a blank at the end for the funeral location and time.

She leaned over, reached for the pen. His brow furrowed, but he gave it to her. Her fingers inadvertently brushed his, and she felt another rush of sensation similar to what his quiet compliment had given her. She froze for a split second, not understanding. Then she grasped the pen and filled in the blank spot.

She set the pen down, realized he was staring at her.

"It's set?" he asked.

She nodded. "I chose the smaller chapel. I hope that's all right. You need to go in and confirm everything and sign some papers, but it's set for Saturday morning at ten. Oh, and you need to call to okay the release of… the bodies to them."

"Gemma, I—"

A startled woof from Flash snapped both their heads around. The girls were giggling, and the stuffed rabbit lay half atop the big dog's head. Lucia was waving her arms, looking proud. Zita had rolled over on her back and was kicking her legs in apparent delight.

"Oh, one thrower, and the other is going to be crawling soon," Gemma said in mock horror. "You'd better look out."

He burst out with a laugh, and it was the most wonderful sound she'd heard in ages. The weariness, the worry in his eyes vanished with it, and she had her first glimpse of what he must have been like, before. He was gorgeous enough already—he must have been a stunner before the weight of the world had come down on him.

"How on earth are you still single?" she asked before she thought.

The smile that had lingered after the laugh slowly faded. "I could ask you the same thing."

"Oh, it took a while to find someone I was certain wasn't after money or a connection to my father."

Dev wasn't—he hardly needed either. And they would put it back together, perhaps sooner than she'd expected. Dante just looked at her for a moment, and she wondered if he was considering giving her his opinion of Dev again.

But in the end he only shrugged and said, "Just as hard to find somebody who can handle being married to a cop." Almost visibly the weight descended on him again. "And now, with two babies in the mix, I'd say that would be a useless search anyway."

"But they're adorable!"

"I thought twins were twice the work."

"Well, yes, but they also entertain each other a lot. You have to see them when I set them both in front of the mirror in the bedroom. It's fascinating to watch them try to figure it out."

He was staring at her again, so intently, with such a bemused look on his face that it made her feel awkward. And she was not used to feeling awkward. The silence spun out, oddly tense, until she grabbed at the first thing that popped into her head. She gestured at the finished obit.

"Are there people you need to call? Any of them I can handle?"

The mental shake he gave himself was almost visible. "I… No. Any of his friends I know about I…wouldn't call."

She thought about that for a moment. Then realized. "Are you thinking you could get in trouble?"

"The department frowns on socializing with criminals."

"But…this is hardly socializing, is it?"

"Maybe." He let out an audible breath. "It was in the news. This—" he gestured at the obituary "—will run tomorrow. Word will get out. And if it doesn't, so be it."

"All right." She glanced over to be sure the girls were all right. Apparently Flash had nudged the rabbit back to them, because they had it between them again. "What about them?"

"What about them?" he echoed her words rather blankly.

"They're just babies. But it's their parents' funeral."

His gaze shifted to the twins. "You mean...bring them?"

"I mean, you need to decide if you want them there. Not the service itself—I'm sure you wouldn't want them to disturb it if they started crying or giggling. But... one day, will they wonder? Wish you'd taken them?"

"If I live that long, one day they'll probably hate me for something. Maybe a lot of things. This funeral will be the least of it."

The almost bitter note in his voice told her just how apprehensive he was about all this. The oddity of it struck her. He was a cop—he'd no doubt gone into life-threatening situations, where he could be badly hurt or worse. And yet these two tiny beings had him scared.

"I think you might be underestimating them," she said softly. "And I'm sure you're underestimating yourself."

The look that came into his eyes then was a visual echo of that compliment he'd given her. And Gemma Colton suddenly felt, oddly and unexpectedly, that she was exactly where she was supposed to be.

Chapter 18

The twins were looking around with great interest, and Gemma was pleased. It was a nice morning, seventy degrees out, and taking them out had been a good idea. Dante had been a little edgy this morning, comparing a printed list with some kind of schedule on his laptop. He obviously wasn't happy about something—whether it was what he was seeing or having to do it at all she didn't know.

She knew he wasn't thrilled about having been put on half days at home, and while she had calls to make to confirm some things for the upcoming funeral, she could finish that this afternoon, so this morning she'd decided she would corral the girls and vacate for a while. After all, he'd hired a nanny for a reason, and just because he was working at home now didn't mean he wasn't working and didn't need peace and quiet to do it.

And so she had loaded the girls into their stroller and proceeded to walk the two blocks to the park. She'd even offered to take Flash, since the dog park was right there, but Dante had declined.

"I wouldn't want you to have to choose between reining in the girls or the dog," he'd said. "Plus, he could drag you halfway to Sioux Falls if he got fixated on a trail."

She was beginning to see that dealing with a bloodhound was rather different than even other police K9s. They had always seemed so well mannered and obedient, but Dante had said bloodhounds had a mind of their own and could be very stubborn about using it. He also said they were big on passive resistance, and for all his lolling about, Flash looked very powerful.

She heard a loud squeal, the sound of an excited and happy child. She looked and saw there was a fairly large group at the small playground, on the swings and clambering around the large cedar structure that served as playhouse and nexus for the several slides and ladders and other apparatus. She'd done a fund-raiser for that project, but somehow she'd never seen it in use. It made her smile now, and she wondered why on earth she had never made this simplest of trips and come to see delighted children playing on this thing she'd worked toward.

The girls seemed to be interested, too, so she began to wheel them in that direction. All the while she pondered the simple realization she'd had. She'd begun working on fund-raisers because she had at last found something she was very good at. It had been such a joy, after feeling so aimless since turning twenty-one, that she hadn't looked much beyond that. She truly enjoyed helping worthy causes, and since she didn't need the money a professional organizer would make, she was happy to donate her time. But her enjoyment had only gone as far as the successful event itself and the fact that she usually exceeded the fund-raising goals.

She had never realized that seeing the final result would make her feel so good.

As she neared the playground and studied the sturdy cedar structure with the slides, currently festooned with kids clearly having a wonderful time, she had a vague memory that RRPD had, after the money had been raised and the materials purchased, built the thing.

Dante? Had he been part of that? He didn't seem the carpenter type, but what did she know? She never followed through to the down and dirty part of the projects she raised money for.

...he's the first guy you go to if you need a favor.

Juliette's words echoed in her mind. And Gemma decided she wouldn't be in the least surprised if he'd been right in there with a hammer, a saw or whatever.

Now that's something I would like to watch.

The idle thought struck her as rather odd, because she'd never before been interested in such things. But now, people who built things, good things, seemed like people she should know.

The girls were jabbering nonsensically back and forth. Nonsensically to her, anyway, because they certainly seemed to understand each other. But they were obviously quite entertained by watching the kids play, so she settled down on a bench to let them, as she saw a couple of other mothers or caretakers had done. She found herself smiling, and she wasn't quite sure why.

She leaned back on the bench, closing her eyes and tilting her head to let the sun warm her face. Soon enough winter would be here and—

Her eyes snapped open. Winter.

In just a couple of months, the temperatures would be about twenty-five degrees colder and well below freezing at night. A month after that, breaking freezing during the day would be considered warm, and nights would plunge into the teens if not lower.

In just a couple of months, she would normally be off to a warmer clime, maybe to the house in St. Croix.

She hadn't even thought about that when she'd pushed her way into this job. She'd sort of given Dante a timeline of six months, although she hadn't really intended to.

If you haven't gotten it together by then, you may need to get a real mom.

This time it was her own words that rang in her mind. A real mom. Like Dev wanted for a wife. The kind who are so good with kids you marry them just for that.

Getting married just to have someone to help take care of them would be the worst thing I could do for them...not to mention the insult to that woman if, for instance, I asked her to prove she could take care of them before I'd marry her.

Back to Dante. And what he'd said stung even more now than it had when he'd said it.

Another happy squeal from a little girl on the swings. Grateful for the distraction, Gemma watched her go higher and higher. Wondered how old the girls would have to be before they could start to play like this. She tried to picture it, tried to imagine them and how much more chaotic life would be when they were independently mobile. They—

Her thoughts broke off as someone on the far side of the playground moved. It was a woman, carrying a baby in a sling in front of her. Her dark hair was short, in that pixie kind of way it was hard to carry off, but this woman did it. Gemma watched the woman watch the children, much as she herself was doing, and wondered if she was thinking the same thing, of the day when her own baby would be big enough to join in the fun.

At least you've only got one to deal with.

She smiled wryly to herself. The woman looked toward the play structure as a boy atop it trumpeted out his triumph in a Tarzan sort of yell. Gemma started to look as well, but her gaze suddenly snapped back to the woman.

The sunglasses, she thought. They were exactly the same ones she'd bought for that disaster of a Christmas when several of the family insisted all the branches of the Coltons get together. A Secret Santa project had been part of it, and the sunglasses had been her gift. They were French, very distinctive—she'd bought them on a trip to New York City and doubted there was another pair just like them in South Dakota.

And the name she'd drawn had been Demi Colton.

She stared at the woman's profile. Tried to picture

her with long red hair, as she'd known her. She knew the latest description said Demi had either cut and dyed her hair dark or had been seen wearing a wig. Gemma studied her nose, her chin, her shape, the way she held herself. Her stunned mind tried to process what her instinct was already telling her was true.

She was standing less than fifty feet away from the woman all of Red Ridge was searching for.

Demi.

The instant the name formed in her mind the woman's head turned back toward the kids on the swings. Gemma rose to her feet. The movement must have attracted Demi's attention, because she looked. For an instant she simply stared. But it was long enough for Gemma to know that Demi had recognized her.

Demi spun around and ran.

"Wait!" Gemma called out, even knowing she was already too far away to hear. "Wait," she repeated, barely whispering this time. "I don't believe you did it."

And she meant it. Demi might be a little rough around the edges, and yes, she had a temper, but a killer? No. Gemma could not believe that. She didn't care how much evidence they had.

And the baby. So that had been true, too. Demi had had a baby. While she'd been on the run. Gemma couldn't even begin to imagine what that must have been like.

She sank back down on the bench. Looked around at the other adults. None of them seemed aware in the slightest that they had been within feet of the woman most believed was the crazed serial murderer they called the Groom Killer. They either hadn't seen her or hadn't recognized her.

One of those, a woman holding the hand of a rather grubby little boy—the one who had yelled from the top of the tower—was passing, headed for the parking lot. But she paused to coo over the twins.

"Oh, they're beautiful," she said. "How old are they?"

"Six months," Gemma said, rather absently since her mind was still absorbed with what had happened.

"Such pretty girls you are," the woman said, bending over the two.

"Girls," the little boy muttered, making a face.

His mother straightened, looked at her son. "Hard to believe someday you might like them, isn't it?"

The boy made a worse face, and for a moment Gemma smiled, distracted. But the moment the woman and boy had gone, her mind leaped back to what had happened.

If she'd been alone, she might have gone after her. But she had the twins, and there was no way she could abandon them to chase Demi.

Chase. Like the cops were chasing her.

She'd just seen a fugitive. A multiple-murder suspect.

But she was family. Not the closest, but family.

Family that Dev put out a $100,000 reward on, don't forget that.

She shoved away the fact that had bothered her since Dev had done it.

She should call the police.

But Demi was innocent. She was sure of it. The police, including some of her own relatives, seemed sure she was guilty, though. They'd haul her off to jail, and she'd end up in prison, maybe for life.

The baby. How could Gemma report seeing her when Demi had a baby even younger than the twins?

How could she *not* report it?

She shivered despite the mild weather. Wrapped her arms around herself.

She looked at the twins. "What should I do?" she whispered to them.

Lucia, who had been trying to reach the brightly colored ball that hung above her from the stroller's handle, shifted her gaze to Gemma. Zita helpfully said, "Ba ba ba."

She got out her phone. Stared at it for a while. Minutes ticked by. She felt torn, uncertain. It just seemed so cold, so heartless, to sic the police on family. And Demi had a baby...

She didn't know what to do. Twice she punched in 911 but didn't send it.

Maybe she should call Finn Colton. He was also family, after all. But she found the chief of the K9 unit rather intimidating.

Brayden. She could call the other Colton cousin who was a K9 officer. He was Demi's half brother—surely he'd be more open to thinking her innocent? She'd even heard that he didn't believe she'd done it. Gemma wished now she'd paid more attention to all the stories circulating.

She called the K9 unit and asked for him, without saying why she needed to speak to him and hoping her name and the family connection would do it. She was put through, but it went immediately to voice mail. This was not something she wanted to leave a message about, so she disconnected.

God, she didn't know what to do. Time was passing, Demi was running and she had to do…something. Tell someone. But someone who would give Demi a chance. She didn't think she could bear it if she turned Demi in and she ended up dead. But if she couldn't reach a Colton cop, who could she—

Zita chimed in again, this time with an equally helpful, "Pa pa pa."

"Thanks, kid," Gemma said. "But—"

Dante.

She could call Dante. He would understand. Of all people, he would understand.

Feeling like a fool for not having thought of it sooner, she grabbed her phone again.

"How long ago?"

Dante knew his voice had gone up a notch, but he couldn't believe she'd waited twenty minutes to call him. Loading up Flash and getting here had added another ten, which he had spent alerting the department.

"Just after ten thirty."

"Damn it, Gemma, she'll be long gone by now! Especially if she got in a vehicle."

"I know. But…she has her baby with her, and…she didn't kill anyone, Dante. I just know she didn't."

Her eyes were glistening, and he reined in his temper. "That's for the court to decide."

"No! The truth is the truth, and the court doesn't always get it right. You know that."

Dante smothered what he wanted to say, because he knew it would come out in a yell. The twins were already restless and looked as if the slightest thing would set them off into those ear-piercing wails.

"I tried to call Brayden right away, but it went to voicemail," she said.

At least she'd tried, then. Dante calmed down a bit.

"You're absolutely certain it was her?"

She nodded and told him about the sunglasses Demi had been wearing.

"All right," he said, rather grimly, "if she's still anywhere around here on foot, Flash can find her." *If I can get him on her scent. Big if, with no scent article on hand.*

Her eyes widened. "You're going to sic him on her?"

"He's not an attack dog, Gemma."

"But—"

"Just figure out how we're going to explain why you waited so long to call," he snapped. "Now, tell me where she was."

"Over there, next to the playhouse thing. Where all those kids lined up to climb the big slide."

He'd been afraid of that. "Did she touch anything?"

Gemma blinked. "What?"

"Did she touch anything? The slide, that fence there, anything?"

"I…don't think so. She was just standing there, watching the kids play. Then when she saw me, she ran."

"Which way?"

"Toward the parking area."

"Did you see her get in a car?"

"No. I couldn't see from where I was. But I didn't see her after that."

She was starting to look a bit harassed. He was sorry for the barrage of questions, but he didn't have time to be polite—too much time had already been wasted. He wasn't on the Groom Killer case officially, but in effect every cop in the county was.

"Did you see or hear a car leave after that?"

"Yes."

"About the right time for her to have gotten to it?"

"I… Yes. I heard a car start. And then the bus."

His turn to blink. "Bus?"

"With the children. It must have been a field trip or something, that's why there were so many here."

"How many?" he asked, his energy suddenly ebbing.

"Twenty or so. Maybe more."

Twenty kids all over the parking lot, leaving fresher scents than Demi, and him with nothing with Demi Colton's confirmed scent on it to use to home Flash in.

"What?" she asked. "You changed all of a sudden."

"Twenty kids," he muttered, surprised she'd noticed.

"You mean he wouldn't know who to follow?"

"If I had something she'd touched—we call it a scent article—he could sort it out, pick out her trail infallibly. But I don't. Flash is brilliant and a tireless trailing dog, but he can't start from nothing."

"But she was right there—"

"Along with a couple of dozen others. No way to isolate which scent is hers for him. And in the parking lot, with maybe thirty other people and a bus likely putting out carbon monoxide? That'll contaminate scent for even the best trailing or tracking dog."

"Aren't they the same thing?" she asked.

He wondered why she'd fastened on that. "No. Most tracking dogs are trained to follow a specific trail, footprints or whatever, to the end. A trailing dog follows the scent he's given, whether it's on the trail or on the wind."

Gemma was looking thoughtful. "So...that must be useful if somebody doubles back or something. He'd go after the scent, not the tracks."

He looked at her, startled. She'd gotten that quickly. "Exactly."

He heard the sound of vehicles approaching, saw the troops had arrived. He tried to marshal his thoughts, what he was going to say. Logically he knew it wasn't his fault she hadn't called immediately upon seeing Demi Colton, but he still felt responsible somehow. He wasn't sure why—they'd never even talked about the Groom Killer case.

But they were going to ask, the cops who were on the case. Why she'd waited. Wonder if it was because of her family connection to the suspect. He'd have to convince them that being related to a criminal didn't make you one.

And that was something he'd had practice with.

Chapter 19

In the end it took almost two hours for him to extricate them from the process, between Gemma being questioned and him having to explain why using Flash wasn't feasible, and then the inevitable arched eyebrows and lewd suggestions when they learned Gemma was his new nanny. He knew he was on edge when he snapped at Collins, who ribbed him once too often.

"I only need a nanny because my brother is freaking *dead*, so back the hell off."

The man looked surprised, putting up his hands. Dante didn't know if it was because of the uncharacteristic flash of temper or that Al had simply forgotten why Dante was suddenly the guardian of two babies. He found he didn't care. He'd had enough.

"We're out of here. You've got my number."

He went and rescued Gemma, who was looking more than a little harassed and had been saying to the other detective, "I've told you three times," when he got to her.

"And if you want a fourth repetition, you can call me later. We need to get my nieces home."

As if on cue, the girls began that wailing. Every head turned, some in rueful recognition—likely those with kids of their own—and some in horror at the decibel level, or maybe the pitch.

They walked back to Dante's car, where he opened the back and greeted Flash. The animal looked woeful, and Dante could have sworn he winced at the barrage of sound from two obviously healthy sets of lungs.

Zita spotted the dog first, and her wailing stopped abruptly. "Ah ew ah," she said.

Flash's head came up. By now Lucia was curious about her sister's change of mood and stopped wailing to look around. She also spotted Flash and began to smile.

"A miracle worker," Gemma said. "Now if he could only change diapers."

"Tired of that already?"

"You're not?" she countered. "You've done your share."

He appreciated the acknowledgment, although his efforts in that arena were undeniably second-rate. How they ever did it with cloth and pins he didn't know.

"Thanks. Figuring you'll quit when I get the hang of it?"

"If you ever do," she came back at him quickly. "And I won't quit. You'll have to fire me."

Something in her voice told him she meant it. She wouldn't quit. And he filed that away in that place in his mind where he'd been putting the numerous Gemma surprises.

Since she'd walked the twins here and the car seats were in her vehicle, she had to walk them back.

"I'd walk them and let you drive, but—"

"That?" she said, glancing at the big SUV full of police equipment and Flash's gear along with the dog himself. "No, thanks. Besides, isn't there a rule against civilians driving police vehicles?"

"Probably. It's never been an issue before, so I plead ignorance."

"Think that'd fly?" she asked, and he saw the corners of her mouth twitching slightly.

"About as far as Flash's drool," he said with an exaggerated sigh.

"Gross!"

"Only when it hits your plate."

She looked as if she didn't know whether to laugh or gag. But more importantly, she appeared to have put the last couple of hours out of her mind—for now, at least. Which had been his intent.

It was much later, after they'd gotten everyone and everything home, he'd fed and groomed Flash while she fed and bathed the girls, and they had mutually decided frozen lasagna would do fine for dinner. She wasn't above such things, he'd already noted, which had been yet another Gemma surprise for the file. They were waiting for it to bake when he saw her expression shift and he knew she was thinking about today again.

"I understand," he said quietly.

Her gaze shot to his face. "What?"

"Why you…waited. To call, I mean."

"Oh." She looked down again, as if there were some secret code in the pattern of the granite counter.

"I had to rat out my uncle once."

Her head came back up. "Why?"

"He pulled an armed robbery right in front of me. A woman got hurt. I was fifteen. I had to testify against him."

Her eyes widened. "My God. Why on earth would he do that in front of you?"

"I think it was a test. Of my family loyalty."

She stared at him. "You mean…they expected you *not* to turn him in?"

"That's who my family is. So you see, I knew he was guilty and it was still hard as hell to do it. But you're convinced Demi Colton is innocent. So I get why it took you a while."

She was still staring at him, but he thought he saw her eyes glisten a little more, as if moisture were pooling. He didn't want her to start crying, even if he didn't understand why she would. He'd had enough female crying from the younger set today. Instinctively he reached out and put a hand over hers where it was resting on the counter.

For an instant he felt as if he'd touched a live electrical wire. The snap made his fingers tingle, and all he could do was stare at their hands. She'd turned hers until her fingers were curled around his. Not gripping, or hanging on, but there, touching, and it felt…right. So very right.

Uh-oh.

He risked a glance at her face. She, too, was staring at their hands and looking almost as stunned as he felt.

Double uh-oh.

It took everything he had to gently disengage rather than yank his hand away as if hers were that live wire. He stood up abruptly, and for lack of any other idea he walked over to the oven on the pretense of checking on the lasagna, which had a good twenty minutes yet to go.

He wanted to turn back and look at her. He wanted to see her face, her expression. He wanted to go back to her. He wanted to ask her if she'd felt it, too. He dared do none of it.

He stared at the timer. Watched as it clicked over another minute gone.

Another minute of his life gone.

The hand that had reached out to hers clenched into a fist. He let his fingernails dig in, trying to replace one sensation with another. Wipe out pleasure with pain.

He nearly groaned aloud at his own thoughts.

He had to be losing his mind.

Gemma lay in the dark, staring at nothing.

She had never expected him to understand. But when he'd told her why he did, her heart had almost broken.

She had never expected him to stand between her and the other cops, the suspicious one. He did.

She had never, ever expected the mere touch of hands to send a jolt through her like that.

She held up that hand, some part of her swirling brain surprised that it wasn't somehow glowing in the darkness. It should be. There should be some sign of that connection—surely something that strong, that instant, should leave a mark?

For a long time she lay awake, trying to make sense of it all, trying to see the path she had once thought so clear.

When she finally fell asleep, she was more confused than ever.

Chapter 20

"Do you think there will be very many there?"

Dante looked over at Gemma as he strapped Lucia into her car carrier in the luxury SUV. Saturday and the funeral were finally here, after a relatively quiet morning that had still managed to have a steep learning curve. Lucia liked carrots, Zita did not. Since they were only starting on solid food, they ended up wearing as much as they ate. Which resulted in the knowledge that Lucia squealed at cold water on a washcloth, but Zita did not. And on it went.

They had finally agreed on taking the girls, but only to the quiet, private room in the chapel, and if they started to fuss, Gemma would take them outside to the peaceful, tree-lined garden beside it. Then, if that someday came, he could tell them they had at least been there.

"I can guarantee there will at least be a police presence," he answered.

She looked startled. "Why?"

He didn't tell her it had been his suggestion. "They never miss a crook's funeral. You never know who on the wanted list might turn up."

She stared at him. "You…really grew up with this?"

"All my life."

"Until you walked away from it."

"Yes."

She seemed to ponder for a moment. "Is that why you decided the twins could come? Because there will be police there?"

"No other way I'd take them into what will likely be a den of thieves."

Again she looked at him thoughtfully. "That's why you wanted me to drive them separately, isn't it? You might get into something…police related and I'll need to get them out of there?"

He straightened up from fastening Lucia's carrier— why did they make the damn process so tricky?—and looked at her. Anybody, he thought, who dismissed this woman as a pampered airhead heiress would be making a serious mistake.

"What?" she asked at his look.

"Just thinking you'd make a hell of an undercover operative."

It was a moment before she smiled. "I've the perfect cover, haven't I? Silly, spoiled rich girl, and throw probably stupid into the bargain."

"Exactly. They'd never know what hit them."

She gave him a look that reminded him of how she'd looked when he'd asked why Harrington didn't ask for her help on everything. It warmed him in a way he didn't quite understand, and he bent to double-check the seat belt fastening to keep from letting his disconcertment show.

"Dante?"

"Hmm?"

"Don't worry about the parenting thing. You're already getting it down."

He couldn't stop the pleased smile that curved his mouth, but he couldn't think of a thing to say and so said nothing.

They started on their way, Dante in the lead. He was already thinking ahead, wondering if Flash would alert on anybody at the funeral. Dante might even let him out after for a round of sniffing, just for that reason.

About a mile out his cell rang, and he used the car system to answer.

"Mancuso."

"Hey, man, it's Duke. Just wanted to give you a heads-up. Collins and I will be there this morning, and we'll be set up for video."

"I knew somebody would be. Sorry you got the short straw." Just because it was sometimes productive, nobody enjoyed feeling like a vulture clustered around the dead.

"I volunteered. Figured it'd be easier on you if it was a friend."

He didn't know what to say. All he could manage was "Thanks, buddy. I appreciate it."

"No prob. And you don't know us."

He supposed Duke thought he might be unsettled enough not to have realized he, the known cop to just about anybody who might show up—Dominic's rebel brother was well known by his colleagues—shouldn't tip off that there were other cops present. Personally, Dante figured the bad guys knew it already, but they couldn't know which people they were, so he only said, "Got it."

When the call was disconnected, he automatically checked his mirrors. Noted the attractive woman driving the luxury SUV behind him. Realized with a little jolt it was Gemma. Smothered his reaction; his life was complicated enough just now—he wasn't about to spend any of his limited time and energy dwelling on the obvious, that she was a beautiful woman and he responded to that. And the even more obvious—that it would be utterly, totally insane to let his thoughts wander one more step down that path. She was Gemma Colton, for God's sake.

They arrived early, as planned, to give them some time to deal with the girls and for him to get Flash set up with water, although it wasn't at all warm today. He left windows partway down anyway.

Gemma parked beside him, and he went to the back of her SUV to get out the twin stroller. It occurred to him as he lifted it out that she had to be stronger than she looked; this thing wasn't light, and even collapsed it was awkwardly bulky. But between them they got it done quickly and walked toward the chapel.

They were met by a tall, soft-spoken man, and Dante

wondered if he'd developed the low-key persona for his work as a funeral director or if he'd been born with it. He saw the man glance at the twins and quickly assured him they would not be dealing with wailing babies during the service. The man smiled serenely.

"Whatever you wish," he said.

"We'd like to take them to the chapel," Gemma said. "Is the photo up?"

The man nodded. "It is. This way."

"Photo?" Dante asked her in a whisper as they followed his lead.

"They have the service available, and I found a nice one in the girls' baby book," she said.

He stared at her yet again. And had no idea what to say. "You think of everything" sounded far too cliché for what she'd done. In the end, "Thank you" was all he could get out. And her smile made it seem like almost enough.

The funeral director left them alone in the chapel. Dante stared at the enlarged photograph that sat on an easel next to a spray of flowers. He'd never seen it before, but that wasn't surprising. What was surprising was how…happy his brother and sister-in-law looked, formally dressed and holding two tiny babies not even recognizable as the two here now, except for the point on Zita's eyebrow.

At the same moment, they both leaned down to pick up the girls, and Gemma's head bumped his shoulder. He nearly jumped at the contact.

"Sorry," she said.

"You all right?" he said simultaneously. They both

let out a low chuckle, muted by the intentional solemnity of this place.

He picked up Zita, she Lucia, and they walked to the front of the chapel, to the picture. The girls both looked at it, but if it registered he couldn't tell. He had no idea at what point babies recognized images as something familiar. But that wasn't why they were here. They were here for that day when they might ask.

If I live that long.

It struck him anew. How could he do this? How did other people do it, have kids and still be a cop?

"What a life they brought these two innocents into," Gemma murmured, staring at the photograph.

It hit him with a jolt that she was right. Again. Dominic and his wife had brought these two pure, innocent souls into their world—one full of petty crime and dodgy characters.

"I wondered," he said slowly, "when they were born, if he'd change. If he'd go legit, clean up his life."

"But he didn't," Gemma said quietly.

"No." He looked at Zita, who smiled that sweet baby smile and reached out as if to pat his cheek, although the gesture was a little short on coordination yet. He hugged her a little tighter. "And I don't understand how he couldn't."

"And that," Gemma said, "is why you'll probably be better for them, in the end."

His gaze went to her face. There was nothing but a quiet sincerity there. "I'll settle for not being bad for them."

"Not a chance of that."

"I wish I was so sure."

She gave a shrug, as if the answer was obvious. "You're a good and honorable man, Dante, and you'll love them. That's a lot more than some kids have."

For a long moment he just looked at her. His throat was a little tight at the unexpected praise. He was surprised at her words and wondered if she felt that way because her father had fallen short on all those fronts.

"How did you get so wise?"

"Given who my father is, you mean?" It was close enough to what he'd been thinking that he was sure he looked guilty. But she didn't call him on it. "I had my brother and sisters. And," she added with an arch look, "we had that really great nanny."

He couldn't help smiling at that. "So that's where you learned."

"Only when I was old enough to notice, since I was the youngest. But Mrs. Hicks is a wonderful person. I adored her and still do. I tell her if I ever have children, I'm luring her out of retirement."

Lucia started to squirm as he said, "If? I thought this whole thing was in preparation for that."

For an instant she looked startled. Almost as if she'd forgotten. It was a mere flash of expression, but Dante was almost sure he'd seen it. And then her cheeks pinked, and he was certain.

"I think the girls have reached the end of their quiet capacity," she said, rather briskly. "And people are arriving. I should take them outside while you…do what you have to."

It was time, he knew that, but he felt a powerful urge

to postpone going inside the main room. But Zita was also getting restless now, and he knew Gemma was right.

He gave the little one a kiss on the cheek and she giggled. Dante gave an exaggerated sigh as he settled her back in the stroller. "Story of my life. I kiss a girl and she laughs at me."

"A grown-up girl wouldn't," Gemma said.

His gaze shot back to her face. There was still the slightest trace of pink in her cheeks, but he decided it had to be left over from before, not because they were talking about kissing.

Him kissing, specifically.

If this were some other situation, if she were someone else, he might have asked her if she was offering. But this was Gemma Colton, and he was a Mancuso. Besides, the girls needed her, so he'd best not send her running the first week.

But she thought he was good, honorable. And that he'd have a line of potential dates if he went looking.

And why the hell was he thinking about what she thought of him, personally? All that mattered was that she took good care of the girls, and so far, with a few inevitable stumbles, she'd done that. Surprisingly well.

But then, she was full of surprises. So many that he knew the fault had to be in his assumptions.

He'd vastly underestimated Gemma Colton. In more ways than one.

He watched her wheel the stroller out carefully— she had to, it was wide and barely fit through some doors—and wished he could go, too. Nothing to do with Gemma, of course. Just that he'd much rather take a stroll through the admittedly beautiful garden outside than head into the main room here and spend an hour swimming with bottom-feeders. But he had no choice.

Dante hadn't been in the midst of so many lowlifes since the last time he'd had to go to interview someone at the state prison down in Springfield. He recognized several but saw no one RRPD was actively looking for. Nor did he see anyone he suspected of being connected to the Larsons; Dominic's criminal world and theirs didn't overlap much. And not, he was sure, because he'd once warned his brother to stay clear of them—Dom had scoffed at that—but because his brother had kept his own activities out of Red Ridge.

He smothered the instinctive assessment. He'd been pulled off the Larson case. Not that that would have stopped him if he'd seen someone connected to the brothers, but he'd have some explaining to do.

The service was short, because no one had much to say. Him most of all. But outside afterward, he was awash in a sea of curious—or suspicious—gazes. Some gave him words of condolence, while some who had apparently known Dom better expressed surprise that he was even there. Only one asked him if he was finally going to take up the family business. The guy got a cold stare in answer.

He hated this. He'd often wished Dominic had lived somewhere else, where he didn't have to face the knowledge of both their estrangement and his brother's chosen life every day.

And now he didn't.

Careful what you wish for.

A deep, loud baying snapped him out of his thoughts. Something had set Flash off. He looked toward the SUV. Some people were walking by to their own cars, but no one was close enough to really disturb the dog. In fact, the only person at all close to the car wasn't even looking at it—he was looking at the garden. Dante frowned. The man seemed not familiar, but as if he'd at least seen him before. Not just now, in the service, but somewhere else. But he was too far away for Dante to pin it down. He started that way.

Flash was building momentum now, and heads were turning all around him. He wondered for a moment if any of these guys ever had nightmares of a bloodhound on their trail. Given their activities, he wouldn't be surprised. No wonder they were starting to look uneasy at the sound. Dante locked gazes with Duke, who was still back near the chapel, for an instant. He gave the barest of shrugs to indicate he had no idea, and Duke went back to scanning the mourners.

The man he'd noticed glanced nervously over his shoulder toward the SUV and Flash. Dante noted he had a bandage on his cheek and a black eye. Dante tried not to let that throw him off as the man began to walk quickly away. In that instant, at that distance, that angle, and with the sudden hurry…

It clicked. Dante's breath stopped. His pulse kicked up. It had only been a glimpse, just as it had been that day, but he knew. As Flash, who could scent on the air as well as the ground, had known. The dog never forgot, and he had had this scent in his nose before. And Dante knew where.

The crash.

This was the man who had fired those shots, resulting in Dom hitting that pole.

This was the man who had killed his brother.

Chapter 21

It had taken Gemma a moment to realize what she was hearing. The sound sent a shiver up her spine, as if it were some primitive reaction she had no control over. All the cultural references ran through her head—the baying of hounds, a bloodhound on your trail... How very odd, she thought.

She looked at the twins, who appeared to be on the verge of either laughing or crying at the sudden howls. In the hopes she could tip them into laughing, she laughed herself.

"Isn't that wonderful?" she cooed at them. "That's your friend Flash. Who knew he could sound so...so impressive?"

Zita, who had begun to squirm and look worried at

the first howl, suddenly shifted to smiling. "Ah eh oh," she said.

"Exactly," Gemma said, and happily Lucia seemed to find conversing with her twin in that long string of sounds more important than the louder noise coming from her canine friend.

She looked up in time to see a man she'd noticed earlier outside the chapel, apparently watching, now walking quickly away. Then she saw Dante walking toward the SUV; obviously he'd heard Flash and was—

He was running. After the man who had been watching the mourners. She'd assumed he was one of the officers Dante had told her would be there, but that was obviously wrong if Dante was chasing him.

There was no chance he would catch up with him. Dante was obviously fast, but he was too far away. Even as she thought it, the man jumped into a car and sped off. Dante made a quick move with one hand and for a moment her breath caught; was he going to shoot at the guy?

She breathed again when she realized what he'd pulled out was not a gun but his phone. He seemed to snap a photo of the fleeing car, then made a call as he turned to walk back. Flash's howling had slowed, but the dog still didn't sound happy. Then again, she wondered if the serious, sometimes mopey-looking dog was capable of sounding happy.

Not that he'd had much to be happy about, she thought as she looked back at the girls. His life had been turned inside out just as Dante's had. The only bright spot she could see was that the girls were too young to understand what had happened. They had to be confused, though, that their parents, those familiar faces, were gone. She'd done some research and found that at six months they would know those faces.

"Let's go see your uncle," she said to them brightly and began to wheel the stroller that way. Dante had stopped at his vehicle to calm the dog, but he was headed toward them now. "Who was that?" she asked when he reached them.

He hesitated, and she could see he was trying to decide what to say.

"He was watching the people coming out of the chapel," she said to explain her curiosity.

He went still. "Did he see you?"

She frowned. "I suppose. He was there the whole time I was sitting on the bench in the garden. I only really noticed because he had a black eye."

His voice was sharp now. "Did he ever approach you?"

"No. He came from over there," she said, pointing toward another small building where some people were gathered.

"How was he looking at you? Like he wanted to hit on you?"

"No. He barely glanced over."

"You're sure?"

"I always know when a man is thinking about that." She was rather irritated, and it showed in her voice.

It was a moment before he said, sounding almost rueful, "I think you probably miss one or two here and there."

"What's that supposed to mean?"

"Nothing. He was watching the people coming out of my brother's funeral?"

She didn't believe it was nothing, but something about the way he was firing questions—like a cop—bothered her enough to just answer.

"Maybe he just wanted something else to think about, if he just came from another funeral."

"Or maybe he went to the wrong one," Dante muttered, almost under his breath.

He was making her really nervous now. "What is this about? Should I be worried?"

"Only if you see that guy again," he said flatly.

He made a brief call. As he spoke quietly, she looked around at the few mourners who were left. Odd how ordinary they all looked, for the bunch of petty criminals Dante had said they were. The cops must still be among them, and she tried to guess who they were. The only one who looked like he fit the bill was the big, powerful-looking man with the unibrow. So that probably meant he was one of the cops, she thought wryly.

Then, abruptly, Dante said, "Let's get out of here. I've had enough of this place and these people."

She couldn't blame him for that. Nor could she seem to quash the desire to soothe him somehow. When she looked at it all, she realized what a horrible week this had been for him. And he'd handled it with much more grace than a lot of men would have. Certainly more than Dev would have.

The traitorous thought formed in her mind before she even realized it. She tried to shove it away, but it rang with a truth she couldn't deny. Dev would not handle this well. He didn't handle anything that didn't go his way very well.

She thought about that all the way back home. And didn't realize until they were almost there that that was how she was thinking of it—as home. She felt heat rise in her cheeks. Again. She'd blushed more in the last week than she had in years. Funny, Dev never flustered her like this.

And there it was again, negativity about the man she loved and wanted to spend her life with. What was wrong with her?

I think you probably miss one or two here and there.

What had Dante been saying? That she had so many men panting after her—too often for her money, or a connection to her father—that she didn't notice them all? Maybe that was true—she'd grown so used to that kind of attention she barely paid attention any longer.

Or had he been saying she hadn't noticed…him?

She tried to laugh at the thought. She might not have known him long, but she knew he wasn't the type. Odd, it had taken concrete knowledge of Dev's wealth and position for her to be sure of that about him, but she'd only had to spend a week in Dante's company to be utterly certain he had no interest in a connection to her father or her own wealth. In fact, she was reasonably certain it had been a drawback in his eyes, part of the reason he'd been doubtful about giving her the job in the first place.

Which in turn was part of the reason she'd been so determined to prove him wrong. Which was odd in itself, since she usually didn't trouble herself much about what people thought about her. She'd cared too much, once, had hated the way people made assumptions. Yes, she'd had a gilded upbringing, had had few worries in her life. But just because she'd had few cares didn't mean she didn't care.

But what he'd said still niggled at her, especially because if she eliminated her father and her money, it would leave only that he was interested in her herself. And there was no way that should make her blush or her pulse pick up. She should be immune. She loved Dev, didn't she?

And there it was again, the doubt. And with it came the fear she'd buried the deepest—that not only did Devlin not love her the way she loved him, but…he loved someone else.

A solid alliance with the Coltons would make our fathers very happy.

She remembered so clearly the night he'd said that. He'd covered for it quickly, making a joke of it, but she'd never forgotten. She'd told herself of course it was a joke, because his father was already engaged to—and quite smitten with—her sister Layla. The wedding had had to be postponed because of the maniac running around killing would-be grooms, but once he was caught, things would proceed as planned. So there was no need for Dev to start dating her just for that. Just because his father approved?

As for her father, she wouldn't put much past him. He'd been very worried about the business lately, and so had Layla, although they didn't talk about it in front of her. She'd tried to bring it up once, because she knew a lot of green-energy companies were struggling, but her father had brushed her off. But she hadn't missed the glances he and Layla had exchanged. And she couldn't help suspecting Layla was less than enamored of the elder, very wealthy Harrington, but had agreed to marry him anyway, and that made her uneasy. But no one would talk to her about any of it.

She smothered a sigh. She was ever and always the youngest daughter and little sister, and they didn't take her seriously. Even Blake, whom she was closest to, had laughed at the very idea of her being able to do even this, take care of a couple of sweet babies.

She remembered that thought in the dark hours of that night, when the girls began to wail for the third time. They had seemed distressed all evening and utterly unable to settle after she'd put them to bed. As if the funeral had affected them in some way they hadn't expected.

Sleepily she got up, wondering as she yawned at what point you left them to cry it out and hopefully go back to sleep on their own. She'd have to research that. She stumbled out her door and toward the den, pulling on her robe, and was nearly there when the screeching began to ebb. When it did, she heard something else.

Music.

Dante must have gotten up and turned on the sound system she'd seen in the den. The song was something slow, sweet and lulling. And it was apparently lulling the twins. And she smiled when she realized the lovely, deep male voice was singing in Italian. So he wasn't completely severed from his heritage, she thought, if he had that music to play. She should have thought of that before, playing lullabies for them.

Oddly, as she reached the door, the recording seemed to skip, and when it picked back up again, it was without words, only humming of that pretty, soothing melody. Then the words picked up again, as if the singer had forgotten a phrase but then remembered it. A recording of a live performance, perhaps? But there was no accompaniment—that was puzzling.

But the girls were deliciously quiet now, the only sound that wonderful, deep voice, and she peeked inside. And realized it wasn't a recording at all.

It was Dante.

"You can sing."

Dante shrugged as he eased out of the den, mission accomplished. "I'm not sure you can call it that when I don't know half the words."

She waved that off. "You know what I mean."

He shrugged again, embarrassed now. But at least he'd taken time to pull on sweats and a T-shirt or he'd be even more embarrassed. "I was desperate. And I remember my grandmother singing that to me when I was little and wouldn't go to sleep."

"Obviously it still works."

"Seems like."

"Your voice is amazing."

"It's…decent."

"It's a lot better than decent. Why aren't you out there with a singing career?"

She wasn't the first one to ever suggest that, and his answer never changed. "Because I can't imagine a career I'd want less."

She looked startled. "Doesn't every kid dream of being a star?"

He grimaced. "Not me."

"But you could be the next—"

"If you name some Italian opera singer, I'm going to bury you in poor little rich girl stereotypes." He gave her his best glare.

She stared at him for a moment. Then the corners of her mouth—that damned, luscious mouth—began to twitch. When the laugh came, it was the best yet, that rich, wonderful thing that seemed to envelop him in light and warmth. She stood there, looking up at him, and he wanted… He wanted…

Damn, he wanted to kiss her.

Dev Harrington was a fool.

"I'm completely awake now. Buy a girl a drink?" she asked, still smiling widely.

He couldn't help smiling back. "Sure, if you don't mind that the bar's a bit thin."

"I had something more like hot chocolate in mind," she said. "One of us should probably stay conscious."

"Done."

They were sitting in the living room a few minutes later, sipping at the warming brew. Only the kitchen light was on, so the light in the adjacent room was muted, and where he sat in his usual chair was nearly dark. Maybe it was that—that he could see her but she likely couldn't see him very well—that made him say it.

"So, tell me…is the main reason you want Harrington back because you love him, or because he hurt your pride?"

She stopped in the midst of taking a sip. "I love him."

She said it quickly. Almost too quickly. He'd learned to read people's answers fairly well in his years as a cop, and she sounded as if she were trying to convince someone. He suspected it wasn't him.

"Not what I asked."

"What you asked," she said, her voice chilly now, "is none of your business."

"It might be, if you pull it off and I have to find a new nanny."

"Then maybe that's what you should have asked, if I'll quit when Dev and I are back together."

"Oh, if that happens, you will."

She drew back slightly, but her chin came up. "Assuming again?"

"From what you've said, he wouldn't want you taking care of somebody else's kids." He saw her glance toward the den, where the girls were. Her brow was furrowed. "He'd want you pregnant with his as fast as he could manage it."

Assuming he can, speaking of assuming.

He was a little startled at the fierceness of that thought. But he couldn't deny he didn't like the image his words had conjured. Only because he didn't much like what she'd told him about Devlin Harrington.

"I think I might have something to say about that."

"You're doing this to prove to him you'd be a good

mom, because that's his requirement to marry you, and you don't think he's going to want that right away?"

She waved a hand. "I'll stall him."

Something chilly was working its way through him, despite the warmth of the chocolate. Something in that blasé dismissal rankled. It took him a moment to realize it was exactly the kind of thing he would have expected from her before he'd met her and spent a rather intense week—damn, not even a week yet—with her.

How could it have been only five days? It already felt as if they'd been doing this forever.

"You do that," he muttered, standing up. He walked to the kitchen, rinsed out the mug and put it in the dishwasher. Paused for a moment when he realized it was nearly full. Amazing how fast three extra people could fill the thing up. Not to mention the laundry.

He went back to bed, even though he already knew he'd be a long time going back to sleep. Because all he could think about was that moment outside the den when he'd wanted to kiss Gemma.

Chapter 22

Gemma didn't think she'd ever been so tired in her life. She had to look at her phone to find out it was Sunday. She was bleary-eyed when she got up to deal with the twins, and if she later found their clothes—or her own—were inside out, she would not be surprised. Not after she'd found herself drying off after her shower with the blouse she'd meant to wear today.

All of which, she thought rather acidly, could have been avoided had she been able to go back to sleep last night. But her mind had refused to shut down, careening from Dante's startlingly beautiful singing to the way he'd made her laugh to watching him fix them both hot chocolate, and then slamming full force into his snarky comments about Dev and his abrupt departure.

Is the main reason you want Harrington back because you love him, or because he hurt your pride?

Of course she loved Dev. And it wasn't pride. It hadn't been pride when she'd had to become the pursuer to get him to ask her out in the first place, either. She'd just been…intrigued. Not many men she showed an interest in didn't respond. Of course, she never knew how often it was because they knew who she was; even if she kept it secret, her face was fairly well known in Red Ridge, especially since she'd starting doing the fund-raisers.

She yawned. A moment later she yawned again.

I think my next fund-raiser should be for an organization to give new parents a break.

She nearly laughed at her own thought, but it died in her throat when, after the girls were settled in the playpen, she walked out to the kitchen desperate for coffee and found Dante already there, slouched wearily over the coffeemaker, his hands braced on the counter next to a mug ready and waiting.

Wearing nothing but a pair of boxers.

She stopped in her tracks. For an instant all she could see was the line of his body, the broad shoulders, long, muscled legs, narrow hips, and…that sweet, tight backside. Her imagination easily provided what the boxers almost concealed.

She should, she told herself, be thankful he hadn't strolled out here naked. The memory of that bath towel slung low around his hips slammed into her. And she found herself wishing he'd done that instead; one tug and it would be gone and she wouldn't have to rely on her imagination.

She barely managed to smother a gasp of shock at her traitorous thoughts. He turned his head to look at her over his shoulder. His eyes, bloodshot and sleepy, probably mirrored her own. He looked as tired as she felt. She felt a little spark of what she denied was pleasure at the thought that he'd had as sleepless a night as she had.

With a tremendous effort, she said lightly, "Good morning."

"It's morning," he acknowledged.

The coffeemaker began to drip the restorative fluid into the pot. He quickly turned back, yanked the pot out from under the stream, replced it with the mug, held it until it was full, then reversed the procedure. And despite his obvious exhaustion—a feeling she could relate to all too well—he did it sacrificing only a couple of drops to the heating plate beneath.

"All yours," he muttered, gesturing at a second mug on the counter. He'd gotten it out for her, she realized with a little jolt of what, this time, she acknowledged as pleasure. But it spiked into an altogether different kind of pleasure when he turned around and she confronted that chest and ribbed abdomen again. Damn, but the man was built. And she couldn't help thinking that while Dev was trim enough, he was just slightly softer.

She tore her eyes away from that expanse of sleek skin over taut muscle and focused on the coffee.

"Are you working today?"

He nodded. "A bit, at least. I haven't done much all week."

"Understandable."

He grimaced, and she guessed he didn't agree. She

thought about making some comment about how no one could do it all, but didn't. Instead she said, "The girls are up and dressed. It's a nice day, so I thought I'd get them out. Maybe take them over to the park where they could watch the other kids again. Or play in the sandbox. I think they'd like that. And we'd be out of your way while you work."

She was chattering, she realized. But it seemed that's what it took to keep her mind off the nearly naked man just a couple of feet away.

"Then I thought we could—"

"I don't need an itinerary."

She gave him a sharp look. "I would have thought you would want to know what I'll be doing with your nieces."

He ran a hand over his hair, rubbed at his eyes. It showed her he was indeed as weary as she was, but somehow all she could think about was the way he moved and how well muscled he was. Not bodybuilder huge, but very masculine and solid.

"I didn't mean it like that. I meant I trust you."

"Oh." Yet another kind of pleasure welled up in her, a warm, happy kind. She couldn't remember the last time she'd felt anything like it. If she ever had.

"And that will help. I'm going to drop Flash off at the training center this morning so he can wander for a while. He's been a bit cooped up since all this happened."

She glanced over to where the dog was sprawled in front of the hearth. Only to see that he'd quietly moved.

"He's in his chair!" she exclaimed, startled anew by how much that pleased her.

Dante smiled at her. "He is. Looks like you have the Flash stamp of approval."

"And the girls," she added, smiling widely back at him. "You think he's resigned?"

"Maybe. But he'll milk it, try to guilt you with that long-suffering demeanor he's so good at."

She laughed. And it suddenly struck her how seldom she laughed with Dev. He was always so serious.

This was beginning to get very unsettling, this comparing Dante with Devlin and having Dev come up short. How could that be, when she loved Dev? If she truly loved him, shouldn't she see only the good in him? To cover her tangled emotions, she walked over to Flash, who lifted his head.

"How on earth do you curl up small enough to fit in that chair?"

"He's in boneless mode," Dante said, and she smiled again.

But she kept her attention on Flash. She stroked the soft silk of his long, droopy ears. And was touched beyond what she could have ever imagined when the dog leaned into her touch.

"Definitely approval," Dante said. Then he added in a teasing tone, "I'll give you that, Colton. You may have grown up clutching the proverbial silver spoon, but you're no quitter."

The pleasure expanded inside her. So much that it almost scared her. Again. At this moment, with the girls jabbering in the den, a dog's acceptance and Dante Mancuso's smile, her life felt fuller than it ever had. She fought for equilibrium. Looked over at him. Grabbed at the only retort she could think of.

"It was a gold spoon, thank you very much," she said primly.

He stopped mid–coffee gulp. Swallowed. Lowered the mug as a crooked grin curved his mouth.

She stared at that mouth she'd seen so many ways— tight, smiling, frowning, under pressure from his fingers steepled against them…and suddenly she was wondering what his mouth would feel like if it were her lips instead of his fingers pressing against it.

She nearly gasped aloud again. What was *wrong* with her? Why was she thinking such things?

Because he's standing here practically naked and he's damned hot?

She quashed the thought even though she couldn't deny the factual truth of it. All of it. And try though she might, she couldn't deny that this man stirred things in her she'd never felt with Dev.

And where that left her, she wasn't sure.

Dante helped her maneuver outside with the stroller. He'd kissed both girls before they'd been strapped in. They had both giggled. He'd glanced at Gemma, but if she was thinking of his earlier joke he couldn't tell, because she wasn't looking at him. Or maybe wouldn't look at him. And that made him think maybe she did remember.

Damn, he was tired. Even his thoughts weren't making sense. He smothered yet another yawn. Gemma still didn't meet his gaze. In fact, she'd barely looked at him since they'd had that discussion over the coffee.

What did you expect? She'd faint dead away because you pulled on only boxers?

No, she was made of sterner stuff than that. And she'd probably seen her share of guys in that state of undress. And more. Besides, she'd already seen him in just that towel, when he'd been unable to control his body's reaction to her.

That thought sent his mind careening down a path he did not dare follow. And he didn't like the amount of effort it took to get his unruly brain to behave, to get his thoughts under control.

"Gemma?" he said when he thought he'd done it. She did look at him then. "If you happen to see the most wanted person in the county, the one every cop in the state is hunting for, call a little sooner, okay?"

He intentionally didn't say it accusingly, or even sharply. He sort of drawled it out jokingly, and after a moment she clearly decided to take it that way.

"Right. Copy that. Isn't that what you guys say?"

"Too much TV. It's usually just 'Copy.'"

She smiled at that. But her expression changed to that look of curiosity he'd come to know. "You don't sound worried that we might see her again."

He gave a one-shouldered shrug. "You hardly fit the profile of the victims."

"But I saw her, recognized her."

"So have others. If she wanted to go after them, she's had the chance often enough."

She hesitated, then asked, "Do you really think she killed all those men?"

"Doesn't matter what I think."

"It does to me."

Something had changed in her tone, something that made him feel a tightness in his gut. He answered carefully. "She's a tough girl. With a temper."

"And that makes her a serial killer?"

"No. Look, Gemma, I can't talk about the case, especially since I'm not on it. But I can say every bit of physical evidence they've got points directly at her."

"Wouldn't you think that someone smart enough to elude capture for months would have been smart enough not to leave any evidence?"

In fact, he had thought exactly that for some time. It was the big question mark that had been hanging over that case for him. But he still couldn't tell her anything that wasn't already public knowledge. "Like I said, what I think doesn't matter."

It wasn't a direct answer, but it wasn't a denial, either. And she seemed to understand that. But she shook her head slightly, looking at him with a bit of awe that made him feel almost awkward.

"I never thought of that," she said slowly. "That you have to do things you don't like, or that you disagree with."

"Of course we do. Our job is to follow the leads even if we don't like where they take us, and sometimes enforce laws we don't agree with."

She studied him for another moment. And he had no idea what she was thinking. But he had no doubt that she was, because as he'd also come to know there was always a lot going on behind that pretty, rich-girl facade.

Chapter 23

Gemma left with the girls without saying anything more. A little while later he loaded Flash up and took him to the training center. The dog looked delighted for a change, knowing he was going to get to simply follow his nose off harness. Dante checked in at the desk and told them barring anything unexpected, he'd be back for him this afternoon.

Then he went home and settled in to do one of those things he didn't like. Really, really didn't like. Namely, trying to find a dirty cop.

Once more he watched the video feed the chief had sent him, correlating whom he saw coming and going with the duty roster and the cases caught for the time between when Ron, the property officer, had booked in the phone and when it had been discovered missing. No one who shouldn't have been there appeared. Nothing that didn't match up with the reports, paperwork and time elements appeared. He'd watched the video run at least a dozen times, and nothing unusual happened. There was no gap in time or action, and the only hiccup at all was a few minutes during a power failure an hour after the phone was booked in. There had been a twenty-second delay before the standby generator had kicked in.

That would normally be suspicious, especially since the property officer had been at lunch, but it hadn't been just the department but the entire neighborhood. Ironically, the utility company said it had been an intentional outage, while they repaired damage done by a vehicle that hit a power pole. His brother's vehicle.

Was it enough time to get in, get the phone and get out? He supposed so, if you knew exactly where it was. But you'd also have to know exactly when the power was going to be shut down for the repair, because you'd only have that twenty seconds before the generator fired up and restored the power. Maybe another couple of seconds while everything came back online and settled.

Whoever had done it would have to have been right there. Waiting. Had to have had the security code to get into the evidence room. That pretty much limited it to sworn officers and the property officer, who had already been cleared by several people who had seen him at lunch at the time.

Dante watched the video yet again, at normal speed. Saw Duke joking with Ron as he handed over the sealed plastic baggie holding the flour-dusted phone Flash had

found, and Collins tapping his pen on the counter restlessly. Moments later saw Duke sign the form on Ron's
clipboard as the other man filled out a number on the
ID tag. As Ron went to put the phone in the locked evidence room, Duke and his partner turned to go. Collins realized he'd left his pen and turned back. Reached
to pick it up off the counter but somehow missed and
pushed it farther away so he had to lean over and grab
it before it slid off the other side. Got it, straightened up
and stuffed it in his jacket pocket as he again turned,
and this time left the room, stepping out of the frame
just as Ron came back. Dante again watched Ron call
out something, probably goodbye.

Once they were all out of frame, he sped the video
up. He'd already made note of what time stamps showed
visitors to the room. There weren't that many, only a
couple of cases that had physical evidence that had to
be booked in. More that had forensic evidence listed,
fingerprints and the like, but that was handled in the
lab, not here.

He sipped at his third cup of coffee as he watched.
His frustration was growing; there was nothing here
that he hadn't seen multiple times already. Nothing that
didn't correlate with his list, nothing that couldn't be
matched up to a corresponding case. There was nothing out of the ordinary.

Except that damned power glitch.

He fast-forwarded to that spot on the recording. Since
the power had gone out, there was no blank spot in the
recording, just a barely perceptible hiccup and a jump
in the time stamp when it had begun again. Showing

the same empty room it had been showing before. He
froze the image.

He sat thinking. Closed his eyes. How would he have
done it? Skip the part about knowing exactly when the
power would be cut for now. How would he have gotten in and out with the phone in under twenty seconds?
He pictured the layout of that part of the building and
walked through it in his mind. It would be better if he
could do it on site, but right now he was working on
the quiet, and being caught timing things would make
his assignment pretty obvious.

He opened his eyes. Stared at the empty room on
his laptop screen. And finally he picked up his phone
and called the chief. Finn didn't seem surprised to hear
from him on a Sunday, although something about his
voice made Dante wonder if he'd interrupted something.
Which made him wonder if Darby Gage, who bred dogs
for the K9 center, was with him.

Isn't she always these days?

He smothered a pang of envy and made his request
for the videos of the hallways leading to the property
room. Finn said he'd have them first thing tomorrow.
"How are your nieces?"

"They're alive," Dante answered wryly.

Finn laughed. "You're doing your job, then." Then,
in a different tone, he asked, "How's my cousin working out?"

He wasn't sure what the change in tone meant. "Uh…
fine. Sir."

"Really?"

"Better than I expected," Dante said, then hastily amended, "I don't mean I thought—"

"Stand down, Mancuso. I'd probably have thought the same thing if I hadn't seen the way she works on those fund-raisers. She's got more grit than I ever expected in Fenwick Colton's baby girl."

Dante breathed again, reminded of why he liked working for this man. "Yes. Yes, she does."

"Personally, I'm of the opinion the less Fenwick had to do with raising them, the better his kids turned out."

Dante couldn't help laughing at that. "I understand there was a nanny involved who kept them all fairly sane."

"Ah. So she had someone to model on."

"Yes. Sir."

Finn laughed, told him to ease up for the rest of the day. The man sounded…happy. After they'd disconnected, Dante sat for a moment, pondering the oddities of life in Red Ridge lately. Seemed almost every cop from the K9 unit had found whatever they'd been looking for in a life mate and were settling into lives with them, albeit holding off on marriage until this killer was caught.

Well, except him. Other than the twins now, he had no one in his life. But he wasn't looking. Still, it was making him feel…something. Not quite bothersome, but close. It somehow made him feel alone. Isolated. Left out.

He gave an inward, mocking laugh at himself. *Poor, poor, pitiful me.*

And for some reason he thought of Gemma saying,

so very prissily, "It was a gold spoon, thank you very much." And that made him grin. Stupidly, at a room empty even of Flash.

That his mind had gone from thinking about mates to Gemma was beyond unsettling.

He stood up, yanking his mind out of that track by muttering, "I'll start worrying when Nash goes down." Fellow K9 officer Nash Maddox was in a similar boat to Dante's, raising his four half siblings, and he had no time whatsoever for a life of his own.

And neither did he, now.

But Gemma's already in it.

He shook his head sharply. Realize he was pacing the living room. Stopped.

Maybe he'd go pick up Flash. The dog would give him that mournful side eye for cutting his wandering session short, but maybe he'd make up for it with a game of tug-of-war with his favorite rope toy. That'd probably do them both some good. Maybe if the big bloodhound yanked him off his feet and dragged him a couple of yards, as he'd done once before, he'd be just scraped up enough to keep his mind straight. Or maybe nothing would help.

And why was his life suddenly full of maybes?

He was in civilian clothes, so he got the Springfield XD and clipped the holster at the small of his back. He grabbed a jacket and pulled it on to conceal the weapon, grabbed the long, knotted rope toy from the basket near the door that held miscellaneous Flash-related items, and headed for the car. He was just pulling out of the condo parking area when his cell rang. He glanced at the screen. Quickly hit the button on the steering wheel.

"Gemma?"

"Dante, please, you have to come. To the park."

She sounded a bit breathless. Like she'd been running. "What's wrong?"

"Please, hurry."

It hit him then. She wasn't breathless because she'd been running. She was terrified.

"What happened? Are the girls okay? Are you?"

"Yes, but—" Her voice broke, and he heard her gulp as if she were taking a huge breath, trying to steady herself. "Dante, somebody tried to kill us."

Chapter 24

For a moment time seemed to freeze. And rather inanely, Dante realized he'd been wrong. There *was* someone else in his life now.

Gemma. And it made no difference how or why, because she mattered. A lot.

He made a violent U-turn, then drove as if he had lights and siren on, even though it was only two blocks. He tried to keep her talking, even knowing his time would likely be better spent calling in reinforcements. She rather chaotically told him the man was gone now, but they were still hiding, just in case. She told him where they were, sounding more shaky by the second.

The tires squealed as he pulled into the parking area. He slammed on the brakes and threw the SUV into Park. Leaped out, killing the engine with the key fob as he went. His off-duty weapon drawn, he took a split second to scan the area, searching for any sign of a still-active threat. He saw nothing, no one else even in the park this Sunday morning.

"Gemma!" he yelled as he ran toward the wooden play structure, where she'd told him they were. He spotted the stroller standing lopsidedly, half on the walkway and half in the sand of the play area. The girls were not in it, and his stomach knotted violently.

"Dante!"

Gemma sounded steadier than she had on the phone. He was taken aback for a second when she stepped out of the small cedar building; he hadn't realized she'd meant they were *in* the thing. He shifted direction, still running. A few feet later and he could see the girls, in the sand, apparently too fascinated with this new environment to care about anything else.

And then he was there, and Gemma threw herself into his arms. She was shaking so hard that he knew he wasn't going to get any information out of her yet. He holstered the Springfield at the small of his back and wrapped his arms around her. Held her.

"It's all right, you're all right now, it's over, everything's fine," he whispered to her, smoothing her hair. She buried her head against his chest, and he heard her gulp in a breath again. Then he realized she was crying. She hadn't been, but now she was. As if she'd been waiting for him before she let go. He wasn't sure how that made him feel except…good.

He held her close, saying whatever soothing thing

came to him, and had the odd thought that if anyone came at her now, he'd take them out without hesitation.

As it triggered by the realization, the cop in him kicked back to life.

"What happened?"

"He…shot at me. Us."

Dante's blood suddenly ran cold, and he nearly shivered with the force of it. It was all he could do to keep his voice even.

"Did you call 911?"

"I… No. You were the only one I could think of to call."

Those quiet, shaky words almost put him on his knees. He made the call for reinforcements himself, warning them of a possible shooter still in the area, but he never let go of her.

"What happened?" he asked again. The answer came in pieces.

"I heard the sound, but I didn't realize… I thought it was a car backfiring, but then…it came again and I saw a chip of wood fly off that post—" she gestured vaguely toward the play structure "—and realized what it was."

He looked, spotted what looked like a fresh graze on one of the upright support posts.

"Then what?" he asked, trying to keep his voice calm.

"I looked where the sound came from—" another gesture, toward the trees on the north side of the park where, Dante noted, there was the most cover "—but I didn't see anyone. But…he kept shooting."

"Gemma, it's okay. You're safe now," he said softly,

tightening his hold. She nodded against his chest. "What then?"

"I grabbed the girls and ran in there," she said. "I didn't know if the logs would stop the…the bullets, but it was the only place I could think of."

And only now did she fall apart, after she'd done what was necessary.

She's got more grit than I ever expected in Fenwick Colton's baby girl.

He'd have to tell his boss just how right he'd been.

"You did good," he said, letting both his thanks and his admiration echo in his voice. "Really, really good. You took yourself and the twins out of his line of sight. You saved them, and yourself."

He felt another, stronger shudder go through her. But after that she seemed steadier.

"Did you ever see the shooter?"

She shook her head. He felt the tiny movement more than saw it. But then her head went back and she looked up at him. "But I saw his car. It had to be his. There was no one else here. Dante, it was the same kind of car that guy at the funeral was in."

It didn't take much for him to put it together. The trigger-happy clown who had capped off those rounds at the apartment had shown up at the funeral, must have seen Gemma with the girls there in the garden. What Dante didn't know was whether the shooter had just happened upon them now or had somehow discovered where he lived and staked them out. That thought made him so furious it was all he could do not to let out a string of oaths that would turn the air blue.

But he knew what this was now. A warning. *I know who matters to you, and if you don't back off, I'll take them out.*

"I don't understand," Gemma said, sounding as if the shock of it was receding now. "The girls, they're just babies. Me, maybe. Dad always said we had to be careful about getting snatched, but what good would shooting me do him?"

Dante felt a little jolt as he realized for the first time that despite that silver spoon, Gemma had grown up with her own set of problems. He looked over at the twins. Something tickled the edge of his mind, but he was too grateful they were all right to formulate the thought right away. And again he was nearly swamped with the enormity of being responsible for these two.

And if Gemma hadn't thought so quickly, either or both of them could be dead now. He tightened the hug, and this time she hugged him back.

And suddenly it hit him, what he'd noticed. His head snapped back around to stare at the girls. Zita. "Wait... was she doing that before?"

Gemma looked over. Her eyes widened. "No! Dante, she's sitting up, on her own! And look at Lucia."

The other girl was apparently too fascinated with the sand to care that her sister had hit a milestone. She was trying to grab tiny handfuls of it and then watching as it slipped through her fingers like...well, grains of sand.

For that moment, even though Dante heard the approach of the sirens, he just stood there, still holding Gemma, looking at the two creatures who had brought them together.

"If I had to guess," she said, and there was a trace of her old humor in the words, "I'd say we've got the makings of maybe an athlete and a scientist here."

A bit to his own shock, Dante laughed. At the sound of it, both girls looked over at them.

"Ba ba ah eh," Zita crowed, reaching out toward them with her arms up. Lucia giggled, as if reacting to his laugh.

As if instinctively—and perhaps it was—they both moved at once, toward the girls. It seemed the most natural thing in the world to Dante to pick up the baby who was reaching out to him, and he wondered if it really was in the DNA to react to tiny, helpless humans like this. Gemma picked up Lucia, and she giggled again.

For a moment their gazes locked. Something alive and warm seemed to flow between them as they stood there, something he couldn't quite put a name to.

And then the cavalry arrived, and he knew the next couple of hours would be chaos. But in this moment he simply stood there, staring at this woman who had been so much different, so much more than he'd ever expected.

And when she smiled at him, he wanted nothing more than to hang on to this moment, this feeling, as long as he possibly could.

Gemma had never been so glad to get home.

And there it was again. *Home.* Who'd have ever thought she would come to think of this place as home, this condo she'd at first thought small but now thought cozy, convenient and rather charming. At first she'd caught herself thinking she'd like it better with a few of her own touches, but now, with the girls' things scattered about, Dante's laptop here and his work boots by the door, and even puffs of Flash's fur here and there, it felt more like home than her own big, glamorous, top-floor place ever had.

Dante had offered, after she'd been interviewed by a detective and her cousin Finn had—to her surprise—shown up to make sure everyone was all right, to have an officer take her and the girls home. She'd refused, not even sure why at the time. But later she'd realized she didn't want to be separated—she wanted them to go home together. And so she'd waited until finally he was free, they went to get Flash, and all five of them went together.

But now she was starting to get worried. Dante had been pacing since they'd put the girls, who had finally surrendered to sleep, into their crib. He looked edgy, his jaw tensed and his mouth—that damned mouth she couldn't seem to stop thinking about—tight. He and Finn had had a long conversation at the scene, and he'd been like this ever since.

She stood it as long as she could but finally went over and put herself in his path. "What is it? Should I be worried? Is that man going to show up here?"

He stopped barely an inch short of bumping into her. Started to say something, then stopped.

"I have a right to know, don't I? If we're in danger here?"

"We don't know that he even knows where we live."

For an insane moment all she could think of was that

we. It was a moment before the logical part of her brain told her he meant himself and the girls.

"You think he just happened to see us at the park?"

"I don't know." He drew in a deep breath and really looked at her for the first time. "But we're not taking any chances. You go nowhere without me. If you have to go somewhere, I go with you. When we get back, I check the house before you or the girls come in. And there'll be a marked unit around most of the time."

Gemma blinked. "So you're my bodyguard now?"

"Sorry. That's the way it's got to be."

"That wasn't a complaint," she said mildly.

"Good. Because until we nail this guy, we're joined at the hip."

Joined at the hip.

She knew, *knew* it was just a turn of phrase, an idiom, and yet when he said it, her mind went haywire, darting into places she'd spent a lot of energy denying existed in the last week. All the ways a man and a woman could be joined at the hip flashed through her mind with vivid clarity, and heat blossomed in her, head to toe.

"Damn, Gemma." It came out low and harsh. And she knew what she'd been thinking—and trying not to think—had shown on her face.

And suddenly she had to know. For so many reasons, many of which were only half-formed in her mind, she had to know. She tilted her head back, looked at his mouth, that mouth that fascinated her. Her own lips parted, and suddenly they were unbearably dry and she had to moisten them with the tip of her tongue.

He went rigid, staring down at her. This time her name was a question. "Gemma?"

"Yes," she whispered.

And then his mouth, that mouth, was on hers, and his lips were everything she'd thought they might be, hot and alive, firm yet soft enough to be coaxing, but they were more, so much more, and he was setting her on fire.

She leaned into him, hungry for even more of this wonderful, glorious heat. This, this was what had been missing from her life, what she'd been longing for even while she was unaware it was possible. *The heart wants what it wants*, her cousin Quinn had told her. Well, apparently hers wanted Dante Mancuso.

She brushed her tongue over those lips, both heard and felt his sharp intake of breath. And then he returned the action, and it was as if he were tasting the finest of delicacies, gentle yet insistent.

And then it changed, shifted from a tentative exploration to a fierce demand. She was suddenly pressed against him, his hands at the small of her back, her hands on his shoulders, pulling him even closer. She wanted more of him and pushed the kiss deeper. She heard a low sound, a groan coming from him as their tongues danced, touched, tasted.

She wasn't certain when her hands had moved, but suddenly she was feeling hot, sleek skin under her fingers. Only then did she realize she'd tugged his shirt free and that tight, ridged belly was bare to her touch. She felt as well as heard him suck in a breath, and the muscles beneath her fingers clenched.

. And suddenly he pulled back. Put his hands on her shoulders and pushed her, albeit gently, away from him. She made a tiny sound in the back of her throat, a protest that was utterly heartfelt. She felt a chill, as if he'd been the only thing keeping her warm. And alive.

She opened her eyes to find him staring down at her.

His rapid, unsteady breathing was the only thing that heartened her; he couldn't deny he'd been as affected as she had been. His lips, those lips that had driven her mad, parted, as if he were going to speak. But then he stopped, closing his eyes and giving a sharp shake of his head, as if to clear it.

He put up his hands between them, palms toward her. She couldn't think, so wasn't sure if he meant to ward her off or push himself back. He turned away, and she still couldn't get her mind to work. She watched silently as he walked across to the front door. She saw him touch his waistband, realized sluggishly that he was checking for the handgun in the holster she now saw was clipped to it. She hadn't even realized it was there, but of course it was—he was a cop, even off duty.

He pulled the door open. Seemed to realize something, and stopped.

"I'm going to check around outside," he said, his back still to her.

He was gone without ever looking at her again.

Chapter 25

He'd done some pretty stupid things in his life, Dante thought, but it would be hard to top kissing Gemma Colton.

He tried to concentrate on the task he'd set himself, making sure every outside access point to his front unit was secure and setting up various entanglements for anyone who'd try to use them. If it was just himself, he'd count on the alarm system to alert him in time.

But it wasn't just himself anymore. He had the girls to think about.

And Gemma? What about the woman you just kissed, and who kissed you back so hotly you about boiled over right then and there?

He was insane. He'd turned into a walking cliché, the guy who got the hots for the nanny. Hell, he was a half a dozen clichés, from falling for the nanny to falling for the rich girl. A Colton, for God's sake. Insanity was the only explanation.

His own words hit him suddenly, and he straightened up from carefully checking the front window. Falling for? No. No, no, no. He wasn't. He couldn't. He'd just been too long without, that was all. He'd been gunshy ever since he'd caught his woman of the moment slapping Flash when the dog had inadvertently brushed against her in passing, leaving a couple of strands of hair on her black slacks.

The moment he thought of it, the image formed in his mind of the times he'd seen Gemma petting the dog, talking to him much as she did the twins, and the way Flash had come to accept her with surprising speed.

Dogs know, isn't that what they say? They have good people judgment.

Come to think of it, Flash had never taken to anyone from the beginning, not like he had to Gemma. Of course for Flash, "taken to" only meant he went back to his normal routine of sprawling in his chair and letting out the occasional woeful sigh. But for him, that was tantamount to a trumpeting welcome.

Trying to focus, Dante walked over to his department SUV and opened the equipment locker in the back, next to the big, flat cushion for Flash. He got out the ever-useful duct tape and some thin wire and walked back to the condo. He strung wire, about ankle height, from shrub to shrub at the sturdy trunks, across the most likely approach to any window. He tore off thin strips of the tape and fastened them from the underside of branches to the windowsills. None of this would really stop anybody, but it would let him know if anyone had prowled around without getting close enough to set off the alarm. He also adjusted the motion-detector lights near both the front and back doors to activate farther out.

He'd have to watch that Flash didn't get entangled, and he'd have to show Gemma so she didn't—

Gemma.

He couldn't stay out here making up work much longer. He was going to have to go back in there and face her. She'd said yes, but that didn't make it any less foolish.

Or cliché.

He heard the back sliding door open. "Dante, I need help."

He spun around, his hand halfway to his holstered Springfield as he scanned the area, looking for a threat he'd missed. But she was in the doorway, looking perfectly calm. At least, she was until she realized what he'd done. Then she paled a little.

"I just meant with your washer. I'm sorry, I—"

"No." He started toward her. "Don't be."

"I should have thought to say something else first." She managed a smile. "Something without the word *help* in it."

He came to a halt in front of the sliding door. Noted that Flash had come up beside her. And saw her fingers brush over the dog's head, as if automatically. It made something tighten inside him all over again.

"Not your fault." He sucked in a deep breath, let it out, jamming a hand through his hair. "It's mine."

"What's your fault? Reacting like a cop?"

"That guy coming after you. Hell, in a way, all of this is my fault."

The woman who lived in the condo next door was heading out to the dumpster enclosure with a bag of trash. She waved at Dante through the open gate in the back fence, then glanced at Gemma with speculative interest. Her expression changed to thoughtful, as if she found Gemma familiar. Entirely possible, given how often her picture had appeared in the local news.

Gemma smiled graciously at the woman but said to Dante, "Perhaps we should continue this inside."

He'd slid the door shut and locked it, with both the latch and the more secure foot-activated lock at the base, and reset the alarm when she spoke again.

"Why is what your fault?"

"That guy from the funeral coming after you. It was a warning. From the case I was on…before."

"But you aren't on it now."

"I guess he didn't get the memo."

She smiled, but it was fleeting and followed by a frown. "How can you be so sure?"

He walked into the living room, realized he was about to start pacing again and made himself sit down instead. Gemma followed and sat down beside him. Close.

Too close.

"He's done it before." She simply waited, silently. He hesitated, then decided she had to know, to be fully aware of the danger. "He did a drive-by on an apartment where we found some evidence in the case. Took out all the front windows."

Her eyes had widened as he spoke. "He tried to kill you?"

He grimaced. "Not that much finesse. I was in the kitchen—no way he could have seen me, let alone hit me unless by accident."

"What about Flash?" she asked with a glance at the dog, who had returned to his comfy chair.

Dante heard the concern in her voice, even though it was obvious the dog hadn't been hurt; he could have been, and she cared. He remembered that moment at the door when she'd touched the dog without even thinking about it. And Flash had let her. Had bestirred himself to get out of his chair and come with her in the first place, even after his morning of romping freely at the K9 center.

He wanted to kiss her for that.

Hell, he wanted to kiss her again for any damned reason he could come up with. And it would be so easy—she was so close, he'd only have to move a matter of inches and—

"What did you mean when you said in a way all of this was your fault?"

He stomped down on that impulse to kiss her, although his gut knew it was only temporarily quashed. What had happened that day was hardly a secret, nor confidential, like his so far failed effort to find the infiltrator who had stolen the phone.

When he finally told her, it came out in a rush, as if it had been building for a long time.

"He came after me that day. But he ended up killing my brother and his wife."

Gemma drew back, clearly startled. "But...didn't they die in a car accident?" He saw understanding quickly dawn in her face. She was many things, Gemma Colton, but slow was not one of them. "Drive-by, you said. He caused the accident?"

He nodded. "Hit them and smashed them into that power pole, completely destroying the car. They never had a chance."

He saw her look toward the den, where the girls were napping. "Thank God they weren't with them."

"Yes."

She looked back at him. "But you can't really think that was your fault?"

"If he hadn't come after me, the accident never would have happened." His mouth tightened. Dom and Agostina might have gotten arrested for the stolen car, but they'd still be alive.

"You were doing your job."

"And it got them killed."

She was silent for a long moment. Then she said, quietly, "If your job was building roads, or maybe installing power poles, would you feel responsible for a crash?"

His brow furrowed. He thought for a moment. "Roads yes, poles no."

"Explain?" she asked, looking surprised at his answer.

"Roads, I'd wonder if it had been done right—no unevenness in the surface, no potholes or weird slant that might have contributed. Poles aren't in the road, so under normal circumstances there's no way they'd get hit."

She gave him a slow, odd little smile as she nodded. "All right. But if you knew your job had been done right?"

"Look, I see what you're getting at, and—"

"You are not responsible. Any more than that road builder is. There's only one person at fault here."

He let out a compressed breath. "I know that. In my head. My gut, not so much."

"And that, Dante Mancuso, is why you're a good cop."

He stared at her. She just smiled at him. After a moment he said, "Tell me, do you cultivate that rich glamour girl thing to hide who you really are?"

He saw a tinge of color rise in her face. Wished he knew if she was embarrassed or pleased.

"It does have its uses," she said.

"Like lulling people until you get what you want?"

"Doesn't seem to be working on you."

He couldn't believe what appeared to be showing in her eyes as she looked at him steadily. It took an effort to say lightly, "Depends on what you want."

"If you can't tell, obviously I'm not doing it right."

Oh, you're doing it right.

And I just might be stupid enough to fall for it.

What was *wrong* with her?

The words kept running through Gemma's mind. Not because she couldn't seem to focus on Dante's explanation of the washer, which included a laugh that anyone would ask him about laundry when he'd once ended up with a batch of light blue T-shirts after washing them with a new pair of jeans. Or on sorting the small pile of tiny clothes with various stains. Or even on something as simple as measuring out the liquid detergent.

Even Dante's teasing, "You ever even done this before?" didn't focus her. Because all she could think about was what she hadn't thought about. She hadn't had one single thought about Dev since...since...she'd come out to find Dante at the coffeemaker. As good as naked.

And when he'd kissed her, Devlin Harrington might as well never have existed.

She was so lost in the contemplation of what this meant that it took her a while to realize Dante was scrupulously avoiding her, at least as much as was possible in his relatively small condo. If she spoke to him she got short, polite answers. He sat in a chair with his laptop, not on the couch with his feet up, like he always had before. As if he wanted to be sure she couldn't sit down within three feet of him. And even if she walked right in front of him, he never even looked up.

When the twins woke up—something they seemed to do in unison—she busied herself with them for a while. They were apparently none the worse for the chaos in the park, and she was glad of that. She suspected it had a bit to do with their fascination with the sand, which she had found everywhere when she'd changed them.

"Be glad, little ones," she said to them. "Time enough for you to worry about the problems in the world. For now you just enjoy what you can in your own little world."

"Ah ew oh," Zita said wisely. Her sister giggled.

"Truly?" Gemma asked, smiling at her as she picked up Lucia. "That might just be the answer, my girl. It certainly makes as much sense as what's going on."

And more sense than your uncle is making right now.

As if her thought had conjured him up, he appeared in the doorway just as she turned around. For an instant silence spun out between them. And then, determined to be as cool as he was, she said in the cheery tone that coaxed wallets out of wealthy pockets, "Oh, good, you're just in time. Bring Zita, will you?"

He looked a bit wary. "Bring her? You're not going anywhere—"

"Without you. Yes, I got that."

She smothered the unsuitable thought that she wished he meant that because he wanted to be with her personally, not as a bodyguard. And she felt a nudge of guilt that she truly had so completely put Dev out of her mind. Of course, she had been shot at…and Dante had ridden in to the rescue.

She knew she was kidding herself even as she thought it. Because Dante had been the only thing in her mind well before that had happened.

"I meant," she explained, in the same kind of polite tone he'd been using, "out to the living room. I presume we're allowed to go that far?"

"I… Sure."

"Or," she said, driven by a sudden need to prod him out of whatever this mood was, "I can keep them cooped up in the den all day. That should make for a restful night."

He looked pained and quickly went to pick up Zita.

She cooed at him, again reaching out to pat his cheek. He dodged a tiny finger in his eye by grabbing her hand and kissing it, somewhat noisily. Lucia giggled again. His gaze shot to Gemma's face, and she somehow knew he was thinking of the joke he'd made about girls he kissed giggling.

"I didn't giggle." The words were out before she thought. But when she saw the sudden flare of heat in his eyes, the sudden intensity that came over him, she couldn't regret them. Mr. Dante Mancuso wasn't as immune as he was trying to show.

And why that pleased her so was yet another thing she had to think about. When she could think again.

Chapter 26

"If you were any more stiffly polite, you'd shatter."

Dante looked up at Gemma, who, after spending the hour before putting them to bed getting both girls playing with some sort of big plastic toy—playing apparently consisting mostly of putting the thing up to their mouths—had come to a halt before his chair.

He'd been sitting here for that hour, plus the time it had taken her to get the girls settled in the crib, trying to focus on work and failing utterly. He'd ended up surreptitiously watching her sitting on the floor with the girls, talking to them quietly in that way she had, as if they were old enough to understand, yet with that kind of singsong cadence that seemed to delight them, even when she took them in to bed.

He'd been idly wondering how she knew to do that,

if that kind of knowledge really did come built in in women, when she came back out of the den and confronted him.

"In fact," she went on, not waiting for him to answer, "you're being a total—" she glanced back toward the den, and when she went on he was pretty sure it wasn't with the word that had come to mind "—jerk."

"Working?" he suggested, gesturing at his laptop.

"Right. You keep hiding behind that, then," she said and started to turn away.

Irritation flashed through him. "What do you want from me, Gemma?"

She went still. And very slowly turned back to look at him. And then, bluntly, she said, "I want you to kiss me again."

He stared at her. "What?"

"You heard me." He let out a sour chuckle as he looked away from her. "Are you saying you don't want to?"

He closed his eyes, fighting the memory of that kiss she was saying she wanted a repeat of. Fighting the heat, the need and the way his mind was screaming at him not to question, just do.

"What I don't want," he said carefully, gesturing toward the room where the twins were sleeping, "is to tangle this up. Besides, I don't poach."

"Poach?"

"Dev? The guy who's the reason you're here in the first place, the guy you're in love with, remember?"

He saw color rise in her cheeks. "He's why I want you to kiss me again."

He would never, Dante thought, understand the female mind. The only thing he could think to say was "Why?"

He realized suddenly how tense she was. And he didn't understand that, either. And then a burst of words came from her, tight with confusion but ringing with honesty.

"Because I haven't even thought of Dev all day, even before the park. Because I can't get you out of my head. Because you sang last night. And," she went on with a gulp, "because I have to know if it really is...how I remember."

He wasn't sure he understood any better now than he had before the flood of words. But the only words he could seem to say, rather thickly, were "I've wondered that, too. If it could have really been that...good."

"All right, then," she said, moving even closer, as if his words had sealed the deal. And only then did he realize he'd stood up, his body apparently making the decision before his mind could tamp it down.

All the reasons this was wrong, that it would be a mistake, jammed up in his mind. All the cliché ones, all the practical ones—along with the simple fact that she was a Colton, one of *those* Coltons, and way, way out of his league—couldn't seem to get past the fact that this woman who had surprised him at every turn, who had already proven she was much more than the rich girl most people thought her, who had already nearly put him on his knees with one kiss, wanted another.

He made a last-ditch effort, one that his body protested mightily. "Gemma, look, it's just the adrenaline hangover from this morning. It's normal, but...you don't want to do this."

"I told you," she said with an air of long-suffering patience, and he wondered inanely if she'd picked it up from Flash, "I was thinking about it long before that crazy guy came after us." She smiled then, and the soft warmth in it oddly made him shiver. "And then you showed up, all brave and fearless."

"Fearless?" He nearly laughed. "I was scared to death you'd been hurt." Something flashed in her eyes then, something that made him add hastily, "Or the girls."

"I would never let them be hurt." There was a quiet determination in her voice, and he knew she meant it. "I think I understand now why women will do anything to protect their child."

"And you call me fearless?" he asked softly.

Her gaze snapped back to his face. She whispered his name, and the warmth in her voice matched the heat in her eyes and he was lost.

And then she was in his arms, her mouth was on his, and the feeling flipped crazily.

He wasn't lost, he was found.

She had truly only wanted this one kiss. Had had herself convinced she couldn't possibly be remembering that first one right. In a way, that turned out to be true, because it was much, much more than she'd remembered.

She felt as if every bit of who else she was had been seared away. She wasn't Gemma Colton, of the wealthy Red Ridge Coltons, she wasn't the effective fund-raiser who practically kept the K9 unit going, she wasn't even the nanny to the twins she had just put to bed. Right now she was only one thing—the woman who wanted this man more than she had ever wanted anything or anyone.

She tasted him, savored him, savored even more the low groan that came from him as their tongues brushed, touched, danced. She slipped her arms around him, wanting him even closer. A little recklessly, she slid her hands down his back to cup that taut, muscled backside she'd so admired. It felt even better than it looked.

And the other pleasing discovery she made in the process—that he was completely aroused—made her feel a new sort of heat, a kind that pooled low and deep inside her. And this time she did think of Dev, but only to realize he had never, ever made her feel this way. And she and Dante had only just begun.

Or at least, she thought they had.

He broke the kiss. But it was only to say, rather breathlessly, "Gemma…if you don't want to take this all the way, you'd better stop."

"Stop? Oh, no."

The very idea was chilling. She emphasized her answer by pulling him harder against her and stretching up to kiss him again. She felt his hands move, sliding up her rib cage. Then he was cupping her breasts, and the heat of his touch arrowed through her. Her nipples were achingly tight long before he ever shifted his thumbs to rub over them. She heard a tiny cry, realized it was her, at the fierce, hot sensation of it.

She tugged at his shirt, freed it enough to slide her

own hands under it, to actually touch, caress that ridged abdomen. She felt as much as heard him suck in a breath then let it out in another low groan as she fumbled with the button of his jeans.

His hand was suddenly over hers, halting her movement. "Gemma, wait. I'm not sure I…have anything."

"Have…?" Belatedly it hit her what he meant, that he didn't have protection. That he wasn't sure he had a condom immediately handy for any opportunity warmed her somehow. He didn't make a habit of this. That he didn't find a small package until the third place he looked warmed her even more.

She spent the time he was searching looking at his bedroom with interest. She'd thought it would be masculine, maybe all neutral colors, dark ones, but instead it reminded her of the library in her father's mansion, walls a dark hunter green, the bed covered with a thick comforter in a matching tone with tan stripes, and a wingback chair and footstool in the window bay. Beside it was a small table with several books stacked on it. So the man read at night, perhaps. She could picture it. But only one chair, although there was room for two. He must—

And then he was there again. "Door number three," he muttered. Then, as if he was afraid the interim had given her too much time to think, he cupped her cheek with one hand and asked, "Change your mind?"

It was significant, she supposed, that she had not. But she would think of all the ramifications of her own certainty later. Right now all she cared about was relighting that fire they'd begun.

"No way," she said, reaching up to touch his mouth, those lips she'd had dreams about.

His mouth came down on hers fiercely, and within ten seconds he'd done just that, rekindled that fire. It was as if they'd never stopped. Then he was pulling free of his clothes and ridding her of her own. She shivered, not from cold but at the sight of him naked before her. He was even more beautiful than she remembered. And the heat in his eyes as he looked at her stoked the flames even higher.

"You are so beautiful," he said, sounding as if he could barely get the words out.

"You're pretty hot yourself," she murmured and stroked a hand down his belly. She wanted to savor the feel of sleek skin over muscle, but it seemed Dante had run out of patience. And she was glad, in fact gloried in it when he swept her up and took them both down to the bed, as if he couldn't wait any longer.

"Gemma?"

He was, she realized through the sweet, luscious haze that had enveloped her at the feel of his naked weight atop her, giving her one last chance to change her mind. She nearly laughed at the very idea.

"If you don't hurry, I'm going to scream."

His voice went rough, low as he said, "Hang on to that scream. You're going to need it later."

"Promise? I—"

Her words turned into a gasp as he drove into her. She marveled at her own readiness, proven by the slickness of her body's welcoming of his. He went deep in one stroke, filling her, stretching her, and she cried out his name at the sheer pleasure of it.

He braced her shoulders with his hands and began to move, faster, deeper. She shuddered under the impact of sensations she'd never experienced. He slammed into her, she gasped again, and he stilled.

"Too hard?" She felt a tremor go through him, as if it were taking every bit of his strength to stop. And yet he had. To be sure she was all right.

"No. More."

It was all she could coherently manage, which was another new shock for her. She'd never been so driven out of her mind that she could barely speak. Nor had she ever been so moved by that sign of tender care amid the heat and power and glorious rush of pleasure.

He began to move again, long, powerful strokes that drove her near to madness. And then he reached between them to swirl a finger over that taut button of flesh at the same time.

He'd been right. She needed that scream.

Chapter 27

In a million years, Dante never would have pictured a Monday morning like this one. The absurdity of it warred with an odd sense of rightness, and even though he knew it was foolish, he let the rightness win.

Him, in bed with Gemma Colton, after a night spent discovering just how incredible what had unexpectedly flared to life between them was. She was wearing his T-shirt—and it had never looked better—and he had pulled on his boxers after a brief hunt through the discarded clothes on the floor, because to complete the rightness, she had brought in the twins when they'd begun to fuss upon waking.

So here Dante was, with the woman who lit a fire in him unlike anything he'd ever felt, and the two babies who had so quickly become so important to him, and he felt so connected to all three of them that it was stunning. He'd never felt that before, either, that kind of connection.

She looked up, caught him staring at her. "Regrets?" she asked softly.

"No," he said instantly. "God, no. I just was afraid... you might have them."

"I thought about that when I woke up this morning. Couldn't find a single one."

He could suddenly breathe again. He had no idea what would happen now, but at least they didn't have that to deal with. Because he had no regrets, either, the only worry the pressure of wondering what would happen, where they would go now.

"Ah ooh da ee," said Zita, grabbing at his hand and pulling herself toward him.

"I believe she just said, 'I love you, Dante,'" Gemma said with a laugh.

Dante didn't dare look at her, afraid the tumble his gut had taken at the words *I love you, Dante* coming from her mouth, even if she was just teasingly interpreting a baby's babbling, would show.

With an effort he reined in his crazed imagination. He'd known this woman exactly a week. And he needed her to do what she'd proven surprisingly good at—help take care of the twins.

If she was anyone but Gemma Colton...

And if she didn't fry his circuits when they touched, if every move she made didn't remind him of the night they'd just spent together, he might be able to think more clearly.

He had to look away. Saw that apparently Flash had, at some point, decided it was safe to come in and was sprawled lazily on his own bed in the corner.

Get used to it, partner.

He caught himself, realized he wasn't just thinking of now—he was thinking of a long, long string of nights like last night.

Zita had worked her way up to him now, looking rather pleased with herself. Instinctively he reached out for her, lifting her just under her arms. She got her feet under her quickly and started to bounce.

Gemma, sitting on the bed with Lucia in her lap, who was tugging at a lock of her hair—that hair that had slid so deliciously over his skin last night—laughed. "She may skip crawling and go straight to walking."

"Not any time soon, I hope," he said, rather grimly thinking of the chaos there would be once these two were more rapidly mobile. Then Zita began to coo happily. And rather melodically, he thought.

"Not only that," Gemma said with a smile, "she might have inherited your beautiful singing voice."

For an instant he was embarrassed at the compliment, but the feeling was quickly pushed out by the way she'd said it. *Inherited.* And again it hit him, that sense of connection. And the panic started to rise in him again.

"I don't know anything about this," he said, feeling helpless. "I'm just their uncle—I've barely seen them before now. I can't raise them the way my brother would have."

"I should hope not," Gemma said acerbically.

He blinked, for an instant startled at her adamancy. But then he realized how what he'd said sounded. He'd been thinking of the twins not having their parents; Gemma was thinking of them being raised by petty criminals. And in the larger scheme of things, he couldn't argue the point.

"You're right," he said, looking once more at the delighted, bouncing Zita, who was smiling at him joyfully. "If I were to stay true to the family heritage, I'd start them off now on a life of crime. They could be diversions while I rip somebody off, or devices to gain somebody's confidence for the same purpose."

She was staring at him now. "That's absurd. Who would do such a thing?"

He shrugged. "My parents did."

Her eyes widened in obvious shock. But then she smiled. "Boy, you're a whole different kind of rebel, aren't you?"

He laughed in spite of himself.

"You'll do right by them, Dante. I can already see that."

"Even though I said let them cry last night?"

"It worked," Gemma pointed out. And it had—when the twins had started to fuss in the wee hours and Gemma had stirred, he'd held her close and whispered to let it go, see if they'd settle on their own. And after a while, the girls had, and quiet reigned anew.

And they had once more, like two explorers who had discovered a land of untold beauty, turned to each other and found new ways to touch, to learn and to fly.

"You know," he said casually over Zita's head, "for

as little sleep as we got last night, I feel pretty da—" He caught himself and finished with, "darn good."

Gemma gave him a smile that threatened to kindle that blaze all over again. "So do I."

He fought down his response to that look. With effort regathered his thoughts. "Look, I know this complicates things," he began. Zita squirmed to be let down, as if she didn't like what he'd said.

But Gemma merely looked at him innocently. "Does it? I thought it clarified things. It certainly did for me."

He blinked. Let Zita go. "It did? Like what?"

She held his gaze steadily then. "That I was a fool for ever thinking I loved Dev." He drew back then, a little stunned. "Oh, don't panic, I'm not saying I expect you to…to propose or anything."

Since that was rather a moot point with the Groom Killer on the loose, he focused on the other part of what she'd said. Or hadn't said. Had implied? Had she really? Just because she'd said she'd been wrong about loving Dev Harrington didn't mean she was saying she loved…him.

His pulse slammed into high gear at the mere thought. This was insane. Beyond insane. He'd known her a week. And this was still Fenwick Colton's baby girl he'd just spent the night ravishing.

And been thoroughly ravished by in return, don't forget.

Heat exploded in him as the memories hit—the feel of her, the taste of her, Gemma kissing him in turn, caressing him, using her hands and mouth on him. He fought it down; it wasn't like they could indulge again with the girls right here and so wide-awake. But he wanted to. Oh, he wanted to.

He cleared his tight throat. Swallowed. Managed to speak. "A little risky these days, proposals."

"Exactly."

Wait, what? Was that what she was saying, that she simply didn't expect him to propose with a serial killer running amok? That if it wasn't for the guy out murdering grooms, she'd expect it?

He started to ask, then stopped himself. He didn't want to ruin this wonderful feeling by getting into some heavy morning-after discussion. So he said nothing, hoping she'd let it drop. And then Lucia intervened by picking up something shiny from the bed and passing it to her twin. Zita reached for it, had it, and he wondered rather foggily when they'd perfected that maneuver.

Then he realized what it was. A condom wrapper.

"Damn," he said, forgetting any language caution, and grabbed it away from Zita. The tiny girl gave a start, then her face scrunched up. Dante knew a wail was forming and nearly panicked.

Gemma laughed, full throated and genuinely amused. Zita looked at her, the momentum of her wail interrupted by the cheerful sound.

"You startled her with that quick move," Gemma said. Then she laughed again, and Zita changed course and began to giggle herself. "Really, Dante, you acted as if you thought she knew what it was."

"I…" He felt rather sheepish now and crumpled the wrapper in his hand.

"I think you have a few years before you have to have *that* conversation with them."

He stared at her, then the twins, horror-struck. A conversation about condoms? His imagination spun dizzily, but he could not picture that. Or a million other things that now awaited him.

But for now Zita was chattering, not wailing, at least.

He looked back at Gemma. "Thanks for…forestalling that storm."

"They respond very well to laughter, if you get to it soon enough. But once they're launched, you're done for a while. Especially that one," she said, nodding at Zita. "She's harder to talk down than this one."

For a moment he just looked at her. Then, slowly, he shook his head in wonder.

"What?" she asked.

"A week ago I couldn't have told them apart on a bet. Now…thanks to you, I can guess right half the time without even checking that eyebrow."

She colored slightly, looking pleased, but she said only, "They have different personalities."

"And a week ago I would have laughed at the idea of six-month-old babies having personalities at all."

Lucia, on her stomach on the bed, lifted herself up with her arms, tried to balance on one and reach out toward him.

"Yes, Lucia, your uncle Dante is silly, isn't he, thinking you don't have a personality all your own," she said in that singsong voice the twins obviously loved.

"He's silly, period," Dante said wryly, but he reached down and picked Lucia up and smiled himself when she cooed delightedly. Even Flash got into the act, rising and coming over to rest his wrinkles, as Dante frequently teased him, on the bed. He glanced at Gemma, who looked over at the dog and laughed. God, he could get used to that laugh.

"Is he allowed?"

"Sometimes. Special circumstances."

"Well, I think this qualifies."

"Can't argue that. Come on up, my furry friend."

It was a king-size bed, but the five of them filled it to near overflowing. And Dante was starting to feel like a commercial selling…something. But it felt good. Really good. And when Lucia babbled happily at him, he grinned at her and babbled back nonsensically.

When he looked up and saw Gemma smiling at them both as she took her own turn cuddling Zita, he was seized with an urge stronger than anything he'd known since the day he'd become determined to make it as a cop. The urge to hang on to this moment, this treasure of a moment when four disparate people—and a dog—had come together so unexpectedly.

The fiery joy of last night merged with the quieter joy of this moment, and he didn't even know what to call the result.

Except a family.

Chapter 28

As if to make up for the night they'd been allowed to spend so blissfully together, the girls seemed determined to make the next week as hard as possible. Between Zita's growing mobility and Lucia's growing dexterity, watchful eyes were required at all times. Yet Gemma found she didn't mind at all, even though she was tired. Instead she found herself admiring their ingenuity in exploring the world around them.

As for her and Dante... It had been a bit awkward that second evening, because Dante wouldn't talk about the amazing night—and the surprisingly pleasant morning—they'd spent. It had taken her most of the day to figure out he didn't want to assume anything. But she knew what she wanted, and, once the girls were down for the night, she had gone after it in a very Gemma-like way.

"So are you having regrets now?"

He'd given her a startled look, and his immediate "No!" assuaged her concern.

"You had me worried."

"How could I possibly regret…that?" he said, glancing toward his bedroom door.

She'd given him her best slow smile. "It was pretty amazing."

"It was," he'd said solemnly, "the most amazing night of my life."

She'd felt herself blush and didn't care. She, who had always tried to come off as light, airy and not caring, didn't care if this man knew just how much she was feeling.

"Does that mean you want a repeat?"

His answer to that had been to drop everything he'd been doing and sweep her literally off her feet and carry her to his bed. Where she had quickly discovered it had not been a fluke, the circumstances or some odd alignment of the planets—it had simply been that she and Dante were incredible together.

And they'd proven it time and again over the last week.

A movement on the floor now tugged her out of the hot, vivid, luscious memories. She resisted for a moment, savoring the memory of waking up with Dante's arm holding her in the curve of his body, but then realized some action was needed.

"Oh, no, you clever little widget," she said with a

laugh as Lucia managed to reach Flash's rope toy on the floor and immediately directed it to her mouth. She quickly swept the tiny girl up in her arms and spun her around, making her laugh before she could cry at the removal of her fascinating discovery. Gemma grabbed the toy and tossed it back to Flash, who was in his chair.

"Here you go, boy," she said.

The dog merely gave one of his patented long-suffering sighs, but he added a small whuff of sound.

"Nice job." Dante's voice came from the couch, where he was once more ensconced with his laptop, although it didn't seem he was doing much but watching the same pieces of video over and over. "That was as close as he gets to *thank you*."

She laughed again. It was funny how much she was laughing when she was so tired. She turned to Flash. "You're welcome, sir," she said in the poshest accent she could manage. "I'd curtsy, but I'm afraid I'd drop your cousin here."

Dante laughed then. She remembered the first time she'd heard that genuine, pure laugh, for the first time not tinged with an undertone of worry that she guessed was from what had happened to his life.

"That was nice," she said to him.

He blinked. "What?"

"That laugh. I'd like to hear it again."

"I..." He stopped, as if flustered. She just smiled at him.

"Know what else I'd like?"

She leaned over and whispered a very sexy suggestion in his ear. She heard him suck in a harsh breath, followed by a muttered oath.

"Nap time," she promised.

"Wear them out," he said. "Fast."

"You sure? You look already worn-out."

"I'll manage," he said with a crooked grin.

She grinned back, then turned herself to indeed wearing out the girls, but kept up a conversation with him as well. "I thought they pulled you off that case you were on."

"They did." He glanced over at her. "And put out a press release that I'm on leave, with my...changed circumstances as the excuse." His gaze flicked to the girls, then back to her. "So the shooter will hopefully think it was message received."

"You mean he'll think you backed off and back off himself?"

Dante nodded.

She smiled wryly. "Shows what he knows."

"Meaning?"

"You are not the kind of guy who backs off."

He stared at her. "But he came after you and the girls. That makes it different."

"I won't say I wasn't terrified—I was. But I knew you'd come, just like now I know you'll do what you have to in order to keep us safe."

She said it simply, because she knew it was true. This was the kind of man Dante Mancuso was.

Unlike Dev, who wouldn't do anything that inconvenienced him unless there was something he could get out of it.

It wasn't unlike other thoughts that had popped into her head lately. But this was the first time she had really let Dev into her mind, pictured him, thought about him and felt…nothing. Absolutely nothing. It was as if that wild, mad desperation to make him love her the way she'd loved him had never existed.

Loved. She'd even thought it in the past tense.

"Gemma?" He said her name softly, in that way that made her shiver. She refocused on him. "Where'd you go? You were a million miles away."

"Just in another lifetime," she said. "And wondering how I could have been so blind."

"Blind?"

"About why I was with Dev." Something in the way he was looking at her made her able to admit to him what she'd half suspected all along. "And why he was with me. I think…maybe it was because his father approved. Sometimes I felt like…a front."

"A front? Why?"

"He always wanted us to be seen together. And he always made a point of telling his father every place we went."

"Maybe he was proud of it. Of you."

He said it like a man who was proud of her, and that warmed her more than she could say.

"I thought so, at first. But when we were alone, he was…never really there. Not a hundred percent, anyway."

Dante frowned. "That, I don't get."

And again he warmed her, with the implication he couldn't see how anyone could not be completely with her.

"I started wondering if his father's approval meant too much to him. And there were other things that made me think maybe..." She took a deep breath. "I think he wanted somebody else."

"Somebody his father wouldn't approve of?"

She nodded again.

"Ouch," he said.

And to her own amazement, given how much that suspicion had once hurt, she smiled. "I went to my cousin Quinn, like an idiot, and asked her about it." She put on her snootiest voice. "Her being inappropriate and yet snagging the guy she fell in love with."

"Sometimes you scare me, Colton," he said warily.

"I try not to be that person, really, but I didn't understand then what I do now."

"Which is?"

She fastened her gaze on him steadily. "That Quinn was right. The heart wants what it wants, no rhyme or reason except chemistry."

"And your heart wants...?"

He sounded utterly, completely neutral, so neutral she knew he was working at it. But she saw the tightness of his jaw, and his utter stillness, showing how much that level tone was costing him. And that moved her beyond anything Dev had ever said or done.

"It was my pride that wanted Dev. Because he didn't want me."

"His loss."

She smiled at that. "Yes, actually. But my gain. Because now I know what it feels like to have what my heart truly wants."

He stared at her. She saw him swallow. He was clearly at a loss for words, but unlike Dev, she knew he would find them eventually. And when he did, they would be the sweetest thing she'd ever heard.

She let him off the hook by asking briskly, "Now, what's bugging you so much about those videos—security videos, aren't they?—you keep watching?"

He looked startled, then relieved. Probably that she wasn't going to demand a similar sentiment from him. And it was odd—normally she would have. But with Dante, she was content to wait. It was very unlike her. But she was also finding she liked the person she was with him much better than the person she'd been with Dev.

"Yes. And just…frustrating. Because what I need isn't there."

"Isn't there, or isn't shown?"

"Both." He jammed a hand through his hair in that way he had when he was thinking hard. "And that narrows it down to needing a court order for phone records and a near-impossible amount of grunt work."

"Grunt work?"

He hesitated. She realized she was asking about a police case, and he probably was deciding what he could and couldn't tell her.

"Something happened during that power outage last week. When they did the repairs of the damage my brother's accident caused."

He said it so evenly it took a moment for it to register that he was talking about the crash his brother and sister-in-law had died in.

Justine Davis 267

"And that's why there's no video of it," he finished.

Gemma was surprised at the sudden rush of emotion she felt. For him to talk about it so calmly, when it was that accident that had so totally upended his life… She stared at him with a combination of admiration and an aching sort of…not sympathy, but something deeper. How did police officers do that—see what they saw all the time and stay at all human, let alone go out and do it all over again?

But then she thought about what he'd actually said. "You mean it was just coincidence? That whatever it is, it happened just at that time?"

"I don't believe much in coincidence."

"But wouldn't that mean whoever did it would have to know when they were going to shut the power off?"

"Exactly. Hence the grunt work. Working through who would know, and how."

"But…people call about power outages all the time. That could be thousands of people."

"Yes. But most of them just get the recorded updates, which are pretty general."

"What about on social media? Did they announce the shutdown there?"

"Checked. They did, but they gave themselves a two-hour window in case they ran into complications. Same thing they told our day-watch dispatcher, and he told whoever asked him. But my guy knew down to the second."

"How?"

"Best guess, he knows somebody at the utility and called."

"And that's why you need the phone records." He nodded. "But there would still be a ton of calls to go through."

"Yes, although our tech could do a computer run fairly quickly." He hesitated again, then said, "Especially since there is a...small pool of possible suspects."

Something in the way he said that made her frown as much as the puzzle. "So you'd need to...what, cross-reference the calls they got with your suspects?"

"Yes. And a court order for those call records is going to take a while."

He jammed a hand through his hair again. Gemma felt a tingling in her fingers as she remembered clutching at that thick, silky hair while his body and hands and mouth had been driving her to madness.

She walked toward the kitchen counter where she'd left her phone.

"What are you doing?" he asked.

"Calling my sister Layla." His brows lowered in puzzlement. "Layla Colton, Colton Energy VP?" she elaborated as she picked up the phone.

He stared at her. Then, softly, he said, "Sometimes I still forget who you really are."

"I think," she said, equally softly, "you're the only one who really knows who I am."

For a moment they just stood there, gazes locked, phone in Gemma's hand forgotten.

Then he said, "Maybe because you don't show it to everyone. You just let them think what they think. It's a good disguise. And useful. If people can't see behind the facade, or don't even bother to look, then that's on them."

She wanted to run back across the room and grab him in a fierce hug. Maybe drag him back to the bedroom. But she heard the girls starting to fuss a bit, and that told her time was limited, so instead called Layla's number.

"She should be able to at least get the numbers. Would that help? Without names attached?"

"Of course it would. I have the numbers of most of the…suspect pool."

"So if one of those numbers called the utility…"

"Then I'd have a solid piece of evidence. But it would be inadmissible without that court order."

She thought for a moment. "You can trust Layla. She can keep a secret with the best of them. I'm her sister and I have no idea why she agreed to marry Dev's father," she added wryly.

"I'm not questioning that. If you say she can be trusted, I believe you."

When she had a moment, she thought, she'd savor that simple fact, that he believed her that easily. But for now she just said, "She could run a search on the list. What if you gave her the numbers you have and Layla only said yes or no? Then you'd know if it's worth waiting for the court order."

Again he stared at her. "When did you start thinking like a cop?"

"Maybe since I started hanging around a really good one?" she suggested.

He opened his mouth as if to answer, then closed it. Shook his head, but he was smiling. "Make the call," he said softly. She nodded and called up her contact list. "And Gemma?" She looked up. "Thank you," he said.

"My pleasure," she said, drawing out the word and giving him a look that made it impossible not to see she meant so much more than just a phone call.

Chapter 29

Once Gemma had made the call and he had only to wait and see what her sister was able to access, Dante was hit with a case of cabin fever that had him pacing the floor. He wasn't used to staying inside for days on end.

Finally, once the twins were up from their nap, Gemma suggested that the girls—and they—could use an outing.

If it wasn't for the girls, he could think of better ways to be spending their time inside. And he wouldn't even be thinking about wanting to get out. Uninterrupted hours in bed with Gemma seemed like the best of all possible worlds.

But uninterrupted hours and six-month-old twins appeared to be mutually exclusive.

"Can we stay away from the park?" he suggested.

He thought she suppressed a shiver. "Please. How about downtown?" She put on her most careless tone. "I haven't been shopping in *ages*."

He was sure his expression reflected the instant inward cringe, because she laughed at him. To his surprise, he didn't mind. "If you must," he said warily.

"Actually," she said, "I wanted to get some things for the girls." She looked over at the two, who were carrying on a babbling conversation that seemed perfectly intelligible to them. "And it's never too early to instill the shopping habit."

Dante groaned. Why couldn't they have been boys? He'd have an idea what to do about boys, but girls, all the different stages of girls…nope. Not a clue.

"Mancuso?"

He snapped out of his panicked thoughts. Why was she using his last name?

"Teasing," she pointed out.

He glared at her. Or tried to. "Payback," he threatened, utterly without heat.

"Promise?"

Her voice had gone all soft and husky in that way that awakened every nerve in his body and sent blood rushing to places that were, at the moment, inconvenient.

"Oh, yeah," he muttered.

And so an hour later, after dropping Flash off at the K9 center to ramble under the watchful eye of Patience Colton—who seemed to be eyeing them almost as watchfully, although Gemma merely chatted cheerfully—they were walking Rattlesnake Avenue, the improbably named ritzy shopping district of Red Ridge.

Dante knew it, but only because of various police cases he'd worked in the area; it was hardly his kind of place. He bought most of his clothes at the big outdoor store on the edge of town, and footwear, too, for that matter, since he rarely wore anything but boots or running shoes. Everything else… Well, that was what the internet was for.

It struck him as they strolled—literally, with the girls in the twin stroller—past one of the upscale jewelry stores that there was no way in hell he could afford to buy Gemma the kind of things she was used to. He felt out of place even walking down this street, past stores like that, the designer boutiques and all the rest. It was clear from her clothes and jewelry that she belonged here.

And it was clear from his clothes and lack of even a tie clip—and the fact that he owned exactly one tie in the first place—that he did not.

She'd expect a serious rock in an engagement ring.

He stopped in his tracks. Stood there, staring into nothing, as his thought echoed in his head repeatedly.

"Dante?"

"I—" He cut himself off sharply. No way in hell could he tell her what he'd just thought. "Your favorite store?" he said rather desperately, nodding toward the window full of sparkle.

"It was, once," she said. "But there are more important things."

…now I know what it feels like to have what my heart truly wants.

No matter how many times her words ran through

his mind, the warning always followed. *She doesn't mean you, idiot.*

The door to the jewelry store opened, and a man came out. He looked vaguely familiar, and Dante automatically started running through his mental wanted list. Not that most on that list of suspects in various things would be shopping here, but it was a reflex he figured most cops had.

But then he realized Gemma had turned to look. And gone very still.

"Gemma," the man said.

Dante couldn't read anything in his tone. But he could certainly assess the rest of the guy: the expensive suit, the French-cuffed shirt with cuff links that probably cost more than his SUV, the tie—probably one of hundreds, he thought wryly—that looked undoubtedly silk.

It hit him in the instant before Gemma said, "Dev."

Of course. He should have guessed.

He stayed silent as the other man's gaze swept over them. The strongest emotion he saw—besides an innate sense of superiority Dante found beyond irritating—was a mild sort of curiosity. If that was all he felt at seeing Gemma with another man, she was indeed well rid of the guy. Then he glanced at the twins, and there was no reaction at all. It was as if they weren't even there. And that made Dante edgy.

"I'm glad we ran into you," Gemma was saying. "I wanted to thank you."

Harrington's gaze snapped back to Gemma. "What?"

"For breaking it off."

The other man blinked. "What?" he repeated.

Dante nearly laughed, feeling suddenly better. *Try to keep up, rich boy.*

"It was the best thing you ever could have done for me. It changed my life."

Harrington was staring at her, obviously completely disconcerted. "I... It was?"

"It was," she said firmly. "And I understand. We couldn't have made each other happy."

"No. No, we couldn't." He was looking a little relieved now. "I wish I could have—"

"I hope you get your happiness, Dev," Gemma said, no rudeness in her cutting him off, and just sincerity in her voice when she added, "With whoever she is."

Harrington moved then, to embrace Gemma, and for an instant Dante considered stopping him. But she'd handled this so far—in a way that gave him more hope than was probably wise—so he stayed back.

"You too, Gemma. You deserve it. You truly do."

There was an odd note in the man's voice that Dante couldn't put a name to. Not quite regret, not quite appreciation. A sort of acknowledgment, though of what he didn't know. Maybe simply the fact that Gemma had tried so hard to win him over. But he quickly decided he was giving the guy too much credit, because Devlin Harrington was exactly the sort of person who haunted these environs.

When he'd gone to his car, something sleek and luxurious and with three figures to the left of the comma, no doubt, Dante glanced at Gemma, who was bent over the stroller, adjusting something on Lucia's tiny jacket.

He couldn't stop himself from asking, "That's the guy you had to prove something to? Really?" She straightened up, just looking at him, eyebrows raised. "I mean, I get that he's rich and successful, but damn, Gemma, he's smooth to the point of oily, and it's all layered over with smug."

To his surprise, she laughed and looked in the direction Harrington had gone. "He can definitely be smug," she agreed.

"He was really...what you wanted?"

"He's what the old me wanted," Gemma said, looking back at him. "But I'm not that person anymore. And the woman I am now wants something very different."

"Just like that?" he asked, afraid to trust what he thought he saw in her eyes.

"I was floundering before. Everybody approved of Dev and me, and I thought that mattered the most."

"What about what you wanted?"

"Exactly," she said. "And I did prove what I set out to prove. Didn't I?"

He glanced at the twins, who were happily looking around at everything in this place they'd never been before. "Yes," he said softly, "you did."

"I just didn't expect what I proved to myself."

His gaze shot back to her face. "Which is?"

"That what I felt, what I thought was love, was nothing like it. What I felt for Dev was not even close, just a pale imitation."

Dante stared at her. What was she saying? She couldn't be saying what it seemed like—that had to be his imagination, fueled by this crazy sense of hope that was building in him.

"You're well rid of him," he said carefully. "Now you just need to find someone else who can…afford to shop here for you." He nodded toward the jewelry store.

"I don't need that," Gemma said. "What I need is the man who makes me feel so happy I could burst, even if the only ring he can afford is a—a teething ring."

With that she gave the stroller a push and began to walk again. For a moment Dante couldn't move, torn between wondering what a teething ring was and… wanting to run after her and ask if he was that man.

Gemma felt lighter than she could ever remember in her life. She hadn't really realized until she was face-to-face with Dev, the man she'd thought she loved, how much had changed. Not just her life, but her heart. She truly felt like a new woman.

She felt as if the last puzzle piece had fallen into place, and she suddenly understood why her siblings and cousins who had found this feeling seemed so… different. Because they *were* different. If they felt anything like she did at this moment, they were very, very different than the people they'd been before they understood what it meant to truly love someone.

She was smiling at the twins, amending her thought to *three someones* before it struck her. She'd actually formed the words in her mind but never actually said them out loud. She'd hinted, implied, said it in every way…except those exact three words. And she felt a jab of doubt—why? Why hadn't she said them? Because she was waiting for Dante to say them first? She—

Her cell rang. She dug into the bag hanging on the handle of the stroller, thankful for the diversion. Saw it was Layla and felt a pang. She'd always felt bad about her sister being bartered off to Dev's father, but Layla insisted she had her reasons and Gemma had had to accept that. But she couldn't help wondering if, despite feeling sickened about the people already murdered, and her father's fury over the delay, perhaps Layla was just a tiny bit grateful the Groom Killer had chosen now to go on his killing rampage.

She shivered as she answered. She felt Dante come up beside her, felt his heat, his closeness, and the shiver subsided. She listened to Layla's hurried words—there always seemed to be some sort of crisis at Colton Energy these days—agreed to her suggestion and disconnected. Then she looked up at Dante.

"She has the list of numbers, but she has to run to a meeting. She'll call back tonight, and you can give her your…suspect numbers and she'll run a search."

"Thank you," he said. He reached up to brush back a strand of her hair. "Are you cold?"

So he'd seen the shiver. "No. Just…a grim thought."

"About?"

"I can't help thinking Layla's getting railroaded into this marriage to Dev's father. I mean, I can see he's smitten with her, but… I don't think she feels the same."

"'Sound familiar?" he asked, and he had that carefully neutral tone going again.

She tilted her head back, met his gaze. "Sounds like where I used to be, yes."

"Used to be? Past tense?"

"Yes." She held his gaze, letting him read the truth there, that because of him, she now knew what the real thing was. His expression went from doubt to hope and finally, as she kept looking at him, understanding.

"Gemma, I—"

This time it was his cell phone signaling a text, and for a moment she wished the reception here was bad. But she saw his face change as he read, and her heart sank.

"Bad news?" she asked the moment he ended the connection.

"I have to get back to the K9 center," he said as he shoved the phone into his pocket. "Flash is hurt."

Gemma gasped. "Oh, no! What happened?"

"Little tussle with one of the other dogs."

"We'd better hurry. If he's hurt he needs to be with us."

Despite the urgency that had been in his voice, Dante gave her a long look. Then a slow smile, as if she'd confirmed something for him. "Yes," he said softly.

Chapter 30

They headed back to his SUV and got the girls loaded up quickly, a much simpler process since she'd bought a set of car seats for her own vehicle so these could stay in his.

"I remember when we put these in here," she said, "and thinking that baby seats in a vehicle full of a police gear was kind of an anachronism. But then I realized it was a perfect symbol of what police do—protect the most helpless."

He looked up from strapping in Zita. He knew exactly what she was doing—trying to distract him—but it didn't stop him from smiling despite his worry about Flash.

"Thank you. It's nice that some people remember that, at least."

They were halfway there when his phone signaled again, an incoming call this time. He glanced at the screen, saw it was the K9 center number. Safe enough to answer on the speaker system, he decided, and damn it, he wanted to know about Flash.

"Mancuso."

"Dante? It's Patience."

He felt a chill. "Tell me you're not calling yourself because it's that bad?"

"No, no, I'm calling because I knew you'd be worried. He'll be fine. In fact he's in my office now and we're spoiling him rotten."

He felt the pressure that had spiked ease. "What happened?"

"A little tussle with one of the younger dogs who doesn't know his manners yet. No bites, but a muscle strain. He'll be glad to see you and go home and rest."

Dante glanced at Gemma. "Not much of that going on at home," he said, but he was grinning. And then belatedly remembered Patience was Gemma's sister. Tried to recover it. "Babies are a lot of work," he said quickly.

There was a moment's silence before Patience answered. "Yes. Yes, they are."

After he ended the call, he studiously kept his eyes on the road.

"I admire my sister," Gemma said. "She always knew what she wanted and worked to put herself through veterinary school."

"She's great with the dogs," Dante said.

Gemma smiled, but it was almost sad. "She told me

once she wished she could trust people the way she trusts dogs."

His mouth twisted wryly. "A thought I've had a time or two myself. But they trust her, too. As does everyone in the department. She's really down-to-earth."

"Unlike the rest of us Coltons?" Gemma asked archly as he stopped for a red light.

He looked at her then. Hoped he was right that the glint in her eyes was humor. "I would have said that. Once."

She smiled, far more brightly than he would have thought his comment deserved. "Once," she said, "you would have been right."

When they arrived at the training center, Patience was waiting for them outside. Flash was at her side, looking only faintly aggrieved. Dante saw the woman's eyes widen slightly under her thick fringe of bangs when she saw Gemma get out of his vehicle.

"You have the twins with you?"

Gemma nodded. "Want to meet them?"

"Absolutely," Patience said, but Dante thought there was something…strained about her smile. She shifted her attention to him and handed him Flash's leash. They walked around to the back of the car. "You'd better lift him in."

Dante grimaced. "Glad he's not a show dog, then." As a working dog, Flash weighed a solid eighty-five pounds, but the show ring animals were generally bigger, starting at over a hundred. He got him in the back of the SUV, Flash suffering the indignity of being picked up with a sigh.

"Keep him moving a bit so it doesn't stiffen up, but no more than a walk for a couple of days. He should be fine. If he's still favoring that foreleg after that, bring him back."

Dante nodded. Patience glanced back to where Gemma was leaning into the back seat, keeping the girls amused, then back to him. He raised a brow at her. "Something else?" he asked quietly, recognizing the signs.

"I saw something this morning. Remember the puppy the Larsons stole?"

He didn't bother to remind her there was no proof the Larson brothers had taken the animals—he knew she was convinced beyond talking her out of it. Not that he'd try, given his own feelings about them. So he said only, "Sure."

"I saw him. And Nico." Dante remembered the tough, well-trained protection Malinois that had also been stolen from the training center. "And," she added emphatically, "the guy had the Larsons' two other dogs, the ones Bo Gage sold to them, as well."

Dante didn't like the undertone that had come into her voice and tried for a joke. "A dog walker? What is this, New York City? We're getting too civilized."

She didn't laugh. "I'm going to get those dogs back, Dante."

The cop in him suddenly leaped to the fore. "Patience, stay away from those two. They're really, really bad news."

"You think I don't know that?" she snapped in a tone

he'd never heard from her before. "I know perfectly well what the Larsons are capable of."

She stopped when she realized Gemma was there now, and he left them to chat for a moment while he made sure Flash was comfortable. When they were back in the SUV and ready to leave, Gemma watched her sister walk back into the building.

"She still thinks they stole her dogs, doesn't she?"

"Yes," Dante said, knowing it was no secret. "But I wish she'd keep a lower profile about it. Drawing the attention of either Noel or Evan Larson could have nasty consequences."

"I think..." Gemma hesitated.

"What?"

"I don't know for sure, but I think she might have dated one of them once."

He blinked. "Patience? And one of the Larson brothers?" He was astonished and knew it rang in his voice.

"I saw her with one of them a couple of times, and when I asked she said it was nothing, but..."

Dante stared at the training center building, where Patience had gone back inside. "I hope it really was nothing," he said, and he couldn't help the ominous tone.

Any woman foolish enough to get involved with a Larson was asking for trouble.

This was so...domestic, Gemma thought.

They'd gotten Flash home, and when he'd been about to jump out of the SUV, Dante had instead gently lifted him out and set him down.

"I know, buddy," he told the dog, "it's humiliating, but it won't be long. And if I know you, by the time you're feeling better, you'll have decided you like all this attention and you'll start milking it."

Gemma had laughed but had sneaked the dog an extra treat once he was ensconced in his chair inside.

"Shh," she said, very audibly, "don't tell Dante."

"You mean the guy who already gave him a treat when I put him in the car?"

They'd ended up laughing together and were still smiling now, a couple of hours later, as she played with the twins and he got ready to grill steaks on the small barbecue on the patio. She'd never seen the appeal of these quiet togetherness scenarios before, but now a long, uninterrupted string of evenings like this seemed like the most wonderful thing imaginable. Especially if the evenings were capped off with nights like the last couple of weeks.

In fact, if it wasn't for the girls, she'd be over there luring Dante into stripping down right now, just so she could run her hands over him. How had she ever thought Dev good-looking? He paled to blandness beside Dante. Those piercing dark eyes, that thick dark hair, even the stubble on his strong, masculine jaw… And the rest of him, from broad, strong chest to flat belly to narrow hips, to—

"Whatever you're thinking, don't forget it."

He'd come up behind her and slipped his arms around her. "Not a chance," she said.

There was a long silent moment before he said

against her ear, "Sometimes when you look at me like that, I—"

Her cell rang. "I am," she said crankily, "going to throw that thing into Wyoming."

He nuzzled her ear. "They'd probably just throw it back. Not going to answer?"

"No." She glanced at the screen. Sighed. "Yes. It's Layla."

She felt him go very still, and that quickly the mood was shattered.

This is what it will be like, being with a cop.

When she used to think about why the officers she met through her fund-raisers did what they did, why they were willing to put their lives on the line, she hadn't really thought about the other aspect of it, that their spouses and families had to be just as willing. For if the day ever came when that risk came true, it would be they who were left in pain and anger and grief.

One day it could be her, if she stayed.

On the other hand, leaving him was too high a price to pay for peace of mind.

"Gemma?"

She snapped out of her thoughts. "Sorry." She answered the phone, then handed it over to him. "I'll guard the steaks."

He grinned at that; Flash had been eyeing the two lovely rib eyes since they'd come out of the fridge. Then Dante took her phone and walked back inside to get the list of phone numbers.

He was back in less than five minutes. Looking glum but not angry.

"No luck?" she asked.

"No match," he confirmed. "Only number on the list that hit was from dispatch, and Frank already told me he'd called."

"I'm sorry."

He shrugged one shoulder. "Don't be. It was a big help to have her do that and saved me a lot of time and frustration." He gave her a sideways look. "She's pretty sharp, your sister."

"Runs in the family," she said airily.

He grinned then. "Yes. In various disguises."

They fed the girls, and as usual it was an adventure, since neither of the twins was certain they liked the new, solid food. Once that was cleaned up, they ate their own dinner—Dante had this grill thing down, she thought as she savored the last bite of her steak—and settled into the living room with the babies in their playpen, working hard on crawling.

"My money's on Lucia," he said as he fired up his laptop, no doubt to go to work again; he might have been dealt a setback, but Dante wasn't a quitter. He'd solve whatever this was, no matter how long it took.

"To get crawling first?" she asked. He nodded. She looked back at the two consideringly. "I'd agree. But only because I still think Zita's going to go straight to walking and skip crawling altogether."

She heard him let out an audible breath. "And I'm terrified."

She almost laughed at the idea of the intrepid cop being frightened of two tiny babies, but there had been something in his voice, some sort of undertone, that told her he meant much more than the prospect of the twins being mobile.

"Do your cases always go in a straight line?"

He blinked. "What?"

"They change as you go, don't they? As you learn new things, find new evidence?"

"Of course."

"So you have to adapt, change your thinking about it." She waved toward the twins. "It'll be the same with them. And we'll adapt. Whatever, whenever, we'll deal with it."

He stared at her for a moment. "You have…quite a way of putting things in relatable terms."

She grinned. "It helps."

"It works," he returned.

She smiled. After a moment she said, "I'm thinking about planning another fund-raiser for the K9 unit. My father's always funded it in memory of Layla's mom, but now that Layla's wedding has been postponed because of that maniac killer…"

She regretted saying it, and linking the two, as soon as the words were out. But Dante didn't look puzzled.

"It's that bad at Colton Energy? That your sister has to marry Harrington for the cash infusion?" She flushed. Dante shrugged. "It didn't take much logic." His mouth quirked. "It's a very iffy field."

"He is quite taken with her," Gemma said, but it didn't make her feel much better.

"If he's as…smarmy as his son," Dante said rather sourly, "I hope she wakes up and changes her mind."

Gemma had no idea why Layla had agreed to the

outlandish bargain in the first place, so she couldn't say what it would take for her to do that. "It could happen," she said. Then, giving him a pointed look, she added, "I certainly did."

For a moment he just looked at her. Then, his voice rough in that way she loved, he said, "How do you feel about hot, steamy sex in front of two six-month-olds?"

"Afraid not," she said, her own voice a bit husky. "But just think how it will be if we let it build for another hour until they go to bed."

She was right.

Chapter 31

By morning Gemma was deliciously sated, yet still wondering if they had time to indulge in another round of that glorious connection they had, when her phone rang.

"Definitely Wyoming," she muttered under her breath as she reached to grab it from the nightstand before it woke Dante, who had had a very, very busy night. But she hadn't reckoned on his ingrained reaction to early-morning phone calls; he was awake and sitting up by the time she glanced at the phone's screen.

Layla.

"Hey," she answered, curiosity over the second call clear in her voice.

"I like your cop," Layla said without preamble.

She liked the sound of that "your cop" so much it was a moment before she could answer. "So do I. A lot."

"A lot lot?"

"More."

Layla sighed. It was a bittersweet kind of sound. "I'm happy for you."

Gemma wanted to ask if she should be happy for her in turn, but she knew her sister had to have called for a reason; Layla didn't have time for idle chitchat these days. Even as she thought it, her sister went on briskly.

"Can I talk to him again?"

"Something new?"

"Yes. I found one of his numbers."

Gemma turned to Dante, who was watching her intently. She held her phone out to him. "It's Layla. She found a number."

She saw something flare in his eyes. Realized suddenly that this was a man who did everything worth doing full bore, be it following every trail in an investigation or…making love to her.

Life with him—and his little family of twins plus dog—would be full, challenging, sometimes frightening, but never, ever boring.

She wanted that. All of it. And she let it show in her eyes as she handed him her phone. And knew by the way he just stared at her that he'd read her expression perfectly.

In your court, Dante Mancuso. You know what I want.

He took the phone. But he never took his eyes off her. And before he said anything else, he whispered, "Yes."

Dante was having a little trouble focusing. His life was changing so rapidly and it showed no sign of slow-

ing down. But he also might have just been handed the
thread that could unravel all the way to their crooked
cop.

And all because of another Colton—one who had
gone the extra step and run his list of numbers against
calls not just to the utility, but to its repair workers, who
had company-provided cell phones for callouts, as well.

He pulled in behind the station, parking in the back
corner of the lot that the K9 unit had claimed as their
own. He thought about leaving Flash in the car, but the
bloodhound was already up on his feet, so he opened
the back and lifted him out to the ground.

"I swear you've put on ten pounds overnight," he
said to the animal, who gave him the aggrieved look
the comment deserved.

But Dante only smiled as his mind filled with memories of his own overnight. There wasn't an inch of
Gemma he hadn't explored with eyes, hands and mouth.
That had been delicious enough, but then she'd turned
the tables and taught him how little he had really known
of what his body was capable of feeling.

He wanted this case over and this damned crooked
cop put away so he could spare a moment to think about
the future. A future that had now changed irrevocably
with the twins—and Gemma. Because he wanted her
in that future.

For all his sins, his brother had truly loved his wife.
And in fact, they'd been perfect for each other in their
own dishonest way. It was the one thing Dante had always marveled at, that Dom had found someone so perfectly matched to his view of life and its opportunities.

Gemma came from a very different world. Yet behind that glamorous facade she used so well was a genuine, laughing and loving woman. And despite his doubts, she'd proven herself with the twins, learning fast and laughing at the inevitable mistakes in a way that charmed them…and him.

"Mancuso!"

He snapped out of his reverie at the sound of the chief's voice. He turned and saw Finn Colton heading toward him from his own official vehicle.

"I heard your partner got hurt," Finn said, looking down at Flash.

"A little. He'll be okay."

He liked how the chief was always concerned about the welfare of his troops, human and canine. Wondered what the man would say if he knew he'd interrupted Dante's mental planning of a blissful future with his cousin.

They started walking through the section of the lot where officers parked their personal vehicles. He saw that Finn was watching Flash carefully, and after a moment he nodded. Then he shifted his gaze to Dante.

"Any progress?"

Dante didn't want to have to explain how he'd gotten the piece of information Layla Colton had handed him this morning. Not yet, anyway. "Some," he said. "A good lead, maybe. I'm here to check on something."

Finn nodded and let it go, trusting him. "I'm about to win the betting pool, you know."

"The what?" Then Dante remembered what Finn

had told him—that there had been a pool going on how long Gemma would last playing at being a nanny. "Oh."

"I was the only one who said she'd last a month. She is going to, isn't she?"

"Yes," he said, rather fiercely. Then, when Finn's gaze narrowed, he added with an attempt at humor, "Unless the twins take her out in the next week."

Finn laughed. "I was fifteen when my youngest sister was born. I remember thinking one tiny thing couldn't possibly be so much trouble. I can't imagine what two of them must be like."

"She's doing great with them. And they respond to her."

Finn's expression changed again, now full of speculation. "And you?"

There was no denying the question inherent in those words, and Dante grimaced. "Last I heard, she's already got a big brother."

"Yeah," Finn said, deadpan, "but I'm better with a shotgun."

Dante would have laughed, but he wasn't entirely sure his boss was joking. And when it came down to it, he liked that Finn was concerned about Gemma. So he held the man's gaze steadily.

"You won't need it," he said.

"Glad to hear it," Finn said. "You're a good man, Mancuso. You've had to fight some preconceptions to get to where you are. I admire that."

"Gemma's fought a few of those herself," he said. *Including my own.*

Finn looked surprised, then thoughtful. "Hadn't thought of it quite that way, but you're right."

"I—" Flash's sudden stop cut him off. The bloodhound was next to a silver coupe parked at the end of the row, head and tail up as he sniffed the trunk. Dante frowned. "Whose car is that?"

"Don't know," Finn said. "Why's he so interested?"

"He's not just interested. See his tail, how it's up and to the right like that? That's his tracking signal. He's on to something."

"In that car? What?"

"All I can say for sure is that something he's tracked before is in there."

They exchanged a glance, and Dante knew Finn had reached the same conclusion—that the dog had alerted on an officer's private vehicle when they were looking for a dirty cop couldn't be a coincidence. Finn pulled out his phone and made a call. Waited silently a moment, then came back with a name.

The same name that went with the phone number Layla had given him.

"That's it," Dante said. At Finn's look he quickly explained what he'd learned. The phone number, the power outage, the call made to a utility worker and what hadn't been on those security videos.

Finn frowned. "How you got that number could get tricky, but the way you did it was smart. And I just happen to know a judge who would be happy to get me that court order in a hurry."

"Oh? I figured it would take forever."

"Remember that Ponzi scheme the Larsons were behind but we could never prove it?" Dante nodded; he'd studied every case the Larsons had been even tangentially connected to. "The judge's niece got sucked into that one and lost a chunk of money."

Things happened fast after that. Within an hour, Finn had a court order not only for the phone records, but to search the vehicle Flash had alerted on. Within the next hour, they had the missing phone, secreted inside the spare tire in the trunk; sometimes Flash's nose still amazed him. And with the phone was a debit card from a bank down in Rapid City. Dante guessed a check of that account would show exactly how much the Larsons had paid to have that phone stolen from the evidence room.

Paid Al Collins. Duke's partner. Which likely explained how the shooter had found them, both at the apartment and at home; Duke could easily have mentioned something. And later, all he or one of Larson's goons had to do was follow Gemma and the twins.

And twenty minutes after that they had an at first protesting and then grimly silent cop in custody. The phone itself had been wiped, and the man clearly wasn't about to give up who hired him, but Dante had no doubts. The recent transfer was their guy.

"That's why the whole routine with the pen. So you could lean over the counter and see exactly where Ron put the phone. What, did the utilities guy owe you one? You let him off on a ticket or something?"

Collins made an obscene suggestion. Dante ignored it; they'd find out the whole story eventually.

"I'm glad you're the dirtbag," Dante said as Collins was dragged away. "Better than one of our own."

"Too bad Lambert didn't take you out," Collins snapped, then lapsed back into his determined silence.

But Dante stared after him, the name he hadn't had until this moment echoing in his ears. The name of the man who had fired the warning shots at the apartment where they'd found the phone that this stinking cop had stolen out of evidence.

The man who had attacked Gemma and the twins.

And had caused his brother's death.

Chapter 32

Dante came home as happy as he could be given they'd just found a dirty cop—and walked in on a disaster. Two wailing twins and a frazzled-looking Gemma amid toys and clothes strewn about and…something orange in an artistic streak up one wall in the kitchen. He had the inane thought that if this were a crime scene and that was blood, it'd be classified as arterial spray.

But looking around, he wasn't so sure it wasn't a crime scene.

Flash had stopped in the doorway, taken in the scene for all of three seconds, then turned to head back to his safe haven in the back of the SUV. Dante couldn't blame him. But instead he led the reluctant dog through the chaos and put him out on the patio for the moment. Flash seemed relieved when he slid the door shut.

Then Dante turned around. The girls had subsided to quieter sniffling punctuated by an occasional burst of protest. Gemma looked harassed but determined as she held Lucia, who had been making the most noise.

He looked at the three of them, thinking he should feel like Flash, ready to turn and run. But he didn't.

Instead he went to Zita and picked her up, swinging her up in the air. The weeping turned to excited giggles in an instant. And Lucia subsided into fascinated observation of her sister.

He turned to look at Gemma. "Thank you," he said quietly.

She looked startled, glanced around at the mess, then back to him. "For what?" she began, but then her eyes widened. "You got him? The phone number helped?"

"Yes and yes. And that's what I originally wanted to thank you for. But now that I'm here and see this," he said wryly, gesturing at the room and the twins, "it's that they're still alive."

She grimaced. "I should have known it was pure novelty that got me through these last three weeks."

"And determination will get you through this," he said softly. "You're not a quitter, Gemma."

"I had my doubts this morning," she said. "They've discovered a new level of volume."

"I know it's been hard, cooped up in here. But that may be over soon, too." She gave him a questioning look. "I've got a name for the guy who attacked you and the girls. A last name, anyway."

"You've had a busy morning."

"Thanks to you, your sister and Flash, yeah."

"Flash?" She glanced toward the patio. Dante explained what had happened, without the specifics that he couldn't tell her.

"So now what?" she asked. "Now that you have the guy, do you go back to work full-time?"

"Chief didn't say. He just told me to take the rest of the day off. So," he said, looking around, "I guess I know what I'll be doing. What is that on the wall, anyway?"

"Carrots."

"Who hated them enough to throw them?"

"Zita. And she was quite proud of herself when she saw what she'd accomplished."

"Budding artist, maybe? Or crime-scene investigator." At her look he explained his earlier thought, figuring she'd think it either twisted or gross. Instead she laughed.

"Lucia, on the other hand, decided to smear them on every article of clothing she could reach, including her sister's and mine."

Making a snap decision, he said, "Why don't you get yourself and them cleaned up while I tackle the new wall decor, and washing their clothes before it sets. Then we'll get out of here for a while."

He knew it was the right call when he saw her eyes light up. "Really?"

"Yeah. We'll go get something for us to eat, pizza or something, and take it somewhere these two can make all the noise and get as dirty as they want."

"What about Flash?"

He liked that she thought of the dog. "We'll take

him, too. Maybe stop at the dog park over by the pizza place. He could use a bit of slow exercise. If you don't mind, that is."

She smiled. "I don't. He's such a personality. Even with the drool."

He gave her a crooked grin. "You're just a sucker for his sad-eye routine."

"Lucky for you, I'm a sucker for yours, too."

Caught off guard by the teasing, something sparked inside him, so powerful he had to look away for a moment. "Damn," he muttered.

"Not exactly the response I was hoping for."

His gaze shot back to her face. "What were you hoping for? That I'd say you make me feel things I've never felt before? And not just in bed, great as that is? That I'm so damned glad you walked into my life, and not just for the twins?"

"That's a lot closer," she said, smiling now.

He sucked in a breath. Hesitated. *Aw, hell. Go for it.* "How about… I love you?"

Her eyes widened. Her lips, those eminently kissable lips, parted.

"I know," he said quickly, "it's been less than a month, but—"

He stopped. She was shaking her head. Damn, he'd blown it. She didn't feel it, it wasn't the same for her, she didn't—

"I love you, too," she said a little breathlessly. "I just didn't dare say it."

It took him a moment to get past the declaration to ask, "Didn't dare? Why?"

"Because I came here foolishly thinking I knew what love was, and that I was in love with Dev. And I made that clear, so I didn't think you'd believe me after only three weeks."

"Why not? My entire life changed in ten seconds." Her eyes widened, as if she hadn't thought of it in quite that way. "And it made me a package deal, Gemma," he added, waving at the girls.

She grinned then, and it took his breath away. "News flash—you always were. Mr. Sad Eyes out there."

He grabbed her then, kissed her fiercely. It was a long time before he surfaced. He was looking down at her, savoring the color in her cheeks and the just-kissed look of her lips when the silence registered. He glanced warily at the suddenly docile twins.

"Why are they being so quiet?"

"Probably saving up for an explosion later," she said with a wry smile.

"Then let's eat first. I don't want to deal with that on an empty stomach."

"Good idea. You're going to need your strength later, too."

She said it lightly, but it hit him like a punch low in the gut. Oh, yeah. Tonight. Tonight was going to be something special. He'd see to that.

He was still pondering the ways when they ended up with that pizza—and he was a bit surprised to see she was a traditionalist there, no fancy designer pies for her—sitting on the blanket she'd folded up and stuffed in the back of the stroller before they'd left home. They were on the grass next to the fenced-in dog park with the girls beside them, for now playing happily with the set of brightly colored blocks on a string that Gemma said was their current favorite because they could both play with it at the same time.

There were only a couple of other dogs there, and after an initial get-to-know-you sniff, the trio apparently decided they could coexist and went their separate ways. The two smaller dogs resumed their play, and Flash went about his greatest joy—sniffing.

"It's really amazing what he can do," she said.

Dante nodded. "Especially since we train them to go against their first instinct, which is to follow whatever trail is freshest."

"That makes sense. So you have to train them to go after a specific trail?"

He nodded. "And once they do, they never forget. That's how he found that stolen evidence this morning."

She watched Flash rambling around, glanced at the girls to be sure they were still occupied, then looked at him. "He needs a yard to do that in. A big one."

"Yeah. I've been thinking about that. I've kind of resisted a place farther out, where I could get some land, because of the driving time to work."

"You spend that in taking him to the park or the training center instead of letting him into his own backyard. Not to mention the girls will need more room, inside and out."

He let out a breath. Faced the facts, the most overwhelming of which was who she was. He'd fallen in love with a woman used to the best of everything, which was not something he could provide. Especially now. "I can't afford anything…like you're used to."

She gave him a sideways look. "Was that an invitation?"

"A warning, maybe?"

"There's always your brother's house," she said, rather archly. And then she laughed, and he could imagine what his expression had been. Pure horror, no doubt. But her expression changed then, became serious. "What about your brother? Did he leave anything to the girls?"

"Everything," Dante admitted. "With me as legal guardian. There's some money involved, but… I don't want to touch it. Don't want it to touch the girls."

She studied him for a moment. "Because of how he got it," she said. He nodded. She gave him a smile then, and a nod that seemed to be saying she'd expected that. "You're a genuine good guy, Dante. It must have been hell growing up like that."

"It had its moments," he admitted.

"If your brother had gotten his money legitimately, then what?"

He frowned. "What are you getting at?"

"Just trying to find out if you'd still have qualms about help with the girls from an…honest source."

It finally hit him. He was shaking his head before he could even think of what to say.

"So is it ethics that has you saying no before you even hear me out? Or is it pride?"

"Yes," he said, feeling a bit helpless.

"You know some people are going to say you're with me for my money no matter what, right?"

He winced. Then sucked in a deep breath. "As long as you know different."

"Oh, I do. Because I know you. Dante Mancuso doesn't take anything he hasn't earned."

Her words warmed him, in the way he'd discovered only Gemma could do.

"So here's my plan," she said briskly. "You handle the basics—housing, food, all that manly stuff. And I'll handle the girly stuff. Clothes, shoes, makeup—"

"Makeup?" he yelped.

"Well, down the road, I mean, of course," she said kindly. "Oh, and I can have that talk with them, too. You know, boys and things. I've learned a little about the difference between infatuation and love lately. And by the time they're ready to think about such things, they'll have had a good example in front of them for a long time."

Dante stared at her. Words were beyond him. Finally Gemma gave him a quizzical look. "I know you, Dante," she said again. "You wouldn't love halfway. If you said it, you meant the whole thing."

"I… Yes."

"All right, then."

After a moment of silence, he slowly shook his head in wonder. "Is this how you do it? The fund-raising? You overwhelm people so that they just go down the path you want, and then realize it's the path they wanted, too?"

"Is it the path you want?"

"Yes." He swallowed, said it again more forcefully. "Yes. But you're who you are and—"

"Tell you what," she said cheerfully. "I won't hold your family against you if you don't hold mine against me."

"I don't mind most of your family."

"Except my father. Yeah, he has that effect on people. So take him out of it. I think my siblings make up for that, don't they?"

"Yes."

"And these two," she said, gesturing at the twins, who had apparently discovered the blue flowers on a bottle gentian a few feet away and were working mightily on getting there by squirm or by roll, "more than make up for anything your family ever did."

He looked at the girls, felt that tug of connection again. "Yeah," he whispered.

"Besides, Coltons and K9 officers seem to be a trend," she said. "Bea, Blake, now me."

His mouth quirked. "Something in the water, maybe?"

"Nope," she said, again in that light, teasing tone, "we have good taste." Then, holding his gaze, she added softly, "It just takes some of us a little more time to find it."

His throat tightened so much all he could get out was her name, but he tried to put everything he was feeling into it. And by the look on her face he must have succeeded, because—

A loud baying sound cut off his thoughts. It sent a shiver up his spine no matter how many times he heard it. Flash. He quickly spotted him at the far end of the dog park.

"He looks so funny when he's running, with his ears flying like that," Gemma said affectionately.

He'd appreciate that tone in her voice later, but right now he was staring at the dog. Not because he shouldn't be running on that sore leg, although it was a concern. But Dante was staring because he knew that body language. And he knew what it took to set the hound to baying.

Flash had scented something. And it had to be on the air or his nose would be on the ground. And he was headed their way. Which meant the scent was coming from their direction.

His mind raced through the facts in a split second. He was on his feet before he'd even processed it all. His fingers were curling around the grip of the Springfield at his back as he scanned the area.

"Dante?" Gemma's voice had changed. He took a quick glance at her, and his heart nearly stopped. She had gathered the girls to her and was huddled around them, as if to protect them from the threat she didn't even understand with her own body.

"Get the girls in the car and get out of here," he ordered, tossing her the keys. "Stay away until I call you."

"And leave you here alone?" she asked, sounding so aghast that it warmed him despite the warning bells that were clamoring, waking every instinct he had.

"When you're safe, call 911 and ask the area car to head this way. But get out of here with the girls. Leave everything."

"Dante—"

"I love you," he whispered. "Now go."

He glanced back at Flash, saw the dog still running. He let out another spine-tingling roar. Quickly Dante tried to calculate the angles, where the dog was headed from where he was. *The trees*, he thought. The only cover.

And then he started to move. But he had seen that spark of acknowledgment in Gemma's eyes that told him she understood that *I love you* was…just in case. He wondered if it would change her mind, if she would decide living in a cop's life wasn't worth it. He shoved the thought out of his head and focused on the job. Maybe it was a threat, maybe it wasn't, but he'd gamble on Flash's nose any day.

He walked toward the left of the trees, as if he were headed that way rather than where he was fairly certain his quarry was hiding.

Third time's the charm…

The moment the old saying ran through his head, he was sure. It was Lambert. The man who had indirectly caused Dominic and Agostina's deaths and then tried to kill Gemma and the girls. Something hot and primitive rose in him, and he gave himself an internal warning—this guy could be the thread that unraveled the Larsons and their little criminal fiefdom. It warred with the urge to just take the scum out, and in that moment he honestly didn't know which would win out. All he knew for sure was that he had him, because if he got away now, Dante would go get Flash and the man's fate would be sealed. The bloodhound would track him to the gates of hell.

As he'd hoped, when he got even with the trees, the

guy bought it, thinking Dante was on a wrong trail and he was clear. And he moved. Dante spun around and ran for the trees. He gained a precious few yards before Lambert—for he'd seen him now—realized he'd been had. The man threw him a startled glance and hastily capped off a round. It went wide, hitting a tree to Dante's left and sending bark flying. A piece of it caught him under his left eye, but he never looked away from Lambert. And he kept running.

Lambert spun around and started to run, too. He tripped over an exposed tree root—city boy, Dante thought—and that gained him another couple of yards. But it also sent Lambert careening into the clear, out of the trees. He looked back over his shoulder as if to see if he had a better shot now. Dante ducked behind a large spruce. Lambert hesitated, but only for a moment. He started to run again.

"Lambert!" Dante shouted his name, hoping that realizing he was burned would slow the guy down.

It only made him change direction. Right toward where Gemma and the girls had been moments ago. Dante spared a split second to thank God she'd done as he'd told her and gone; the space the big SUV had been parked in was empty. But he'd realized in that moment when she'd instinctively moved to protect the girls that she would always put them first.

Lambert hesitated by the blanket, as if he hadn't realized they were gone. It gave Dante the extra seconds he needed. When the man realized how close he was, he bolted.

Without even thinking Dante grabbed the handle

of the abandoned stroller. And shoved. It hit Lambert a glancing blow on his right knee. The man staggered. His feet tangled with the stroller wheels. And Dante launched.

He took Lambert down on his right side, pinning him with a knee over his kidneys. The hand with the weapon was beneath them. Lambert squirmed, twisted.

"Yeah, fight me," Dante begged. "So I can say you struggled and your own gun went off and killed you."

Lambert went suddenly still. And a moment later Dante heard the siren.

It was over.

Chapter 33

"Have I got this right?" Gemma stared at him. "You took down an armed man with the baby stroller?"

"Whatever works," Dante said, watching Lambert, hands cuffed behind him, being led to the marked unit. Gemma couldn't help it, she laughed. He turned his head to look at her. Said, rather solemnly, "Thank you."

"For laughing at your method?" she asked.

"For doing what I asked."

Her mouth curved wryly. "You mean for following orders?"

He gave her a wry tilt of his head and a half shrug. "I didn't want to put it like that. But yes. It might not have gone so well if I'd had to worry about you and the twins, too."

"I trust you, Dante. And I trusted you to take care of yourself so that I could take care of the girls."

"And that," he said, "is what I'm really thanking you for. Trusting me."

"And you trusted me, with them." She glanced over to make sure the girls were still secure in their car seats. She'd had to make a quick decision and had driven away with them belted into the front seat until she was three blocks away, then she'd stopped and put them into their car seats.

All the while she'd been playing back in her head the single shot she'd heard. Dante shooting? Or being shot at?

Stay away until I call you...

She had spent a shaky few minutes wondering what she'd do if that call never came. Wondering if she was tough enough to deal with what Dante faced every day. Tough enough to kiss him goodbye every morning, never knowing for sure that he'd come back.

For an instant Dev flashed through her mind. His life had been easy, and now that she could see him more honestly, she knew he was more than a bit spoiled, too used to getting everything he wanted and having things his own way. She knew that because she could see an uncomfortable amount of that in herself, in her own life, and she didn't ever want to end up like Dev, smug and entitled.

Dante will see to that. He'll never let you end up like that. Just the life you'll live with him will make sure you never do.

She had never realized before how much she had always counted on being in control of her life. She would marry whom she wanted, have kids when she wanted, all of it on her terms. Part of this was probably, she admitted, in response to Layla's situation, which she herself would find intolerable.

And yet…here she was, loving the chaos of life with Dante and the girls. She thought of that night when she'd come out of the kitchen after clearing away the dinner debris—her turn, since he had cooked—wondering where he was. She'd found him on the living room floor, Zita asleep on his chest and Lucia cuddled up beside him, also asleep, and he'd given her that rueful, crooked grin that never failed to kick her pulse into overdrive. She'd pulled her phone out and snapped a photo, knowing as she did it that she'd keep that one forever.

She hadn't planned it. But here she was, with two kids and the man she loved, a package deal, as Dante had said. And she realized that while in her life she had almost always gotten what she wanted, what she wanted had changed. And it was right here in front of her.

"You know," she said after they'd gotten the stroller—after a discussion about whether it was evidence—loaded up and were sitting in the car, "you really may have to rethink your approach."

He went very still. "Approach…to what?"

"Life in general and your job specifically."

He looked at her then. "For instance?" His voice was a little tight.

"I only meant you might need to rethink, because it's not like when it was only you. You have to take care of yourself. You have a family now." He blinked. She smiled and went on softly. "A family that will be everything yours wasn't. Loving, supportive—" she grinned then "—honest."

She saw the flicker of a smile. "Now there's a concept."

"And we would be lost without you. So I'm just saying, err on the side of caution now."

He was silent for a long moment before he said softly, "We?"

"Of course we. Oh, and if you can hurry your fellow cops along on that Groom Killer—who is *not* Demi, by the way—that would be good, too."

"Sounds like you have…plans."

"I do. And I tend to get what I want." His mouth twitched. "Of course," she went on in that airy tone that almost always made him smile, "once I was confused about what that was. I'm not anymore."

"I was never confused," he said quietly. "I just never thought I could have what I wanted."

"Well, I'm glad we got that resolved, then," she said briskly. She looked over her shoulder at the twins, who were being oddly quiet. "And you two are going to grow up with your uncle's values, not your parents'."

Before she could turn back, Dante's hands were cupping her face, and an instant later he was kissing her. Deeply, fiercely. And then it changed, to something sweet and gentle and promising forever.

She wasn't sure which of the girls made the crowing sound, but it was Zita who started her little singsong again. Dante broke the kiss to look at his nieces.

"Get used to it," he growled at them.

They both giggled, not in the least intimidated. Gemma laughed. Dante gave her that crooked grin she adored.

A family again, they headed home.

It was a couple of days later when Dante arrived home a bit late. She hadn't been particularly worried—she knew he was entangled in a ton of reports and paperwork—but something about his expression when he'd come in had her looking at him curiously.

He got Flash, who was no longer limping despite his unexpected run, settled in, kissed the girls hello, then straightened to face her. And pulled a box about four inches square, tied with a big gold bow, out of his jacket pocket and handed it to her.

"It'll have to do for now," he said softly.

Gemma tugged on the ribbon. Lifted the lid. Burst into joyous laughter and threw her arms around the man she loved.

It was a teething ring.

* * * * *